"Write down 'no dating.'"

"I'm not putting that on your list, Rhian. Besides, when was the last time you—" Min stopped. "The painter! You meet this guy and all of a sudden you're making a resolution not to date? No way." Min put the cap on the pen and stuffed it under herself. "I won't write it."

"Hey! What happened to 'my resolution, my interpretation'?"

Min shook her head. "That only applies to me. Did something happen this afternoon that I should know about?"

"No. Forget I said it."

"Rhian MacGregor. Say you'll take a shot if the guy asks you out."

Rhian's stomach flip-flopped again. "Taking a shot isn't what you do when there's a kid involved. Maybe I'll date when Jem's in college."

Min rolled her eyes. "Jem is eight. Old enough to understand you deserve a life of your own." She dug around and found the pen. "I know better than to argue when you're like this, though. So let's have your last resolution."

"Learn to play basketball. I promised Jem."

They were giggling as Min handed her the list. She hesitated for the briefest moment and signed her name. This summer her lif̲ ̲ ̲ ̲ ̲ ̲ ̲ ̲ ̲ ̲ ̲ or it wouldn't, an̲ ̲ ̲ ̲ ̲ ̲ ̲ ̲ ̲ ̲ was never going t̲ ̲ ̲ ̲ ̲ ̲ ̲ she should give u̲p̲

Dear Reader,

Wanted Man is my first book. Seriously. (Yes, I still get a big goofy grin when I say that.) In fact, you might be my very first reader. I hope this is as exciting for you as it is for me!

Rhian and Nathan's story went through many versions before coming together in *Wanted Man*, but the two constants that ran through every rewrite were trust and family. These two themes are dear to my heart. (Oh, and basketball and Cap'n Crunch, which show up here, too.)

Nathan is hurting and hiding out from his considerable fame. He's wished for a family and a place in a community his whole life, but every choice he makes leaves him more isolated. Rhian is raising her young nephew and she's convinced herself (but no one else) that eight-year-old Jem is all she needs. She's holding on to old scars and bad memories to avoid the tough choices involved in making a life for herself.

I hope you'll enjoy spending time with Rhian and Nathan as they pass a summer listening to music, playing basketball, eating cupcakes (yum!) and of course figuring out whether they're ready to take a chance on love.

Thank you for taking a chance on a new writer! I hope that this book is the first of many we can share. I'd love to hear from you. You can contact me at www.EllenHartman.com.

Happy reading!

Ellen

WANTED MAN
Ellen Hartman

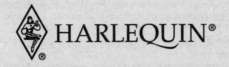

TORONTO • NEW YORK • LONDON
AMSTERDAM • PARIS • SYDNEY • HAMBURG
STOCKHOLM • ATHENS • TOKYO • MILAN • MADRID
PRAGUE • WARSAW • BUDAPEST • AUCKLAND

ISBN-13: 978-0-373-71427-8
ISBN-10:   0-373-71427-0

WANTED MAN

Copyright © 2007 by Ellen K. Hartman.

ABOUT THE AUTHOR

Ellen has been making a living as a writer since she graduated from Carnegie Mellon and went to work for Microsoft, writing documentation for Word. (In those days the company had 5,000 employees, windows were glass things you opened to get a breeze and Bill Gates was still single.) Of her published works, including computer manuals, articles on parenting and a poem about Achilles and Patroclus for her high school literary journal, *Wanted Man* is her favorite.

Ellen lives in a college town in upstate New York, where she enjoys writing romances, forcing her husband to listen to ABBA, and shooting hoops with her sons.

This book is dedicated to The Hartman Group—Ricky, Owen and Cam. You inspire me.

I treasure the support of my family, who encouraged me to write from my earliest days. (Evidence? My parents still have the fairy tale I wrote in second grade. It's a classic—just ask them.)

Finally, my writing group is so awesome you'd think I made them up. Diana, Leslie and Liz are as generous with their time and smarts as they are with their gin. I would be one lonely writer without our late-night sessions.

PROLOGUE

NATHAN STARED at the TV screen in disbelief. Lindsey Hall, the over-the-top star of *Morning Lindsey!* had just launched a nationwide manhunt for him.

It was May seventh, too late for an April Fool's joke. And not the slightest bit funny anyway.

He spoke into the phone without taking his eyes off the screen. "Matt?" He tried to be calm. "What the hell?"

"We don't know. She didn't clear anything with us. I have Jerry checking to see what requests Hall's show put in recently with PR, with legal, hell, with the cafeteria. We'll find out." Matt Callahan, Nathan's literary agent, was talking too fast.

"You sound nervous." Nervous wasn't good. Nervous meant there was something to worry about.

"I am nervous. That psycho told seven million Americans she'd pay them money if they track you down—" Matt broke off when *Morning Lindsey!* came back from the commercial break.

The camera panned across The Hall, a section of the studio audience filled with Hall Heads, Lindsey impersonators wearing platinum wigs and bright lipstick. Nathan looked away but not before registering that some of the faux Lindseys were men.

"Welcome back, fans!" Lindsey spoke in exclamations. Nathan knew about her. Everyone in America knew about her, but he'd never watched the show. Matt had called five minutes ago and told him to turn it on. He was repulsed but fascinated—this was what eighty-nine percent of Americans chose to wake up to?

"Now that you have the Chris Senso Hotline phone number and the e-mail address, I'm going to show you our first clue."

A baby picture of Nathan flashed on the screen. He was about two years old, golden brown hair curled gently around his face and deep blue eyes sparkled with laughter. "We've confirmed with the publisher of the David Dale series that this photo, which we all recognize as the author photo from the back of our most favorite books, is a real baby photo of the person writing under the pen name Chris Senso."

The baby photo was taken down. Lindsey Hall sat at her desk, tapping a pencil on her too-bright teeth.

"Someone out there knows that baby."

"I do," Matt said.

"Shut up," Nathan muttered, eyes glued to the screen. "I didn't meet you until I was seven."

"But I heard stories. Saw pictures." The author photo had been one of Nathan's mom's favorites and had been on their mantel when he was growing up.

Lindsey's voice was earnest. "Think back to kinder-garten. Was there a little golden-haired cutie in your class telling stories and entertaining everyone?"

"Cutie?" Matt snorted.

"Say one more word and I'm hanging up. You're the one who thought it was funny to use the real picture."

"How was I supposed to know your damn books would

turn into a phenomenon? If you'd warned me you were going to break every record in publishing I might have advised against the picture."

"The secret identity of this author can be secret no longer. America needs to know who Chris Senso really is." Lindsey leaned toward the camera, winking and pouting. "*I* need to know who Chris Senso is."

"She needs you, man," Matt snickered.

"One word."

Eyes gleaming, Lindsey stood up and walked to the front of the set. "The long-awaited movie of the second book in the series, *David Dale and the Ice Master*, will be in theaters in six months. The fifth book will be out shortly after that. More than enough time to solve this mystery, people. Put your thinking caps on and look at that baby picture. We can find him and then we'll know everything about Chris Senso, whoever he is!"

Nathan clicked the remote and the room was silent. Matt was quiet on the other end of the phone then, all humor gone, he murmured, "I'm sorry, Nathan. I had no idea."

"I have to get out of here."

"What?"

"I'm leaving. I won't sit here and let them hunt me down. Someone from back home might recognize that picture. If they know I'm in New Hampshire they can put it together and it'll be like last time." He was already shuffling the drawings and notes for his latest book and reaching under his desk for his leather portfolio.

"It's a long shot."

"It's going to happen. Reporters don't let this stuff go."

Matt didn't answer and that was answer enough. Nathan closed his laptop and pulled the plug.

"Where will you go?"

"Away. Somewhere with no trail linking Nathan Delaney to Chris Senso. No roots, no strings, no ties. No nothing."

CHAPTER ONE

Richwoods, New York. One month later.

RHIAN STEPPED OFF the last rung of the ladder onto the roof of her house and paused to catch her breath. There was a puff in the air behind her. She turned and saw the ladder tilting slowly, majestically away from the house. She made a desperate, dangerous grab for it but missed, and then watched as it crashed into the grass below. Good Lord, she was stuck on her own roof.

Lying belly down on the edge, she realized three things: the view from the roof was amazing; the paint looked much, much worse up close; and the housepainter she was hoping to hire would have to rescue her.

Rats.

Before she'd even met the man she'd be the damsel in distress. She hated that. Especially if the man playing Prince Wonderful Rescue was a repairman of any kind. In her experience, damsels, especially of the single-mother variety, were frequently overcharged.

Ten minutes later, just before she started to get bored, an exquisitely clean, midnight-blue pickup with two ladders in a rack made the turn into her driveway. She stood up and squinted, trying to get a look at the driver.

With her luck he'd be some old-timer who'd call her little lady while making bad jokes about women and ladders.

But no, the man who stepped out of the pickup was no old guy: heartthrob handsome was more like it. Rhian blinked. Maybe she was having some height-induced vision problem and he didn't really look like a younger, longer-haired Paul Newman. He whistled softly as he strode up her walk, clipboard tucked under one arm, jingling his keys with the other hand. He moved easily, his walk loose limbed, lean and graceful. Rhian smiled and shook her head in amazement. She'd spent four years learning to ignore men, not fantasizing even about the gorgeous ones. Now, when she truly was in need of a hero, or at least someone with a ladder, fate had sent this, this *specimen* to save her.

He was the only painter in Richwoods who'd even taken her call. Every other painter, including the college boys who strapped a stepladder to the top of their Subaru station wagon and sounded stoned on their answering machine, had been booked for months. But this one, Prince Charming from any number of schoolgirl films, was still available.

There must be something wrong with him. Maybe he was a crook. How many crooked housepainters could one medium-size town support? She knew at least three crooked painters had left town, because the Bobalo Brothers had taken the deposit she'd paid with them when they'd skipped town after ruining her house.

The painter slowed when he saw the ladder lying in the grass and then stopped dead. "Hello," Rhian called. "I got hung up." A beat of hesitation and then he stepped back and looked up to where she was.

He blinked at her and opened his mouth but didn't say

anything. Maybe he wasn't a crook; he might be dumb. That would explain the lack of clients.

She put her right hand up to shade her eyes and took a better look at him. He was looking back at her, his jaw set, and if she wasn't mistaken, his face had gone pale. She hoped he wasn't ill. The house desperately needed to be painted. *Repainted. Whatever.* She couldn't afford to have Prince Pea Brain keel over before he gave her the estimate.

"Don't move." His voice was clipped as he turned to get the ladder. He seemed healthy enough, Rhian thought, as she watched him swing the ladder up in one easy move with a grace she envied. Her head still hurt where she'd bonked it as she wrestled the ladder out of the storage shed.

The painter jerked the ladder once to set it, then braced his legs and looked up at her. "Climb down nice and easy. I'll steady it while you come. Don't worry."

Worry?

She wasn't worried. She was mad that the ladder had fallen, for starters. Mortified by the rescue, maybe. Wishing herself anywhere but on a ladder, progressing bottom first toward a housepainter, definitely.

He didn't step back or let go of the ladder even when she was almost down. He was very tall, six-three at least, and she was hideously aware of him. Passing so close to him that she could feel the warmth coming off his chest, she caught a whiff of shampoo and outdoors. Warm cotton. She jumped the last foot to get some space.

Space didn't help much. He was that attractive. His shoulders were broad and his arms deliciously cut and strong. His eyes were a deep, clear blue. A worn but neatly tucked in T-shirt didn't do much to disguise a lean, muscular body. Rich brown hair was brushed back from his face and clustered in soft curls touching his collar. Who had hair that perfect? It was absurd that this guy was standing in her yard. There had to be something wrong with him.

The Bobalos, the painters who'd made a monstrous joke out of her home and then gone on the lam with her money, hadn't looked evil, either. How on earth would she know if she could trust this guy? Rhian hated when the rules weren't clear.

His voice, low and serious, brought her back to reality. "You weren't on the ladder when it fell, were you?"

She started to make a joke but then realized he was worried. He wasn't making fun of her or trying to make her feel stupid or teach her why women shouldn't mess with tools. What she'd thought was illness on his face had been worry. No one worried about her. It felt…nice.

"It went over after I stepped off. I'm embarrassed, not hurt."

He nodded. Some of the tension left his face. "Why were you up there?"

Rhian turned sideways to gesture at the house. The bottom section was brick, old and faded, luscious peach and red tones blending into sandy browns. It was weathered and beautiful. The upper story was wooden shingles and…well, she hadn't quite come up with the right name for the shade. Pepto-Bismol was close but she thought that was actually, maybe, three shades less pink than her home.

She waved a hand at it. "I wanted to see if it looked better up close." She saw his mouth twitch. He wanted to laugh. Didn't want to insult her, but he did want to laugh, she could tell.

"Did it?"

"What do you think?"

His deep blue eyes danced with humor but he still didn't let the smile appear. "In my professional opinion, it would be hard for it to look worse."

She laughed. Okay, he wasn't stupid. He was funny. Interesting. *Rats*.

"Well, I'm glad you're here, Mr. Delaney."

She stuck her hand out and he shook it. His grip was warm and dry. And then he smiled, his mouth quirking up on one side and his eyes crinkling and she wished for half a second that he would keep smiling at her forever.

"Please, it's Nathan. I save 'Mr. Delaney' for the IRS."

"The IRS?"

"I'm kidding. I just prefer Nathan."

Her laugh was halfhearted. Since the Bobalos had taken off with her money and left her with the Barbie Townhouse her appetite for crime jokes was very small.

"I'm Rhian MacGregor."

"Rhian." His mouth tilted up again in that charming smile. He shifted his weight and folded his arms across the clipboard in front of him. "I like the sound of that. Rhian. Nice."

"So what do we do? Do you look at the house? Do I answer questions?"

He shot a sly look at her. "My first question has to be the obvious one—what happened to your house?"

Rhian shook her head. She still couldn't believe it. "I hired these…these painters, these brothers, Harry, Larry and Dave Bobalo."

"Harry, Larry and Dave?"

"Half brother." Rhian said. "Anyway, they said they'd need a week to paint the house. There was lead paint underneath. I didn't want my little guy here while they were scraping so we left—went downstate to New York to play tourist. When we came back, the house looked like this and every last Bobalo brother and half brother *and* my deposit check for two thousand dollars were gone."

Nathan glanced from the house to her. "They skipped town?"

"Would they have been able to get another painting gig?"

"Good point."

"So that's the story. Now I want it painted over. Painted right."

"No kidding." He flipped open his clipboard and took out a pen. "Walk around with me for a minute, will you?" He filled her name and address in at the top of a blank quote sheet. His hand curved around the pen in the peculiar way left-handed people had. Rhian had always wished to be left-handed. She thought it implied creativity and flair. Would a left-handed painter be more likely to be honest than a righty? She was so caught up in watching him write her name that she didn't notice the plastic Whiffle Ball hidden in the grass. Her stomach dropped as she lost her balance.

Without even seeming to look at her, Nathan shot out a hand and grabbed her above the elbow, steadying her with a firm grip until she had her feet back under her.

"Thanks." She was flustered. His hand had been strong and warm. "You move fast."

"Good reflexes. And you're welcome." He shook his pen gently at her. "That's two times I saved you. In some countries that would put you in my debt."

She'd have to do what he wanted then. What would a sexy-walking, fast-moving, left-handed housepainter want? She shivered and put her hand up to cup the spot where he'd held her arm. "Lucky thing we're here in the good, old U.S.A."

"Lucky thing," he muttered. He squinted at the back of the house then put his head down to the clipboard, making another note. He kicked the Whiffle Ball gently. "You have kids?"

"One. Jem. My nephew actually." She sounded matter-of-fact because she'd trained herself ruthlessly to pull that off. But she never could keep the lump out of her throat when she thought about her sister, Christine, and brother-in-law, James. God, she missed them. Eight years after their accident the pain was still raw.

He glanced at her but then went back to his sheet. She couldn't help watching the slender pen in his long, tanned fingers and the curve of his wrist. How pathetic was it that she thought penmanship was sexy? But being a sucker for lefties didn't mean she wanted to do anything about it. Benjamin Franklin was a lefty and she hadn't ever tried to date him. The dead-for-two-hundred-years thing was a factor, but still. She could control herself.

Just because a left-handed man had come to give her a painting quote, she wouldn't let go of every rule she'd made for her life. She didn't date people. She didn't fantasize about housepainters. She didn't even trust housepainters.

"So what do you think?" she asked, hoping to shift her thoughts firmly back to a professional footing. He was a professional. A professional housepainter and that made him suspect.

"Whatever you do is going to take a few coats. What color was it supposed to be?"

"Blush. Not even that." She clenched her fists when she thought about the Bobalos and how she'd trusted them. "I asked them to add a hint, a tinge, a suggestion of pink to the cream paint. It was supposed to whisper pink once it was next to the bricks."

"And instead of a whisper, Harry, Larry and Dave gave you the Hallelujah Chorus."

She sighed. Her house was so precious to her. It wasn't just a building and certainly wasn't an investment. It was home, the place she and Jem had built their family, the place she'd finally put down roots. She hated that her home had been treated so shabbily. "So what can we do now?"

Nathan shrugged. "Paint it over."

"Again with the professional opinions?"

"Yep." He grinned, making his answer cheerful, not dismissive. "Will you be around tomorrow, late afternoon? I can drop off an estimate."

"Sure, just yell up to the roof."

He shot her a look.

"Joke," she said. "No need to worry. I'll be here, on the ground, ladder-free."

They walked together around the side of the house, passing through the shade of the old oak trees, skirting the enormous hole Jem had excavated off and on since he was four.

"Digging to China?" He jerked a thumb at the hole.

"Maybe originally. Now it's just digging."

"Guy's gotta have a project," he agreed amiably.

She didn't let herself think about how cool it was to talk to someone with an instinctive understanding of little boys. Maybe it wasn't instinctive anyway. Maybe he was married with a half-dozen little boys of his own.

He opened the gate for her and held it while she walked through and stopped near his truck.

"Umm." She hesitated, always reluctant to ask for references because she thought it screamed *I don't trust you*. But she'd already been burned. She could be accused of being naive but she'd be damned if she'd be accused of being stupid. "We didn't talk about references. Maybe I can give yours a call tonight while you work on the estimate?"

For the first time he hesitated. "Local references?"

He tapped his pen on his clipboard. Nervous, she thought. *Great.*

"Yes, people who will vouch for your work. You know people who will say, 'Nathan never painted my house the wrong color and then left town with the deposit.'" She wanted him to pick up the joke. Of course he had references.

"Actually, I don't have any references. Not locally. I'm new to Richwoods." Nathan leaned toward her, sincerity in his posture. "But I can give you my old partner's number in Boston. He'll vouch for my, um, work."

Rhian looked at her feet. One reference from somewhere else wasn't really good enough. Maybe if she called those college boys one more time they'd need some extra cash for beer.

"Listen, Rhian." He put the clipboard on the hood of his truck and put his hands in his pockets. "I know this doesn't sound good and you have no reason to trust me. But I'm being honest with you. I'm starting over here. If you give me a shot with your house, I swear you won't be disappointed."

His eyes were clear and steady on hers and she wanted to trust him, but she couldn't. Now that she looked, she saw that his work boots were new and his truck was much too clean. If he was a housepainter, he hadn't been one for long. "I don't think—"

"Wait, before you say no, what if I do the whole thing with no money down? At the end, you only pay me if you're happy." He made this ridiculous offer sound reasonable, smart even.

"No money until the end?"

"Totally finished, totally happy or totally free. I'll buy the paint and everything."

Maybe he wasn't a crook; maybe he was crazy. "That's the exact opposite of the deal the Bobalo Brothers gave me."

"I promise I can outpaint the Bobalos."

He sounded honest. He looked honest. There was the left-handed thing. She hated to trust an unknown, but what choice did she have? Leave the house the way it was? It only had one coat of paint—it needed at least one more before winter. Besides, everybody had to get their start somewhere, didn't they?

"I can still call your reference?"

"Absolutely."

"Then if you don't mind, I'll think about it. You do the estimate, I'll make my call, and we can talk again tomorrow."

"Done." Nathan uncapped his pen to write a name and phone number on his pad and then ripped off the bottom of the sheet to hand to her.

"All right."

He opened the door of the truck and put one leg in, and then turned, resting half on the seat. Shading his eyes with one hand, he grinned at her. *Oh, Lord, that smile.*

"I'll see you tomorrow, then, Rhian."

She forced herself to use her business voice. "I'll be here."

"Good enough."

Rhian watched as he backed the truck out of the driveway. Despite her strict rule against dating and her total lack of interest in all men for the past four years, it had only taken Nathan twenty minutes to get under her skin. *Rats*. Why did the only housepainter left in Rich-woods have to be him? Hefting ladders, joking about the Bobalos, writing with his left hand, grinning with lethal force. Rhian couldn't imagine where he'd come from. Nor did she know how she felt. All she knew for sure was, tomorrow, he'd be back.

NATHAN SWUNG his truck out of the driveway, his hands clenched tight on the wheel. His stomach was rolling with a mixture of happiness and tension. He'd been in this town for one month and hadn't landed a single painting gig despite going on innumerable appointments like this one. After his crazy offer, though, he had hope that someone was going to hire him. But the someone, that was the problem. Or could be.

Rhian. He'd flirted with her, no sense lying to himself. That had to stop. She was attractive, warm blue eyes, sandy-blond hair, tucked behind her ears and flipped up in the back. He'd watched her come down the ladder, knowing she was embarrassed and doing her best not to show it. He'd appreciated her attitude. Appreciated the view, too.

Which had been a shock. After his fiancée, Patricia, walked out six months before, he hadn't looked at a woman. He hadn't been abstaining on purpose. He'd felt nothing. Noticed nothing. Been nothing. Until today.

Nathan rolled his shoulders and his neck to loosen the knots that were starting to form. His cell phone rang, Matt's office number flashing on the display. He punched the speaker button.

"Hey, buddy."

"Hey, Nathan." Then Matt was silent.

"You call me to listen to me drive?"

"No. No. Nathan, it's something weird and maybe, but not for sure, bad."

He flexed his hands on the steering wheel again, feeling each rounded bump in the leather cover. The knots in his neck were tying themselves up tighter. "Spit it out, Matt."

"Okay. Lindsey Hall has some special guest tomorrow who's supposed to help her 'crack the case wide open.'"

Hell. The knots multiplied, sending tension up his neck and settling in his temples. "Patricia?"

"We don't know. I don't think so. From the way the commercials sound, it's more likely to be a detective or something like that. But the point is Lindsey Hall's not giving up."

"Of course she's not. Hunting me will make her ratings for the year."

"Sorry."

"Hell." Nathan pounded the steering wheel in frustration. "So nothing to do until tomorrow when you and me and the rest of America tune in to see what she's got?"

"I'll keep trying, but probably not. We'll talk tomorrow, after."

Nathan punched off the phone. He had a full-on headache now. He made a conscious effort to relax his shoulders, but it didn't do much for the tension.

Well, maybe it was a good thing Lindsey Hall had picked this moment to kick it up a gear. It made one thing crystal clear. This thing, whatever it had been, with Rhian couldn't go anywhere. He was hiding out, for God's sake. Sure he wanted the painting job. Needed the work to prove he could still function, still live his life. But the last thing he needed, the main thing he didn't need, was a woman. A relationship of any kind. The one constant in Nathan's life since he had gone on the lam was the need to stay disconnected. No connections equaled safety. Safety equaled peace.

CHAPTER TWO

RHIAN WAS LYING on the couch holding the scrap of paper on which Nathan had neatly printed the name Matt Callahan and a phone number. She'd made the call, but had gotten voice mail. Now she was looking at his printing and thinking about his hand on the pen and telling herself to stop being so juvenile. To stop thinking about the house-painter in an inappropriate way. She should be rejoicing that she'd found a housepainter at all.

She'd read about pregnant women who nested just before the baby was born. That was exactly what she'd done when she moved here after Len pitched their lives upside down, except that Jem had been three at the time.

Richwoods, the energetic little Upstate New York town, had folded them in. It was a place for them to be home. Rhian had fallen in love with the house the first time she'd walked through. She'd stripped wallpaper and painted. She'd spent two weeks ripping out the wall-to-wall carpeting and then had the floors sanded and buffed to a warm honey glow. She loved this house like no place she'd ever lived. She hated what the Bobalos had done to it. She needed it fixed. Soon.

Through the screen door she heard the gate open and close. Jem's voice floated in, describing a basketball game to their live-in babysitter and her best friend, Min. The voices faded around the side of the house. They'd gone to the fort Jem had in the forsythia bush next to the fence. It was another few minutes before she dragged herself to her feet and out the door.

The forsythia bush was a monstrosity. It was easily the size of a small public swimming pool and got bigger each year. Half the town dropped by in the early spring to take cuttings and as far as Rhian could tell the bush liked that, growing more because of it.

Some gardeners might have been horrified by such an out-of-control mess, but she wasn't a gardener, she was a person raising a small boy. She knew God's gift to fort-making when she saw it.

Each summer Jem and his friends made the forsythia fort their headquarters, expanding the "rooms" and refining the network of secret passages and booby-trapped exits. She and Min had arranged the picnic table and hammock close by, taking advantage of the shade provided by the bush that ate Manhattan. That was where Rhian saw Min, dozing in the afternoon shadows with a thick book lying open across her chest, her shoulder-length brown hair spread on the hammock pillow. Rhian shook her friend's pink Converse sneaker gently, "Hey, aren't you supposed to be watching my kid?" she joked.

Min flicked one eye open, "Don't you know I can watch your kid and nap at the same time?"

Rhian laughed. Min was right. Rhian trusted her completely, napping or not, to keep Jem as safe as she would herself. Their relationship was far beyond employer and employee.

When Min had moved in, she'd instantly become

Rhian's anchor to sanity. The first night, Rhian had burned the pork chops she'd intended to serve for dinner. She'd scorched the rice *and* the pot she'd been cooking it in. When she'd smelled the smoke and turned to the stove, her hand had slipped and she'd accidentally dumped half a bottle of dressing in the salad. Rhian and dinner were a mostly unsuccessful, frequently dramatic combination. Fires were rare, but not unknown. Even though she knew what a horrid cook she was, it was still surprisingly upsetting each time things went wrong.

On that night Rhian had stared from the smoking chops to the smoldering rice to the ruined salad to three-year-old Jem perched hungrily at the table, and felt so mad and so stupid she'd wanted to scream. And then Min had come in from a study session. She'd taken the situation in with a glance, poured Jem a glass of milk and handed him a banana, opened a beer for herself and one for Rhian, dumped the ruined meal and whipped up a dinner of omelets and toast.

When Rhian had protested that their work arrangement didn't include making dinner, Min had given her the gentle smile Rhian would soon know so well and answered that in the interest of self-preservation she was amending the job description. That had been the start and they'd just gotten closer since.

"Hello, Jem," Rhian hollered into the overgrown bush-fort.

"Hey, Rhian," came the muffled reply. He must be in the very back, the area known as the Secret Sanctum. Good, no chance he'd overhear.

"If I tell you something," she asked Min, "will you promise you won't make it into some big deal?"

"This sounds good," Min said as she moved over to make room for Rhian on the hammock. Min claimed to be five foot four inches on her driver's license but that was stretching things by a few inches. Which was nice for Rhian, who at an honest five feet four-and-a-half inches had never been "the tall one" in any relationship.

"The housepainter came to give me an estimate. Well, not an estimate, but to see the house, measure—"

Min gave her a poke with her elbow and interrupted, "Get to the good part."

Rhian's stomach flip flopped. Nathan—he was the good part and also the bad part. Definitely the confusing part. She lowered her voice to be sure Jem couldn't hear. "He was gorgeous, literally, like Paul Newman. He's got this perfect hair—you've never seen hair like his, wavy and just this side of long." She was gushing but couldn't stop. "And he was left-handed and tall and—"

Min broke in. "First, how sad is it that I was having ice cream with an eight-year-old while this man was here and second, are you mixing business with pleasure?"

Right then Rhian finished being stupid.

"No, no mixing." She shook her head. "You know I don't do that."

Min's cinnamon-colored eyes narrowed and her mouth thinned. "But you could. You've been letting Stupid Len be in charge of your love life for much too long."

"Stupid Len has nothing to do with it." But Rhian couldn't keep a guilty flush from stealing across her face.

"Just because that shallow excuse for an ex-fiancé ran out on you and Jem doesn't mean every man will. Your painting paragon is not Stupid Len."

"We've had this conversation before." Rhian wanted Min to understand. "It's not Len. Everyone leaves. My father left, every man my mother ever dated left, Len left,

Randy left, and Jem is stuck with just me. He doesn't need a revolving door in his life like I had. This so-called paragon of yours—" she took a steadying breath "—he didn't even have a reference. Who knows where he's from or how long he'll stay?

"Anyway, his good looks weren't what I wanted to tell you about." *A smidge of a lie, but nothing major.* "The really interesting thing is he's painting the house for free. If I don't like it at the end, I don't pay."

Min turned to her. "He's the anti-Bobalo!" She held up her hand for a high five. "This must have your crooked painter radar all out of whack."

That's not all that's out of whack.

LATE THAT NIGHT, Rhian was wandering the house. She had finished the last load of laundry she needed to do to get Jem ready for his vacation. He was going on a cross-country trip with his dad's parents, two sets of aunts and uncles and six cousins for the rest of the summer. She could start packing, she supposed, but she wasn't up to that yet. He'd never been away for longer than a week and she was going to miss him unbearably.

She eased the door of his room open and slipped inside. Sleeping heavily, he had one arm flung over his head. Tucked next to his neck was Nestor, his threadbare, formerly white, stuffed cat.

This trip had been hatched over a poker game during a Christmas visit to James's parents' house in Ohio. The plan was to follow the Pittsburgh Pirates, taking in the sights along the way. Jem and his cousins had been delirious at the idea of an RV, of baseball every day, and even more, at spending eight weeks together. She hadn't been able to refuse him the trip—had even felt happy he had this tight connection to his father's family.

Despite that, every time she thought about sending him off she got a pain in her stomach. She could handle a week, but what would she do with herself for eight weeks?

She tugged Nestor out from under her boy's neck and put him on the corner of the pillow. Her fingers traced the oval outline of Jem's face, smoothing a strand of dark blond hair behind his ear. After she spread the light blanket over him, she backed out of the room and closed the door gently. Jem had been her life for eight years. She had no memory of what she used to do before he'd arrived.

She saw light showing under Min's bedroom door. She knocked and poked her head around the door when Min answered.

"Want to see something cool?" she asked.

Min squinted toward her. "Is it after midnight?"

Rhian shrugged. "It might be. But this is cool, I promise. You're not sleeping anyway."

"Not technically, no." Min nestled under a cotton blanket, reading by the light of her bedside lamp.

"Exactly." Rhian waited. She knew Min was coming.

Min put her book down and got out of bed. Her cotton pajamas were covered in lurid pink and orange flowers. "You really think I'm going to get out of bed and follow you around in the middle of the night?"

"Grab some shoes."

Min gave her a hard look. "If you think I'm going *outside* with you, you're nuts."

Rhian grinned and waited.

"If I knew you were going to go crazy I never would have agreed to this summer position in Virginia. How can

I trust you to act normal if this is how you're starting out?" Min muttered while she slid on her sneakers.

Shortly after Jem had made his summer plans, Min had announced that she'd been accepted as a member of a team working on the provenance of some newly discovered paintings at the University of Virginia.

Suddenly Rhian felt a twist of…eagerness? "It's been so long since I've been alone, there's no telling what I might do," she replied. It was true. She could do something, but what? Something outrageous? Something unexpected? Something just for her?

Rhian's bedroom was wide and long, taking up the western side of the house. The built-in bookcases were crammed with her favorite books, Jane Austen and Tolkien sharing space with Louis L'Amour, Larry McMurtry and Julia Quinn. The crazy quilt in shades of purple and green her grandmother had made while her grandfather served in World War II covered the bed.

The walls were pale lilac, and sheer white curtains fluttered at each of the four long windows. Rhian loved the peace she found in her room.

She pushed aside the overstuffed chair tucked into the alcove under the window and climbed out onto the roof.

She stuck her head back into the bedroom. "Aren't you coming?"

"You're joking, right?" Min hadn't moved from her position near the door.

"Didn't you ever sit out on the roof and drink beer when you were in college?"

"No."

"Me either. This is our chance." Rhian gestured with her free hand. "I didn't bring any beer, but I promise it's amazing."

Min sighed, made her way across the room and swung through the window. "I could file an employee harassment case, I'm sure."

"Just look."

They were on the opposite side of the house from where Rhian had sat in the afternoon, but on this side the view was better. The park behind the house stretched out in a dark, impenetrable band. The sky arched overhead and stars glittered at them through the branches of the oak tree.

"Oh! It is amazing." Min still had one white-knuckled hand clutched on the windowsill. But her face was lit by the light from inside and her eyes were scanning the trees and sky and dark spaces as eagerly as Rhian's.

Rhian moved a few steps down the roof and sat. She didn't feel any vertigo, just a wonderful freedom from her regular life.

Her friend carefully lowered herself to sit and then inched to where Rhian sat.

"It's like this isn't part of my real life," Rhian said.

"At least you have a real life," Min said. "I'm a twenty-nine-year old babysitter for a kid who's almost too old to need me."

Rhian was surprised by the bitterness in Min's voice.

"You're not just a babysitter, Min." She thought of the passion her friend had for the work she did on the historical provenance of early American art. "You're getting your Ph.D."

"I've been working on that thing so long, I'm not sure I know how to finish." Tears reflected the moonlight in her friend's eyes. "I've been putting life off. I love you and Jem, but this is *your* home. I need something real of my own, you know?"

Rhian did know. "I feel the same way. When Jem's gone I don't know what I'll do. I don't remember who I was without him. I don't know what's left of me."

They sat in silence while the truth sank in.

"Let's make a challenge," Rhian said, suddenly inspired. "We'll make goals and by the end of the summer our lives will be different."

"A challenge?" Min asked.

"Look," Rhian said, fired up now. "Len and I started *Phases* in college and I thought that would be my life. Len and our hip, literary magazine. *Phases* was everything I thought about, everything I was good at, everything I wanted. When Christine and James died, it was replaced totally by Jem.

"I couldn't leave Jem to be out working and schmoozing and doing everything *Phases* needed. The interviews and PR alone were getting to be a full-time job. When Len split, he took *Phases* with him. I never intended to give up writing. I was going to do technical writing to tide us over before Jem started school. But the first contract ran into more and, somehow, I never did get back to my real work."

Rhian's frustration at the holding pattern her life was in boiled over, and she kicked a stick off the roof. "I've had this halfway life, never doing anything I picked. I didn't even get to dump Stupid Len—he dumped me first. I want a chance to find me." She squeezed Min's hand. "Let's do this together. You saved my life a long time ago. I owe you."

"Come on, I only helped with the babysitting."

Rhian started laughing. "That and everything else."

Min laughed, too. "Well, you *were* a bit of a disaster."

"Remember the potty-training-bribery fiasco?"

"The fingerpaint handprint on your interview suit?"

"T-ball?"

In unison, they chanted, "Coach Jack Johnson, sir!"

Rhian scrambled back up the roof. She leaned in the window and grabbed her notebook and pen from the side pocket of her reading chair.

"Okay. You first. What are your plans?"

"My resolutions," suggested Min.

"Your Rooftop Resolutions," Rhian said as she wrote that heading on the top of a page.

"Quit messing around and finish the dissertation."

"You haven't been—" Rhian protested.

Min held up one finger, "No, no. My resolution, my interpretation."

"Next?" Rhian asked. Min looked up to the sky and sighed. Her hand inched over and covered Rhian's. "I need to look for a job."

Rhian felt her breath rush away. Min was leaving them. This would be another loss for Jem, first his parents and then Len. Rhian wanted more than anything to keep him from feeling any pain. It wasn't fair to her friend to wish she'd stay, but she did wish it. She squeezed Min's hand and managed a smile. She owed her that much. "I guess we all knew that was coming sometime." She'd cry later but not now. "You need one that's not about work."

"Who says?"

"We're changing our *lives*, Min. Not writing a to-do list."

Min shook her head a few times and then snapped her fingers and smiled. "I want to be a blonde."

Rhian burst into laughter. "Are you kidding?"

Min looked sheepish. "Blondes have more fun."

"Look at me," Rhian said as she printed, "Dye hair blond."

"Your turn," Min said, holding out her hand for the paper and pencil.

Rhian could feel herself blushing and was glad for the darkness. But it was now or never. She could commit to herself or give up. She took a deep breath and blurted out, "I want to write children's books."

"Oh Rhian! Prince Kit?"

She nodded, not surprised that Min had made the connection with the long-running bedtime story she'd been telling to Jem. Min clapped her hands. "That's perfect. You've already got us hooked on the story, all you'll need to do is write it down."

"That's all? That's everything." Her voice shook with passion and a twist of fear. "I haven't written anything but computer manuals since I gave up *Phases*. What if I forgot how? What if it stinks? What if I write it and no one will publish it?"

What if it's everything I ever wanted to do and I try it and it doesn't work?

"You won't know until you start," Min answered. "But the writing you did in *Phases* was amazing. You know that. Kids are imitating your style in college workshops. Give yourself a chance. Write a book. Your first resolution."

"And the second has to be that I'm committing all my time to this. I'm liable to get scared and take a tech-writing contract to keep the money coming in. I need to outlaw that. I have enough saved to take the summer off without worrying."

Min nodded and added that to the list.

Rhian read over Min's shoulder. "Write down 'no dating.'"

"What are you talking about—'no dating'? I'm not writing that down. Besides, when was the last time you—"

Min stopped. Her head snapped up. "The painter! You meet this guy and all of a sudden you're making a resolution not to date? No way." Min put the cap back on the pen and stuffed it under herself. "I won't write it."

"Hey! What happened to 'my resolution, my interpretation'?"

Min shook her head. "That rule only applies to me. Did something happen this afternoon that I should know about?"

"No. Forget I said it."

"You are a piece of work, Rhian MacGregor. Your powers of self-denial are truly awesome."

"Is this supposed to be a pep talk?"

"Say you'll take a shot if the guy asks you out."

Rhian's stomach flip-flopped again. "Taking a shot isn't what you do when there's a kid involved."

"No dating ever?"

"Maybe when Jem's in college." Rhian thought that was generous.

Min rolled her eyes. "Jem wouldn't ask you to do this."

"He doesn't have to. He's been hurt enough. Losing both of your parents meets anyone's lifetime quota for loss. And then he got left by Len."

"Rhian, Jem was three when Len left. He doesn't remember. You're hiding behind him."

Rhian interrupted. "He's not three anymore."

"Right, he's eight. Old enough to understand that you deserve a life of your own. Single parents date. You're scared, Rhian. You won't try."

Rhian was frustrated. Why couldn't Min see that she needed to do this to keep *Jem* safe? If she was scared that was beside the point. "I swore when Len let us down that the one thing I'd give that kid was stability. He wouldn't have to grow up the way I did, losing people right when they got to be important."

She went on, "People don't stick around. Remember Randy, the firefighter? We went on three dates. Randy made Jem a junior lieutenant and promised he could go on a real call on the truck. Four more dates and we broke up and the real call never came. Boyfriends aren't dads. They move on."

Min patted Rhian's leg. "Jem's okay, Rhian. You don't give him credit for how strong he is. Trust the life you've built for him."

"Which is my point. He and I have a life and then some guy comes along and, and…remember, after Randy, I dated Sam? But I didn't want Jem to know right away so I could see how things went with Sam before I exposed Jem to him. So I spent three weeks lying to Jem. I hated that."

Min dug under herself and found the pen. "I know better than to argue with you when you're this dug in. So skipping the dating question, let's have your last one, the one that's not about work."

Rhian knew what the last goal had to be. "Learn to play basketball."

Min snorted and Rhian punched her shoulder. "Don't laugh. I promised Jem."

They were both giggling as Min finished the list and handed it to her to sign. She read her resolutions.

1. Write the book.
2. No technical writing.
3. Learn how to play basketball.

Rhian hesitated for the briefest moment and then she signed her name at the bottom of the page in firm letters.

She was committed. This summer her life would change—
or it wouldn't and she'd know for sure that she was never
going to have anything different or better and she should
give up her dreams.

CHAPTER THREE

RHIAN HAD BEEN up early making food for Jem and Min's farewell barbecue that evening. Seven of Jem's buddies and their families were coming to the party, as well as Min's friends from the art history department, and a few people from town who'd become like family over the years including Diane and Chet from the pizza place, Denise (aka Mrs. T, Jem's first-grade teacher) and her family. They were also expecting the RV at some point. Rhian had cringed when she told James's dad to look for the pink house.

Focus on the task, she told herself. Party food was a challenge for Rhian because, well, people expected it to be edible.

Holding the recipe for Green Goddess dip in one hand, she set about pulling out the ingredients. Rhian never cooked without a recipe and still failure dogged her kitchen like the smell of spoiled milk. Which was infuriating, Rhian thought, as she dumped sour cream into the bowl. She made her living writing instructions. She explained how to use intricate machinery and complex software. Heck, she *liked* to follow directions.

The knife in a death grip, she took her frustrations out on the green onions under her blade. Recipes baffled her. One time she'd been trying to make a chicken dish Denise had recommended. Everything went to hell when she reached "Lightly poach the chicken pieces." She'd read the recipe over four times until she'd admitted that the author had not included a glossary. Surely "poach the chicken" didn't have anything to do with off-season hunting of endangered chickens in a nature preserve but that was the only context she knew.

Sweeping the green onions into the bowl, she moved onto mixing. Mixing she understood. That was one of the reasons she was good at dips. Poach, though. She still didn't know what that meant exactly. And that wasn't the only word these recipe writers, these *chefs,* threw around without definition. She had a list she'd been nursing a grudge about for years. Fold, whip versus beat versus mix, deglaze, separate eggs—from what, she'd like to ask. Braise, sear, julienne—bah.

There were two things she could do in the kitchen. She could make appetizers and foods that were assembled rather than cooked. Sandwiches, dip, crudités (which sounded better than calling a carrot stick a carrot stick) and guacamole. She could mash the heck out of an avocado.

And second, she could bake. Not complicated things, but homey stuff like chocolate-chip cookies and brownies, cupcakes and frosting. She suspected her baking skills came from the place in her soul where she had an affinity for chocolate and butter and sugar (white, brown, dark brown—she loved them all).

For parties she stuck to those strengths, meaning she'd never served an entrée, but no one had ever died of food poisoning or smoke inhalation.

As she put a lid on the dip and tucked it into the refrigerator, Jem skidded into the kitchen, all long legs and flyaway hair.

"Lindsey's almost on!" he said.

In Rhian's opinion, obviously a minority opinion in America, *Morning Lindsey!* was one of the most ridiculous shows on TV. Lindsey Hall was an idiot and her guests were flat-out bizarre. But Min and Jem actually liked the show, and with the Chris Senso quest, *Morning Lindsey!* had become a key point in their a.m. ritual. On an ordinary day Rhian wouldn't have watched, but on this last day before Jem left she wasn't missing any chance to spend time with him. Even if she had to share that time with Lindsey Hall.

Rhian and Jem joined Min on the couch and the three of them sat expectantly. "I can't believe you've got me watching this garbage," she said, but in a way that clearly indicated she was partly joking.

Jem grinned at her, the dimple in his cheek dancing into view as his brown eyes sparkled. "You like David Dale as much as me."

"David Dale, yes, Lindsey Hall, no."

"Shh," Min hissed. "We love them both. Now be quiet." Rhian folded her arms.

On the screen, Lindsey's teeth gleamed in a wide smile. She was standing with a map of the United States titled "Senso Sightings" behind her left shoulder. Amber and red-colored lights flashed in almost every state.

"Morning, U.S.A.!" Lindsey shouted.

"Morning, Lindsey!" the audience chanted. Min and Jem chanted with them. Rhian rolled her eyes.

"Chris Senso is proving more wily than we expected. Despite all the tips being phoned in." She gestured over her shoulder at the Senso Sightings map. "We haven't run him to ground." The audience groaned and she held up a hand. "But! We still have untapped resources. Lindsey will get her man!" One perfectly made-up eye winked saucily at the camera.

She walked to her interview chair and sat down gracefully with her legs crossed. One high heel tapped the air. In a practiced gesture, Lindsey flipped her blond hair off her face and behind her shoulders. The camera panned over the Hall Heads who all flipped their hair in unison. Min flipped her own shorter hair, Jem flipped his head, and Rhian crossed her arms over her chest. This was her role in the Lindsey Hall byplay. Min and Jem pretended to be devoted fans and when Rhian watched with them, she pretended to hate every second of it. Actually she wasn't pretending, at least mostly not.

"We've brought in an expert today who might provide a break in our hunt. Everyone, please welcome Sally Monroe, a top developer of age-progression pictures."

The audience cheered as a woman in a forest-green pantsuit came out from backstage. Her brown hair was pulled back in a loose ponytail and she was wearing small, rectangular glasses, the funky kind Rhian always assumed were more for effect than vision correction.

"Sally has been responsible for some of the most famous age-progression work in the fight to find missing kids. Although it's not her usual thing, she's agreed to help us in our search because…" Lindsey turned to her guest. "Well, why did you agree?"

"Because you paid her an exorbitant amount of money," Rhian said under her breath.

The woman leaned forward. "I agreed because I'm dying to know who thought of David Dale—where do those stories come from? And Silvertip. That dog is amazing."

The audience cheered. Many of the Hall Heads barked, in agreement Rhian assumed. Certainly they weren't begging for Scooby Snacks. *They were all nuts.*

Lindsey leaned down and picked something up from the floor next to her chair. "We have a gift for everyone who's helped us with the search." She held up a bright pink T-shirt printed with the words "I Want My Chris Senso!"

"I need one of those shirts," Min said.

"Sally, what do you have?" Lindsey asked her guest.

Sally picked a remote control up off the arm of her chair. "Of course, this is better if there are multiple photos, access to the parents' images, other family members, so we can get all those attributes in the final picture. However, I was able to create what I think is a good resemblance to the adult Chris Senso." She turned to the large screen behind her and clicked the remote. Despite herself, Rhian leaned forward slightly in anticipation.

The picture that came up on the screen showed an attractive man with blue eyes and brown hair styled in a short crew cut. His features were regular, handsome. There was something about the mouth that drew Rhian's eye, probably because she was familiar with that joyous-looking toddler in the author photo on the David Dale books.

Lindsey Hall put on what Rhian thought of as her of-course-I'm-a-real-journalist voice. "Folks at home, loyal Hall Heads, take a good look. I'm quite confident that when we meet Chris Senso, he'll have a startling resemblance to this picture."

"I wonder why she made him have short hair?" Min said. "The kid on the books has curls."

"Maybe she thinks he's ex-military. David's got all those gadgets and he is a superhero, after all," Rhian offered.

"I don't know him," Jem said, sounding disappointed. "I kinda thought he might turn out to be Chet or someone."

He pointed the remote at the TV and turned it off.

Min put a quick arm around Jem's shoulders. "I'll be back later."

He grabbed her in a casual hug around the waist and Rhian's breath caught. He was so open, so trusting. She'd always hoped he'd grow up happy. Originally she'd thought of "happy" as a starter goal. She'd expected to add "bigger" plans like Fortune 500 CEO or World Series MVP or first trumpet for the Boston Pops. But she was learning that happiness was the biggest goal she could have for her boy, and not an easy one to achieve.

"Let's go." Jem grabbed her hand, tugging her toward the stairs. Upstairs in his bedroom, Rhian pulled the pillow out from under the patchwork quilt and stuffed it behind her back. Jem stretched out next to her and crossed his feet at the ankles. When she'd stitched the quilt for him, the year he got a "big boy" bed, he'd looked so small under it. Now he filled up a good half of the bed and was taller every time she turned around.

"You promised a whole hour of stories," he said.

"One complete hour. That's the deal." She reached for one of his feet and started to rub it gently. The kid was a sucker for foot rubs. "Did you decide if you want David Dale or Prince Kit?"

Rhian had promised this special time on his last day and told him he could choose to have her read from a David Dale book or tell more of the adventures of Prince Kit.

"Both?"

Rhian said a secret prayer of thanks—she hadn't been sure she had enough material planned to sustain an hour of storytelling. "Perfect." She reached for *David Dale and the Ruby Tooth* and settled deeper in the pillow.

She read two chapters from the book and then picked up the threads of Kit's story. She'd been telling about Prince Kit discovering a new power. He was keeping this and all his powers secret from the townspeople because he worried they'd decide he was dangerous.

Jem interrupted, "Can I ask you a question?"

She paused, trying to keep the story flowing in her mind while listening to him.

"Do you think Prince Kit's real family is magical, too?"

"I do. We can make sure they are, if that's what you want."

"I guess." He picked up the hem of his shirt and rolled and unrolled it around his index finger as he said, "When I go to Ohio they say I look like my dad. I think I look like you. Don't I?"

She stroked the arch of his foot. His eyes were dark, snappy brown like his father's but he had the same oval-shaped face Rhian and Christine shared and his blond hair had darkened to the same golden-brown Christine's had been, a shade deeper than Rhian's own.

"Your eyes look like your dad's and your hair is the same color as your mom's. But your mouth looks like mine. And you and I think the same jokes are funny."

"But I want to *look* like you. Like that lady on Lindsey said, I want you to be in my picture."

Rhian felt tears in her eyes and bit down hard to keep them in. "What's going on?"

"When they say I look like my dad, it's like they're getting rid of you."

She didn't know what to say. "They miss your dad. Maybe if they see him in you they feel better."

He was paying attention. *Please let me say the right thing.*

"Who you look like doesn't change the fact that you and I are a family. We love each other and are part of each other just like any family."

He nodded. "I like that it's the two of us together."

"I like that, too."

"It's too bad Prince Kit doesn't have backup."

"What?"

"Like you. When my mom and dad died, you were my backup. To be my family. If Kit had an aunt, maybe he wouldn't be stuck where he has to keep his magic a secret. Maybe his aunt would be magic like him."

She didn't know whether to laugh or cry. He was so matter-of-fact.

Jem looked at the ceiling, his eyes unfocused as he continued rolling the hem of his shirt. "You know what's weird, though? You don't have backup. You just have me. Wouldn't it be better for you to have someone else on your team?"

Was it possible for an eight-year-old to break her heart with a sports metaphor? She tugged on his foot, dragging him down the bed toward her. He sat up and she gathered him close.

"You're my team, Jem. You're all I need."

His arms went around her and squeezed. "I love you, Rhian. I won't ever leave you."

She squeezed him back, closing her eyes. When you were eight, you couldn't imagine college or a job or even liking girls, let alone marrying one. He'd leave, and while she hated thinking about it, it was right and good that he'd grow up and move out. If she did her job well, he'd go happily.

She rubbed her chin slowly across his silky hair.

After the hour was up and he'd run downstairs to meet

Min, Rhian pulled the quilt straight and then closed the door of his room. She moved across the second-floor landing, looking at the photos she'd displayed on the walls. She'd framed them all in simple, clean-lined wood frames in shades of blue.

Jem was right. He was everything she had. The people in the pictures from before his birth were dead—her mom, her sister, James, her own grandparents. Her father was dead, too, but he'd never been in any of the pictures. When he'd left, he'd left for good. Her mother had packed herself and her daughters up and moved closer to her own parents, cutting off all contact with her ex-husband's family. Her mother had dated more men than Rhian could remember. But not one of them had made it into the family photos. None of them had stuck around long enough to matter.

If she didn't have Jem, she'd have no one. Which was her choice. Had been her choice since Len. It was safer that way. So why did she have the scary feeling that Jem might have had a point?

NATHAN SAT at the folding table in his rented apartment and quietly but thoroughly ripped up yet another useless piece of junk he'd hoped might become the final chapters for his overdue book. He didn't know why he was even trying to write. It wasn't working today, it hadn't worked yesterday, the day before, or any day since Patricia had walked out six months ago. Leaving New Hampshire hadn't made a difference. He'd landed in Richwoods, hoping to get his life back on track. No such luck. Writing was bad and drawing was worse. It was possible he was going crazy.

He'd hoped the apartment would start to feel like home after a while. But it hadn't. Everything in it was temporary.

He'd shoved a folding table up against the big window of the sunny room that doubled as his living and dining room. The table itself worked overtime as his desk, eating surface and the only place to put a lamp.

There wasn't much else in the front room of the apartment—just an Adirondack chair with peeling paint he'd been given from the backyard of the first house he bid on to paint. He'd lost the bid but the owners had given him the chair and a wooden picnic bench that he sometimes thought of as a couch. The walls were a dingy cream color, filled with nail holes from past tenants. He could easily have bought anything he wanted, but he hadn't. Couldn't muster the interest.

When the phone rang, he jumped at the excuse to walk away from his work. He picked up his cell phone from the mattress on the floor.

"Hello?"

"Hey, it's Matt. You see that thing this morning?"

"Sadly, yes," Nathan replied. "Gave me the creeps."

"Thank God she did a crap job on the hair. She nailed your mouth, though. Weird, huh?"

Weird didn't begin to describe how he'd felt when that picture of someone who was both him and not him had flashed on the screen.

"She's not going to give up," Nathan said. "She's got too much invested in it now." Wandering into the front room, Nathan looked out at the empty street. This was all he'd ever wanted, to be himself, living a normal life in a quiet town. A family and some good friends, if he was lucky. He'd never asked to be famous. After the way his life had gone to hell because of the media in college, he'd retreated. Who would have thought that the comic book–inspired novel he'd dreamed up one night after too many beers with Matt would become this all-time sensation complete with crazy talk-show stalkers?

Matt sighed. "Patricia's the wild card. She's the only one besides me who knows everything. We have to hope she doesn't decide she wants Lindsey Hall's interview chair more than she wants your money."

Nathan's gut twisted. *Patricia missing out on the spotlight? Not likely.*

She'd walked out for good after a fight over his refusal to attend the premiere of the David Dale movie. She took with her the diamond and ruby engagement ring she'd designed for herself, all their household goods and every lick of furniture except the bed. He was beginning to suspect she'd also stolen his creativity, because he'd been unable to write or draw one useful thing since.

Nathan paced. It was exactly ten steps from his desk to the kitchen alcove and ten steps back. He'd walked this route over the past weeks when he couldn't sleep and couldn't work.

"You know what's weird? I don't miss her. We were together for two years and I don't miss her. How did I not see how wrong we were?"

Matt spoke quietly. "You wanted what you imagined she could give you. A family—kids."

"I guess neither of us got what we wanted. She wanted to be Mrs. Chris Senso."

"Her and half the women in America, including Lindsey Hall." Matt sighed. "We'll get through this. So far your money has Patricia happy enough." He paused and Nathan closed his eyes. He knew what was coming next. "Speaking of happy? Your editor? She isn't. She asked me to see how 'things' were going."

Nathan blew an exasperated breath into the phone, not caring if Matt heard it.

"Matt, you've called me every day this week and asked the same question," he snapped.

"I'll tell her it's going bad, huh?" Matt answered.

Nathan resisted the temptation to hang up. His editor was impatient for the book he owed her and he didn't blame her. The movie made of the second book was coming out in a matter of months and the fifth book in the series was supposed to be published shortly afterward. If he didn't get the ending nailed, that carefully orchestrated house of cards would come tumbling down.

"Why don't you tell her the ending I sent last month is the one I want to go with?"

Matt laughed nervously. "Because that's not true."

"No?"

"You can't kill David Dale and his dog. It's a kids' series."

"They're graphic novels, Matt. Maybe it's time for them to turn dark. You're the one who's always telling me more adults read them than kids anyway." He slumped onto the mattress and stretched out his legs in front of him.

"Come on, Nathan. It's not *X-Men*."

"The ending I sent is the only one I can write."

"Technically that's not true. You've written several endings. They just all include hideous deaths for your boy hero and the world's smartest, bravest crime-fighting dog."

Nathan sighed. One of the problems with Matt was he never took you up on an argument—he just kept coming back until you cooled down. "I liked the quicksand."

"Hamstrung on the volcano was my favorite."

"What about the smothering cloud of pine needles?"

"Inspired."

That stopped them. The death scenes had all been inspired. But useless.

"How's the housepainting?" Matt asked. "Still nothing in the fallback career?"

"I need to talk to you about that."

"You want to paint my house?"

"I don't do condos," Nathan said. "But I might have a shot at a house finally."

"You better not be asking me to help you sand."

"I want you to be my reference."

Matt snorted. "Your reference."

"Yeah, vouch for my work ethic."

"Can I mention that you're four months' late with your book?"

"Definitely not." Nathan stood and walked back to the living room. He glanced at the quote sheet where he'd recorded the details for Rhian's house. "The client's name is Rhian MacGregor. Tell her we used to be partners and I'm a good guy. Don't mention books."

"I hope the 'used to be' part of that isn't true."

"I want to finish the book, Matt. But I can't do the superhero thing when all I'm thinking about is how my fiancée left me and that damn Lindsey Hall." Nathan's voice matched the desperation he felt.

Matt sighed. "Talking about this book makes me crazy."

"Try sitting in a room alone with it."

Matt didn't respond right away. When he did, his voice was firm and deliberately upbeat. "There's your problem. Nathan. This is your agent speaking. You need to get out, mingle with people. Drink a beer. I'm giving you an assignment. For one hour this weekend I want you out with people, talking, being normal."

"What?" Sometimes Matt's conversational leaps were hard to follow.

"You're a hermit. A recluse. Next step is bag lady, or bag man, or whatever. You know what I mean. You need some normal in your life. Get your perspective back."

"I'm a hermit?" He wasn't even sure he knew why he was insulted by that.

"Tell me one person you spoke to this week."

"Rhian MacGregor."

"That was work. Give me another."

"I talk to people." The lady at the deli, the guy who had asked him how to get to Maple Street, the kid at the gas station who had to get a *Times* from the stockroom.

"So many people you've forgotten all their names?"

"Where exactly did you get your psychiatry degree?"

"This isn't psychiatry, Nathan. This is agenting. You need to finish your book. You can't because you're dwelling on this crap. So stop dwelling. Have fun. Then finish your book so I can help you collect the rest of your advance."

"You're insane."

"I'm calling on Monday and you better have a story to tell me and it better include beer and actual people with actual names. See you, buddy." Matt hung up.

Nathan stared blankly, holding the phone to his ear until it started beeping. He flipped it closed and set it on the worktable. He leaned over, arms spread, fists clenched on the edge of the table.

Hermit. Didn't Matt understand what it meant to be on the lam?

He stared at the papers in front of him. The worktable was littered with half-started sketches and sticky notes with scrawled ideas. The David Dale books were called graphic novels but they were novels more than comic books. A complex combination of drawings and text, words and pictures woven together to create a scene and a story in one. The focus was on the marriage of art and words. He'd made up his unique style as he wrote the first one, not knowing he was breaking the "rules" for the genre and winding up with a genre all his own.

Even though he'd written them for kids, there was a crossover market for adults and David Dale now had imitators—girl heroes, hero families, boys with different powers, even a dog hero. The first four books had come so easily, and he'd been working steadily through the series for the past eight years without wanting or needing a break.

He had two chapters, maybe three, left in this book. If he could get it done. Something was broken and he didn't know how to fix it.

THREE HOURS LATER, Nathan pulled into Rhian's driveway to deliver the quote. The first thing he saw was the ladder, once again overturned on the driveway. He slammed the door of the truck and was at the ladder in two strides. "Rhian!" he shouted, scanning the roofline. *Not again.*

The front door opened and she came around the house. The panic must have been obvious on his face because she glanced from him to the ladder and started laughing. "Did you honestly think—"

He spoke at the same time. "You said you would be on the ground when I got here."

"Well, I am."

"Barely," he muttered. "What were you doing today, installing a solar panel?"

She came to stand next to him and gestured into the

garage with a quick, irritated wave. "I wasn't *actually* doing anything. What I was *trying* to do was put up that damn basketball hoop."

A tangle of plastic wrap and cardboard packaging stretched across the floor of the garage.

He squinted. "Is that a basketball hoop?"

"At this point, I'm not sure. It might be a very dirty trick perpetrated on me by the sporting goods industry. The directions make absolutely no sense."

He smiled as he walked over and poked at the wrapping with his foot. "Looks like a hoop to me. A better question is what are you doing with it?"

"Would you believe that I want to learn to play basketball?"

He only glanced over because she sounded so embarrassed. But he found himself noticing her, the flush staining her cheekbones, the way her body, slightly less than average height, was trim and athletic looking in jeans and a yellow tank top. Her blond hair was cut above her shoulders and was adorably messy, with soft waves around her ears and in the back. The pink in her cheeks set off the bright blue of her eyes. He itched for a sketch pad, wishing he could draw her. Her coloring was delicately beautiful.

"You need about eighteen more inches if you're thinking about a career switch."

She stretched up on tiptoes, raising her chin to his chest level. "I might be short but I'm tough. Couldn't I be one of those scrappy little guys?"

He laughed. "Rhian, even those scrappy little guys are over six feet."

She crossed her arms on her chest. "Someone watches ESPN."

"I used to play." He squatted and pulled some of the papers aside to get a better look at the backboard kit. "In fact, I've installed a few hoops in my day. My tools are in my truck. Shouldn't take longer than twenty minutes or so."

He straightened with the instruction sheet in his hand and started making a mental list of what he'd need. When her silence registered, he turned to her. She had one hand up to her mouth and her eyes were bright with tears. *Shit. She was crying. What the hell made her do that?* She turned away and he stood still, horrified by her tears.

"I'm sorry." She stood half-facing him. Her voice was muffled as she scrubbed one hand across her mouth and up. "It's so stupid. I've been trying to get this hoop up for two weeks. I have a picture in my mind of how happy Jem will be when he sees it, but I couldn't do it. Today's his last day before he leaves for the summer and then you said—" She took a breath. "Twenty minutes and, well, twenty minutes would be wonderful. I mean, your help would be amazing." Her face was flushed. "This is ridiculous. I don't usually cry."

She was so vulnerable, embarrassed, pathetic and grateful. It would be a small step to offer her comfort, but there was too much between them—Lindsey Hall, Patricia, Chris Senso, hiding out, running away. He couldn't do it. Stick with the practicalities. Get the hoop up. He made himself step away instead of toward her as he said, "It sucks to want something and not be able to do it. Believe me, I know."

She shook her head, her eyes shining with tears. "I can't imagine that. I just met you and you've already rescued me twice." She sniffed and wiped her eyes again.

He was glad to see the tears were under control. That

hadn't been so bad. "No problem." He folded the directions and stuck them in his back pocket. "I'll grab a few tools from the truck and get this thing up."

As he walked past, she reached for his hand and squeezed it. "I don't know how to thank you."

Keep it nonchalant, Delaney. She's grateful, you're helpful. That's it. He eased his hand from hers, putting space between them. "Invite me over for a pickup game sometime. We'll see if I can take on an eight-year-old and a scrappy little guy."

"You're on!" Rhian's face lit up with fun. "Hey, we're having a party tonight, a barbecue, nothing fancy. Jem's going on vacation and it's a farewell. Can you stay? If you don't have other plans?"

His pulse jumped. Plans. His only plans involved going back to his crappy apartment and staring at his crappy book. Matt's voice was in his head. Hermit. Bag lady.

Shut up, Matt.

What Matt didn't take into account in his stupid therapy plan was that Nathan needed to stay hidden. He couldn't risk getting involved. "Um. Maybe." He shrugged. "Let's get the hoop up."

He opened the toolbox and laid out his tool belt. Rhian stood next to him, watching. "You can bring someone. If there's someone you'd like to bring. Your girlfriend?"

She was curious. Damn. When had this changed from a painting job to…whatever this was? He pulled his drill and the box of bits out and put them in his belt. "Thanks." So what if he didn't deny the girlfriend? An omission wasn't a lie.

THREE MINUTES LATER the two of them were standing outside the garage, hoisting the ladder into place.

Rhian wondered what the hell she was doing. She'd been about to give up on the hoop and giving Jem this present he'd love. But then Nathan came along and everything was better. Which was a good thing and a bad thing and also a confusing thing. Again. *Rats.*

Why couldn't she be good at tool stuff? Then she wouldn't have had to ask him to help. She *hated* feeling incompetent. She'd accepted Nathan's help because…what other choice did she have? But in return, she needed to convince him to stay for the barbecue. She'd repay him with cupcakes. It was plain good manners.

"Handyman Delaney at your service, ma'am." Nathan bowed and grinned that fantastic grin at her and then paused at the bottom of the ladder. Although it didn't seem possible, the tool belt around his waist made him sexier. As if he'd needed to be sexier. As if he needed an amazing smile. As if he weren't already the basketball-hoop hero and so damn good-looking it was a joke. Suddenly it was too much for her.

"I'm having second thoughts about asking you to help. I mean, we just met, and if this is an imposition, will you say so and we'll forget it?" she called up to him.

"Halfway up the ladder is too late for second thoughts, Rhian." He didn't look down at her, just kept climbing steadily till he reached the roof. "Anyway, it sounds like your nephew has a basketball obsession that needs to be fed."

"Is that the voice of experience?"

"I'll confess to a youthful obsession," he admitted.

The garage roof had a flat edge near the front. She watched Nathan's easy competence as he hoisted the brace up and positioned it in the right spot. He moved deftly and called instructions to her when he needed help. He was patient but quick and knew exactly what to do with all the metal and wooden bits. He even figured out where to put each item from the pile of parts she'd set aside because she was sure they were extra. Turned out they did have a function.

"You really know what you're doing." She had paused on the top rung after handing him a screwdriver.

He sat back on his heels and pushed his hair off his face. When he tumbled and tugged the soft waves it looked sexier. Rhian's fingers curled harder around the ladder. When she'd touched his hand before, she'd been shocked by how badly she'd wanted to step in and wrap her arms around him.

He tightened the last bolt and then leaned out to untangle the net but the angle was awkward and he couldn't get the last stubborn loop. "Oh, come on," he said. Glancing back he asked, "Would you hang on to my feet?"

Touch him. Hang on to was a synonym for touch. Okay.

She put her hands on his calves, above the tops of his work boots. Through his jeans, she felt his muscles tense under her palms, and she bit her lip. He was rock solid.

He glanced over his shoulder and raised his eyebrows. "You need a better grip if you're going to save me. You're already down three rescues to one. If you drop me you'll never catch up."

She tightened her grip and her stomach swooped even as she concentrated on keeping her hands steady. *Just hold. Do not caress the housepainter.*

He twisted to get a better angle on the basket and his legs shifted so she had to lean closer to him and then suddenly he was swinging back. "Got it." He grinned. "You can let go now."

"Right." She jerked her hands away. It had been so long

since she'd been this close to a man who wasn't someone else's husband or some kid's father.

"Thanks. You hold on very nicely."

She bent her head not wanting him to see her blush, and went down the ladder. She was taking a basketball out of the box when he came down. She didn't know how it had happened, but it seemed her body had developed the ability to sense him. She could feel him behind her without looking. It was a good thing her brain was in charge and not her body because her brain knew she couldn't get involved with this man, psychic-body-sensing powers or not. She had Jem to think about. He was her number-one priority. No matter what her heart or her body said.

CHAPTER FOUR

"PASS IT TO ME, Rhian," he called from behind her. His voice was so warm she grinned despite herself as she stood. He'd put his tool belt down inside the garage door and was standing under the basket with his hands out. She passed the ball to him and he caught it and dribbled it a few times before tossing it back. She dropped it and watched it roll under his truck. She went over to get it out, but he jogged up to her and put his hand on her shoulder. "You don't want to get under there. This is why you hire handymen."

He got down on his knees to reach for the ball and she sucked in a quiet breath. He was so kind. Stupid Len would never have done things for her because he wanted to. He hadn't done much even when she asked.

Nathan straightened up with the ball in his hand. "Ready to christen the hoop?" he asked.

She looked doubtfully at the ball. "You mean, shoot it and make it go in?"

He smiled. "Exactly."

"Want to and can are two different things. How about you take the first shot so we don't start out with bad luck when I break a window?"

He shrugged and shifted the ball in his hands. Then it was like he snapped to attention. Or like the ball did. Every step he took made perfect, fluid sense and the ball responded. He dribbled past her, held up and sank a jump shot. When the ball swished through the net Rhian let out the breath she hadn't known she was holding. She cheered as she retrieved the ball and threw it back to him.

"Do it again!" she commanded.

He grinned, did a quick spin, put the ball through his legs, drove toward the basket and pulled up short to toss in another jumper. He grabbed the rebound, dribbled back a few steps, put the ball behind his back and shot it over his head into the basket.

Rhian whistled as she threw the ball to him again. "Where'd you learn to play?"

"My dad." He kept dribbling and shooting as he answered, only vaguely aware of her—he was in another world. "He loved basketball. It was one of the few things we enjoyed together."

"Looks like you love it, too." She definitely loved watching him play. He was built for the game, tall and strong, and his reflexes were like lightning. When he stopped and spun, she relished the tight control of his muscles and she envied the ball. *Envied the ball? Get a grip, Rhian.*

"Did you play in high school?"

"Captain of the Northside Blues." His voice held a touch of honest pride.

Rhian watched him move from point to point around the driveway, easily making every shot. Clearly he'd spent a lot of time doing this.

For the first time in her life Rhian wished she could have been a cheerleader, specifically for the Northside Blues. It would have been heaven to watch him play on a Friday night in a packed gym. It was heaven watching him in her driveway.

"Captain, huh? What about college?"

He shook his head and moved past her for a layup. "I quit after my freshman year."

"But you did play in college?" This was amazing. He must have been really great. "Where did you go?"

"After I quit basketball I transferred to the Rhode Island School of Design. That's where my degree is from."

He hadn't actually answered her question, which had been about where he played basketball. If he wanted to skip that part she wouldn't push. "I'm guessing the Rhode Island School's not a place that has a basketball team?"

"They do sort of, but I didn't play." His tone had changed subtly and she sensed there was a story he wasn't telling.

"I've never done anything as gracefully as you do this."

"I'm just a housepainter who can beat most people at HORSE."

Rhian stood up and moved closer to the basket, catching his rebounds and passing them back to him. "Um. HORSE?"

Nathan groaned and stopped shooting, holding the ball between his hip and his bent elbow. "How are you going to learn to play basketball if you don't even know about HORSE?"

She smiled sheepishly. He'd worked up a sweat as he shot. Standing close to him, she felt the warmth from his skin and smelled the wonderful combination of fresh cotton, clean skin and layered faintly under that, sweat. It was a tremendously masculine scent.

Her mouth was open and she shut it quickly. Nathan edged closer. She knew he'd noticed her staring.

He took a quick step back and smiled. "Remedial basketball, for all the people who skipped gym in grade school." He tossed the ball from one hand to the other while he spoke. "HORSE is the most basic of hoop-oriented time wasters. I take a shot and if I make it, you have to try the same one. If you miss, you get an H and so on. First one who gets *H, O, R, S, E* loses. See?"

"Spelling. I'm good at that." Rhian put her hand out for the ball. "I'm demanding the first turn."

He held out the ball to her but when she reached for it, he didn't let go. "Demand what you want, Rhian, you're going to need all the help you can get."

There was his wonderful deep laugh again. He was so easy to be with. They laughed at the same things. She didn't even mind making a fool of herself with him. She would like him as a friend, if only her body didn't attempt to complicate things.

She tried to concentrate on how he held the ball and other basketball-related insights, but somehow her main impression was that the man really knew how to wear a pair of jeans.

AFTER HE TROUNCED her in the first game of HORSE he offered a rematch, but she said she needed to get changed before the party.

Why was he disappointed? He put the ball down near the garage door. "Let me give you your quote and I'll get out of here."

"You're sure you can't stay?" she asked quietly.

He reached in the driver's window of his truck and grabbed an envelope off the dashboard. He'd be lying if he said he didn't want to stay. He'd enjoyed their game—way more than he was willing to admit. She was easy to be with, funny, unselfconscious about her lack of skills and normal. She treated him like an ordinary person and he'd relaxed with every minute of the game. But he couldn't get involved. To keep his identity secret he had to be alone. *Thanks for teaching me that, Patricia.*

She took the envelope from him and tapped it against her palm, unopened. "There'll be people here from town. Maybe you can network. Call it a business dinner?"

Was that how he looked to her? Like a guy who had to be persuaded to come to a party by treating it like work? Was Matt right? Was workaholic as sad as hermit? He pushed his hand through his hair, hating that Lindsey Hall and her stupid search had made his life into this narrow cage where all he had left was a book he couldn't write.

"All right." He shrugged. "It sounds fun." If he'd never written a book, if he was still just plain Nathan Delaney, he'd never have hesitated. He liked parties. He'd always thought he'd live in a town like Richwoods with his family and have barbecues with the neighbors. Instead he'd become Chris Senso and started hiding from life. No one here knew anything about that. If anyone got suspicious he could be on the road in half an hour. So screw Lindsey Hall. Screw Patricia. Screw Chris Senso. Tonight he was Nathan Delaney. He'd hang out, drink a beer, prove he wasn't a hermit or a workaholic, have the life he wanted to have and let the rest of it go to hell.

RHIAN LEFT Nathan relaxing in the side yard with a bottle of Harp and a platter of nachos—yes, with the homemade guacamole—while she went upstairs to dress for the party before Min and Jem came home. She wanted to be outside when Jem got there so she could see his face when he saw the hoop. She was passing through the kitchen when the phone rang. "Hello?"

"Rhian MacGregor?" The voice was unfamiliar.

"Yes?"

"Matt Callahan. You left a message about Nathan Delaney?"

It was The Reference. She'd forgotten about him. "Thanks for returning my call. I'm hoping to hire Nathan to paint my house."

"Well, they don't come better than Nathan. Kind of a perfectionist, but he's so damn good at most things it's not a problem for him." Matt chuckled.

Were references supposed to make fun of the referencee?

"Have you known him long?"

"Worked together for years. I haven't seen him in a while. Not since he took off. I mean, relocated."

She hadn't prepared for this conversation, partly because she didn't want to have it. She wanted to believe that Nathan was okay even though he must be at least thirty and had no steady job. Even though he had just this one reference who was alternating between singing his praises and dropping unsettling phrases like "took off" into the conversation.

"I'm sorry. Did you say 'took off'?"

"No." Matt's voice was muffled as if he'd put his hand over the phone. "I said relocated. I, listen, Ms. MacGregor, we have a really bad connection."

She heard a click and the call was over. *That hadn't helped.* It was clear that she couldn't hire Nathan. He wasn't a painter. His reference was no good. She was sure she'd heard the words "took off" no matter what Matt Callahan said.

But how did she reconcile those facts with the other things she knew? He was kind. He was competent. He seemed nice and normal. He knew his way around a set of tools. He was able to use a ladder. He was her only hope for salvaging her house this summer. He wore his jeans *very* well.

She'd decide in the morning. If it turned out that she wasn't going to hire him, she couldn't tell him now. No sense in worrying about it until she could do something about it.

EVEN WITHOUT an entrée on the buffet, Rhian's party was a smash. The right weather, the right people, and suddenly it was a night for memories.

The hoop was an enormous success, and not just with Jem, who was as over-the-top delirious as Rhian had hoped. Shortly after James's family parked their RV, spilling kids and grown-ups full of road-trip energy, the party had shifted to the hoop. The side yard had been lined with lawn chairs filled with spectators cheering on, well, actually *egging* on, the players in a seriously irreverent game of HORSE. Many a wager had been won and lost before the game ended.

Nathan, Jem, and Jem's Aunt Anne were the only ones left in the game, when Chet, who owned the bar and pizza place where they spent every Friday night, bet Rhian that Jem would win. She backed Nathan. She felt disloyal, but she'd seen the guy play. It was an obvious win and she had something she wanted from Chet. If Nathan won the game Chet would buy a new apron and allow her to burn the grungy one he'd had since she moved to Richwoods. Chet's fries with cheese and gravy were almost as important to Rhian as breathing, but the state of that apron had a lowering effect on her enjoyment. If Jem won the game, Rhian would take a waitress shift at Chet's place during the Friday rush.

She didn't know whether to be pleased for Jem or mad

at herself for being dumb enough to bet against him as she watched Nathan ruthlessly crush Aunt Anne and then throw the game, in a very eight-year-old-pride-saving way to Jem. She was sure Jem didn't notice Nathan's maneuvers, but she did. She'd try to remember Jem's overjoyed face when she was slinging French fries and draft beer at Chet's some Friday.

AFTER THE GAME, the kids stayed at the hoop, messing around. Nathan had produced an extra ball from the back of his truck and the Ohio contingent had brought two of their own. Things devolved into a shooting free-for-all.

The grown-ups drifted into the yard, clumping around the picnic table lined with food and the patio, where Min had set up a dessert table and coolers full of beer and other drinks.

Rhian swung on the hammock, kicking her foot gently off the ground when it slowed. She was taking a breather while she decided if she should make more guacamole. Actually, she was savoring. Savoring the night and the party and her friends and family. She wanted to feel this way forever.

There were so many things she wished she could do for Jem. She'd wanted to give him the hoop but had almost decided it would never happen. Then Nathan fixed it. The same way he fixed it so Jem won the game. Jem hadn't put the ball down all night. When she forced him into a chair to eat dinner he'd sat on top of the ball, perched like a leprechaun on a pot of gold.

Cindy and Ned Charles, parents of one of Jem's friends, came over to say goodbye. They were going to extricate their son from the party because they were leaving early in the morning for their own vacation on the Jersey shore.

When Cindy leaned down to kiss Rhian on the cheek, she whispered in her ear, "Nathan is such a great guy. Good luck!"

Rhian was shocked. Did Cindy think she and Nathan were, well, together? There'd been that moment earlier, when she'd come outside and he was on the patio. She'd felt so oddly exposed when he was looking at her, she'd wanted to check that she hadn't forgotten to button her shirt or something. But one moment didn't mean anything. She glanced around and saw that Nathan was out of earshot, near the kids in the driveway. "Good luck with what?"

Her friend glanced at her husband and they shared a sly smile. "With Nathan, of course."

Rhian frowned. She couldn't believe this. Cindy and Ned were so normal. Such good parents. "You think I'm going to pursue a stranger who came to paint my house?"

"When you put it that way it sounds sketchy, but—" Cindy shrugged.

Ned, one arm around Cindy, said, "You should take a shot."

Why did people keep telling her to take a shot? Her life was not a basketball game. Couldn't they see she couldn't do random hookups?

Rhian spoke quickly and firmly. "I know if you didn't have Ned you wouldn't expose Brandon to just random men, dates."

Cindy held up a hand. "The way you say 'dates' it sounds like you mean rabid wolves."

"I don't think 'dates' are fair to a kid who's lost so much."

Cindy shrugged again and took Ned's hand in hers. "Well, you're the one who has to make that decision. But

I can tell you that if I were single, and Nathan Delaney was painting my house, I would definitely consider a few dates, rabid wolves be damned. What can it hurt? Especially if Jem's off on his baseball tour of North America?"

"Oh." She'd been so busy *not* thinking about Jem's vacation that the mention of it made her heart sink.

Standing up, Rhian drew them both into a hug. "Maybe I'll drop by the playground this summer. Meet you and Brandon on the basketball court."

Cindy laughed. Ned crossed his fingers as if to ward off witchcraft. "Don't you dare step foot on the playground until Jem comes home." They started off to collect Brandon but Cindy turned back. "Enjoy your time to be yourself. You deserve it."

By herself. On her own.

Min hugged them as she saw them go by. Then she came up to Rhian, carrying two bottles of beer. She sat in a lawn chair pulled close to the hammock, handed one bottle to Rhian and opened the other for herself. "Are Cindy and Ned consumed with envy over your summer of freedom?" she asked.

Rhian was having trouble speaking. The blood was pounding in the back of her head. "They were trying to get me to date Nathan." Rhian flapped her hand toward the driveway where the rhythmic thud of the basketball continued. "Because Jem won't be here."

"Kind of throws a monkey wrench into your 'protect the kid' objection, huh?"

"Just because Jem's going away doesn't mean I should turn my whole lifestyle upside down. I mean, I'm not going to take up stock-car driving."

"I know Stupid Len hurt you," Min said. "But he's not

a good example of a man. And since him you haven't given anyone else a chance. A couple of dates with Randy and even fewer with that other guy, who wasn't even cute but that's beside the point." She touched Rhian's foot. "Honestly, Rhian, you have issues about being left and you're hiding behind Jem. You're saying you're protecting him but from where I'm sitting you're using him as an excuse. You're scared for yourself as much as for him."

Rhian didn't like the phrase "shut up." but right now she was sorely tempted.

"We should stop talking about this before one of us says something we regret. I don't want either of us to get hurt."

Min let out an exasperated breath. "Stop talking so we don't get hurt. Stop dating so Jem doesn't get hurt. Stop living so no one gets hurt. Life doesn't work that way."

Rhian closed her eyes. Min was her best friend. She'd learned to trust her. Min hardly ever raised her voice; when she did, Rhian listened. When she opened her eyes, Min's expression was hopeful.

"Okay," Rhian said. "I'm not saying this is true, but if you were right and it would be okay to date Nathan this summer, wouldn't he have to be interested in me? I mean, he hasn't said anything to make me think…"

Min smirked. "Who are you and what have you done with my friend Rhian? My Rhian wouldn't wait for a man to ask her out. Go get him if you want him." She slapped Rhian lightly on the leg and walked away.

Rhian stayed in the hammock a few more minutes, eyes closed, beer bottle resting against her bottom lip. Then she got up to go talk to Nathan. Which she was only doing to be polite. A good hostess checks on her guests. It was in *Emily Post.*

She would see if he was having a good time while she decided if she was in the market for a good time.

NATHAN WAS TAKING a breather. The kids had run him ragged on the court for the better part of an hour, and he'd sneaked off to have a beer and another one of Rhian's homemade cupcakes. He was having a great time. The kid, Rhian's nephew, was a trip. His face when he saw the hoop…God, he'd looked reverent. Jem and his friends had taken Nathan right back to his playground days when basketball was pure fun. He should see if he could find a rec league in Richwoods—hanging out with guys on the court again might feel good. It had been too long.

How had he spent so much of his life so isolated? His house in New Hampshire was far removed from his neighbors. He'd never had a party like this.

He took another bite of the cupcake and leaned his head against the frame of the lawn chair. He noticed Rhian, weaving through the party guests, looking for someone. Looking for him, he guessed when she spotted him and her path became purposeful.

He finished the cupcake and lifted his beer bottle toward her. "Cheers to the cook," he said as she sat down in the chair next to him.

"If I could make cupcakes for every meal I'd do okay," she answered.

She was perched on the edge of the chair, her weight shifted forward so the back legs of the chair were raised off the ground. Definitely not relaxed. What could be bugging her? As far as he could tell the party was perfect. He'd been fascinated to see how her effortless hospitality and genuine nature had drawn together the disparate elements of town friends, Min's school friends and the out-of-town relatives. She made people feel at home, valued and included. Matt had been right. He needed a dose of normal in his life. Staying had been a good idea.

"What's up?" he asked.

She shifted. "What? Nothing." Rocking the chair back and forth she looked at him and then away. "Um, your reference called before. And I looked at the bid. It's fine. So if you want to do it, I mean, the painting, that would be great."

Which was weird because Matt was positive he'd messed up.

"Good. Great."

"Good." She put the chair back down all the way and leaned toward him. She licked her lips and he stared, fascinated by the small gesture, by the glimpse of tongue. If he was going to be working on her house day in and day out he'd have to get himself under control. But tonight, in the gathering darkness, with the pleasant hum of the party around them, he let himself indulge. Monday he could resist staring.

She looked as if she was going to reach out to him and his nerves tingled in anticipation, but she didn't move. "I'm glad you stayed," she said. "It's nice."

Nice wasn't the word he'd use for the sparks jumping between them, but before he could answer, he heard a shout.

"Rhian!" Jem ran up and stopped in front of her chair. "Check it out!"

With two fingers, the boy was holding out the hem of the bright orange T-shirt he was wearing. Shocked, Nathan saw it was a knockoff of the shirts Lindsey Hall was giving away. He felt like he'd been punched in the chest. His breath caught as a tight band grabbed his lungs, stealing his air, ripping through the closeness he'd felt with Rhian a moment before.

Block letters printed across the chest declared "I Want My Chris Senso" and underneath was the age-progression picture made from his author photo. The picture had been redrawn in a more graphic style, close to the method he used in David Dale, and the hair had been changed to a big curly Afro style. It was still clearly the same picture, however, and still clearly horrifying.

Min joined Jem. Her shirt was bright pink, and the cartoon Nathan had a beehive hairdo. She had a stack of shirts over her right arm and she tossed one to Rhian as she put her other arm around Jem. "Aren't these hilarious?"

Nathan stood up. He felt disoriented, like he was drunk, and although he'd had three beers, it wasn't alcohol making his head spin. He couldn't believe that this, the chase, the hunt, was here. These people who'd been so astoundingly normal and welcoming, were involved, were treating his nightmare as a joke. He felt sick.

Rhian caught the shirt Min threw and held it up. It was turquoise and the character's hair was long, ropy, Tarzan-style strands. "They're a riot, Min. Who made them?" she asked as she stood up.

"Tara and Neil. I told them about the one we saw on TV and they grabbed the picture off the Lindsey Hall site. I like the hair on yours the best."

"But mine's the closest to what he probably really looks like—the picture on the books has curly hair," Jem protested.

Rhian pulled her shirt on over her checked blouse and then turned to Nathan. "Have you been following this Chris Senso thing? On *Morning Lindsey?*"

She looked so happy, a woman enjoying a good joke.

She had no idea. None of them did. How could they? He had been a fool, a stupid goddamn idiot to think for even one minute he could be here, could be normal. He'd enjoyed himself so much he'd forgotten what he was doing. Forgotten who he was and why he was in Richwoods.

"You want one?" Min flipped through the shirts on her arm. "I think there are some XLs in here. Which hair do you like best? There's one with dreadlocks."

"No. No thanks. I have to go." He set his empty beer bottle down on the table next to him. "Thanks. For everything."

"You're leaving?" Rhian asked.

He nodded. He felt like a jackass when he saw her confusion. It wasn't her fault Lindsey Hall had decided to use his personal life as a springboard to a summer ratings boost. "See you, Jem. Nice to meet you, Min. Good luck with everything. Thanks for the party, Rhian." He raised his hand and then spun around, cutting his way through the party guests. He had to get into his truck, had to get away so he could breathe again.

"Nathan, wait." He heard Rhian following him. He didn't turn around until he was three steps from the truck. He hit the button on his keychain and the lock beeped. She caught up to him and asked, "What just happened?"

If he kept his gaze on her face he wouldn't see the shirt. But he'd see her eyes, see the puzzlement and growing hurt there and know it had been caused by him.

"Nothing. I remembered I have to be somewhere."

Somewhere far from here.

"Are you sure? Because you seem upset."

He couldn't stand there for one more second. Even if he didn't look at it, he knew she had that shirt on. She'd watched Lindsey Hall. Laughed about the hunt. He'd been kidding himself if he'd thought for one second there could be something between them. He was on the run and she was on the other side.

"Nothing's wrong. I should have left a while ago. It's late."

He could tell she didn't believe him but at that moment he didn't care.

"Okay. But painting, is Monday okay?"

Crap. Painting. Two hours ago he'd have jumped at the chance. Hell, yesterday he'd told her he'd do it for free. But that was before. If she was watching the show and following the hunt he wasn't safe. He couldn't stand to be there every day seeing her and knowing he couldn't talk to her, couldn't get to know her.

"I can't." He needed a lie. But he hated lying and he couldn't make himself do it now. Not to Rhian.

"Can't?" She looked confused. She had every right to be confused. There was no explanation. Except the truth and he couldn't tell her that.

"I have to leave town." He hadn't known he was going to say that but after he did, it seemed right. He'd move on, find some place new. Not make the mistake of getting involved. "I'm sorry about the house. But you'll find someone."

He watched the thoughts roll across her face. Her eyes flicked from the yard to him. He needed to be gone before she started asking questions…or asking him to stay.

"But there isn't anyone else. You said you would do it. You gave me your reference." She lifted her hands and then let them fall back to her sides. "I don't understand. If it's the free thing, don't worry. I was planning to pay you."

"No. I can't stay." He climbed into the truck, pausing before he closed the door. "Thanks for the party, Rhian. It was great. You have a nice family. A nice life." He slammed the door and pulled out, willing himself not to look back. He didn't want to know if she was watching him leave. He didn't want to see what he was leaving behind.

THE PARTY WAS WINDING down. Rhian was lying in the hammock again, cradling a plastic cup of orange soda and a final cupcake—a sugary fix she'd hoped would cheer her up but it wasn't working. After Nathan left, everything had gone flat.

Why had he left? Could he have sensed she was considering the possibility that she might, just might, want to date him? Was it possible she'd driven the man out of town with her interest?

Min came up and sat down in the grass close to the hammock. She put her arms behind her and stretched her neck back. "Quite a party, huh?" She rolled her head from side to side. "You figure out what happened with your painter?"

"I think I scared him."

Min sat up and crossed her legs. "What did you do that was scary?"

Rhian thought back. "Nothing. At least nothing I can figure out. Maybe I give off a scary vibe."

"Your vibes are very nice." Min reached out her pink sneaker and gently rocked the hammock with her toe. "Don't second-guess your vibes because of some schmuck."

"Well, the vibes are one thing and then there's the other thing which is I don't think I can stand to live here with the house looking so horrible."

"It's just paint, Rhian."

"I know but it's my *home* and it looks like I don't love it."

Jem ran up and flopped next to her and some of her soda sloshed onto the hammock near her hair. He patted the soda, pushing it into the hammock, getting his hand sticky in the process. "Sorry about that," he said.

She pushed his hand away, trying not to let him know he was making it worse. "Don't worry about it, buddy."

He lay next to her, chin propped on his hands, a faint orange mustache shadowing his upper lip. "Tomorrow's the day." Yawning, he put his head down. He was sweaty and smelled of the outdoors and boy. Rhian's throat felt tight. The house was going to be so empty without him and Min.

"Let's head in, little man."

They walked slowly to the house, Jem in the middle, Rhian and Min with their arms twined around his shoulders. Rhian didn't allow herself to think, ruthlessly shoving upsetting thoughts down as fast as they tried to surface. Instead she watched the rise and fall of her white sneakers and Jem's bought new for the trip. *No. Don't think about the trip.* She stared harder at the ground. Min's pink Converse flashed into view every few steps. *These two people are all I need*, she thought. And yet, somehow, again, she wasn't going to be allowed to have the family she'd found for herself. Min was leaving and there was nothing she could do, nothing she even should do, to make her stay. Jem was growing up, needing her less every year, and again, there was nothing she would change. She'd scared away her housepainter before she'd sorted out her feelings about a fling, let alone been able to start having one. And before one brushful of paint had been put on the house. Maybe Min was right and she had nice vibes but right then, Rhian was pretty sure the only vibe she had was a lonely one.

SUNDAY MORNING they were all up early to let the RV trip get on the road. The first stop was Cooperstown and the Baseball Hall of Fame and then Pittsburgh for a Pirates-Mets home game on Monday.

Jem bumped his duffel bag down the steps and dragged it across the hardwood floor to the front door. She unzipped the bag and laid his washed and folded Pirates T-shirt on top. "I gave your grandpa some money in case you need anything. You might want to buy another Pirates shirt—save you having to wash this one all the time." Or wear it dirty, which seemed far more likely. She zipped the bag back up.

Jem's eyes were shaded by the brim of his black Pirates cap. She pushed it back and searched his face, trying to see what he needed from her. If he was sure about this trip she wouldn't let him see that she was worried. Her boy. How was she supposed to say goodbye?

He flung himself at her, wrapping his arms around her waist, pressing his face to her shirt. She held him tight.

"Don't be sad, Rhian," he said. "I'll be home soon."

Her breath caught. He wasn't sad about leaving; he was worried about her.

"I'm not sad, honey. Well, I am sad, but I'm happy, too." She squeezed him and then slid him around so he was tucked under her arm. "This trip is your adventure. You couldn't skip it. I don't want you to."

She realized that was the truth. She was okay with him going. She scooped up the strap of his bag and looped it across her shoulder. Jem pushed the screen door open and they went down the steps and around to the RV. She kissed him again and held him in a long hug and then he was up the steps and waving from the window.

Sooner than she was ready they were gone, the RV backing down the driveway and then pulling away with a beep.

Min had already left for the university that morning. She'd needed to meet with another student who had an early flight. When Rhian went back inside, the house was perfectly still and quiet. She puttered around trying to savor the alone time and failing utterly.

RHIAN WAS READING in bed when Jem called that night. They'd reached Pittsburgh and were staying in a hotel with a swimming pool. He'd sounded tired but happy. After she hung up, she left the phone on the pillow next to her. She knew he was fine, but what if he called back and she didn't hear the phone?

Min came home around ten, full of last-minute details about her summer project at U.V. She'd be trying to identify the artist who'd done five Civil War–era canvases. The paintings were owned by an elderly woman from Roanoke who swore that two of them were by Thomas Moran. Min's group had found new evidence and she was so excited she'd made herself exhausted. She went off to her room, vowing to sleep for ten hours straight.

Eventually the emptiness of the house overwhelmed Rhian. She dozed uneasily with the beside lamp on the whole night.

CHAPTER FIVE

RHIAN GOT TO HER desk early on Monday morning. From long experience with Min's pretrip frenzies, Rhian did not expect to see her before dinner.

She tried to get started. She and Jem had been exploring the world of Prince Kit for three years. She should have no trouble figuring out what to write. She had a stack of blank note cards to outline the chapters and a selection of colored pens to make her notes more orderly.

The only thing missing was, well, the ability to start. And confidence. And belief that this was the right thing to do for herself at this moment. Why had she ever thought she could write fiction again? Her magazine work was a million years ago. Hadn't she been a different person then?

She pushed her chair back in disgust. Breakfast first and then work. Always best to start on a full stomach.

In the kitchen she grabbed a bowl and some cereal and then flipped on the TV. Anything so she didn't have to think about writing. Lindsey Hall was on. Rhian heard the name David Dale so she turned up the volume.

Seated at her desk, Lindsey was surrounded by copies of the David Dale books. She performed her trademark hair flip as she spoke into the camera. "Chris Senso is on my mind. From the volume of e-mail and calls to the hotline, he's on yours, as well." She waved her hand to indicate the stacks of books. "Normally finding an author who uses a pseudonym is easy. You look at the copyright page and ta-da! The real name." She opened the book she held and tapped the page with one long, red nail. Was she channeling Sherlock Holmes? Rhian was waiting to hear her say "elementary."

"Unfortunately we are discovering that Chris Senso is not your average shy author. His real name is not on the copyright page. The copyright is held by Two Guys Incorporated. The incorporation documents for that company are sealed."

The Hall Heads booed, but Rhian was impressed. It sure sounded as if Chris Senso didn't want to be found. As much as she was curious about the guy she was rooting for him to beat Lindsey.

The TV host leaned toward the camera and winked. "I will not let Mr. Senso deny us the pleasure of meeting him. Which brings me to our two special guests."

Reaching behind her desk, she brought out a cardboard silhouette of a man and propped it in the velvet guest chair closest to her desk. The cutout had the age-progression picture superimposed on its head and a David Dale book taped to its hands. "This fellow will keep Chris's space warm until the real thing shows up." Lindsey smiled seductively, slid a thin arm around the cardboard neck and lowered her voice to say, "Chris Senso, whoever you are and wherever you are, your public awaits you."

She kissed the cardboard cheek, leaving a bright red lipstick print before turning and blowing a kiss to the audience. Her lips and nails were the same hard red—sleek and scary.

"Our other guest is more animated. Let's welcome Anthony Redding, former FBI profiler and current author of the 'Inside Agency' novels."

A short man wearing a dark suit came out and allowed himself to be kissed by Lindsey. His hair was buzzed close and his glasses were serious. He looked exactly like a science teacher from the 1950s. Or like an FBI profiler.

"Anthony. You have expertise on both sides of this question, as a professional tracker and as a professional author, correct?"

"Yes. The anonymous author has done a good job hiding his legal footprints, but the personal information every author stamps on their work is harder to conceal."

"For example?"

"The easiest detail was age. Chris Senso is between twenty-eight and thirty-five, probably at the upper end. We know he published the first book eight years ago so ruling out a prodigy we'll say he must have been at least twenty. Using the text, noting the cultural references, David Dale's sense of humor, the way David thinks about family and popular culture and heroes, indicates that the author grew up in the seventies, definitely post-Vietnam, post-Watergate."

"Fascinating. What else?" Lindsey breathed.

"Language analysis gives a ninety percent certainty that the author is from the North, white, college educated." The man paused. "We can run some more regressions and probably come up with better details, religious background, ethnicity, etc."

"You're very good," Lindsey said, drawling the words appreciatively. The Hall Heads let out a few suggestive whistles, but Anthony Redding just nodded his head. For

FBI men, a compliment was a compliment and not a come-on. "Anything else?"

"David Dale is a seventh-grader and a geek. Not a traditional hero. He falls into this 'profession' of his, superheroing, because he's a failure at everything else. Your author is also on the outside of society, looking in. He values connection but has trouble finding it for himself so he gives it to this kid. David Dale is a superhero who doesn't want to be one. Chris Senso equates 'normal' with 'super.'"

Lindsey Hall was rapt. When her guest finished speaking she put her hand to her heart. "A reluctant hero. Anthony, what a gift you've given us." She applauded and her Hall Heads followed suit. "We turned a corner today. I just know that soon, our man will be sitting here in person."

"Jeez." Rhian blinked. That was weird. "Run hard, Chris Senso," she muttered as she turned off the set.

Back in her office she stared at the index cards some more. The phone rang and she leaped to answer it. A phone call! Just what she needed.

Until she heard the voice on the line. Mario Vorhees was the writing manager at BinTech to whom she'd mailed final changes to his product manuals on Friday. BinTech made receipt printers for corporate clients. Mario wanted one more pass through the books.

She surprised herself by saying, "No."

"Rhian, you know how this goes. The client wants changes. It's a deal breaker. I wouldn't ask if I didn't have to."

She sighed. Of course he wouldn't ask if he didn't have to, but he *always* had to. Her sleep was haunted by nightmares about calls like this.

"No."

"Do you have something else already?"

Rhian looked at her note cards and colored pens. "Yes. My new project is going to take all my time for a few months."

Mario laughed nervously. "But you have time for my changes, right?"

"No," she answered. She didn't trust herself to say more.

"Rhian? Please?"

"Mario, no. Look. I'll e-mail you my friend Nick's information. He's good and he's fast. You'll like him."

It took a bit but she convinced him. Almost before the phone was back in the cradle, she picked up a pen and started making notes on the first card. She'd outline the whole book she decided.

As she scribbled a title onto one card and then flipped it to start a stack, she felt the stirrings of excitement.

HE HAD PACKED his damn stuff. Packed. His. Damn. Stuff.

So why couldn't he leave?

Yesterday he'd had a lot of reasons. Perfectly valid errands. Clean out the fridge. Secure his tools. Sort the recyclables. Wait for Rhian to call him and beg him to paint her house.

But today there was nothing left. He could leave. He should leave. Was, in fact, leaving.

Nathan closed the door of the apartment, turning the key in the lock and then dropping it in the mailbox. He'd call the landlord from the road and break the lease.

As he was getting into the truck his cell phone rang. His pulse sped up but he glanced at the caller ID and froze when he recognized Patricia's number. What the hell could she want? He shouldn't answer it, but he knew she'd call Matt next. He couldn't do that to his friend.

"Nathan! I thought you might have changed your

number now that you're in hiding or whatever. Where are you anyway?"

Since she'd left, everything about her irritated him. It was like a switch had been flipped. Her voice made his skin crawl. He had no idea how he'd stayed with her for two years.

"What do you want?"

"No need for hostility, Nate." She knew he hated to be called Nate. When they were together she'd done it to be cute, which it never had been, but now she did it to bug him, which it always did. "I saw Lindsey Hall this morning. She's not making much progress is she? She must be getting desperate."

He hadn't heard from Patricia in several months and the first thing she brought up was Lindsey Hall? Not good. He leaned back against his truck and grunted noncommittally. He'd stay on the phone, but he'd be damned if he'd engage her in conversation.

"Well, aren't you as talkative as ever? Do you watch that show?"

"Patricia." He kept his voice flat. He wanted to know what she wanted and then he wanted to hang up.

"Nathan." The honey dropped from her voice. He couldn't decide which he hated more, the falsely friendly tone or the one she used to sound threatening. "I'm just chatting. I mean, we were engaged. Don't you ever wonder about what ifs?"

"What if you tell me what you want?" he snapped.

"What if you try a little harder to be nice to me?" she snapped back. "You need me, Nathan. Don't you forget it."

"I'm aware of what I need. How much do *you* need?"

Her voice changed again and he could imagine her pouting at herself as she spoke. "Why do you have to be mean? You promised you'd support me until I got on my feet. You don't have to be a bully about it."

She'd nailed him. He had promised. It had been when he'd still thought there was a chance she'd come back. He'd been worried about her and had wanted to leave her options so she could work out her problems and come back to him. Now all he wanted was her gone for good.

"I didn't promise to be a bottomless well of cash for the rest of your life."

Patricia pressed on, building her case for pity. "Matt won't talk to me. He wants me to sign some paper about your privacy and Lindsey Hall and you know I want to do that. But Nathan, I can't sign until I know I'm safe. You're the only person I can count on and I'm not giving you up until I have something else."

Someone else was far more likely, but he kept that to himself. No need for them both to be petty.

"Okay." He bit the word off harshly, her threats making him sick. How had they come to this? He'd always known she had a mercenary side. In the beginning he'd gotten a kick out of buying her things and seeing her pleasure in his ability to be extravagant. But when indulgence became more an expected tribute than a fun surprise, he'd stopped enjoying the game. "Okay. I'll call Matt. There'll be money. No more threats, though. This is my life, Patricia. I know you don't want this life. But I do. I'm asking you to please respect that."

Even as he said it he knew she didn't care. She'd reveal his identity in a heartbeat. He had to keep her happy. She didn't want him, but maybe his money would keep her quiet.

"There's the introvert I love. Ta-ta, then, dear," she said.

He smacked his phone shut and stuck it in his pocket.

As he climbed into his truck he thought about Rhian. If Patricia had been in her position, she'd have begged him to paint the house and then probably refused to pay him when he finished. But Rhian hadn't begged. She'd looked at him, hurt and confused, and let him drive away. He was so used to assuming people wanted things from him that her silence threw him.

He'd left his tool belt at her house. He'd swing by and get it. As he put the truck in gear he knew he was being stupid. Rhian had that T-shirt. She watched Lindsey Hall. But…she hadn't begged. She hadn't tried to use any tricks. She'd stood back and let him go. And because of that he was reluctant to leave even though he knew he should.

SURPRISINGLY the college boy painters had answered their phone when she called on Sunday in her last-ditch attempt to find a painter to replace Nathan. They'd agreed to come by Monday morning at nine.

At precisely twelve-thirty, the doorbell had rung. She was currently "negotiating" with the boss or team captain, class president, whatever he called himself. His name was Seth. Tall and thin, he had a head of wild curly hair. Jeans hanging low on his hips bunched around the tops of flip-flops. His mint-green T-shirt read Yes, I Can. Unless it was referring to napping or using the word "dude" in new ways, she didn't buy it. Seth didn't seem much like a doer. In fact, she was beginning to suspect he was either stoned or still drunk from the night before. He reeked of leftover party, stale smoke, stale beer, stale college boy.

She couldn't help comparing him with Nathan. Seth came up short in all categories. He was right-handed, too skinny and unlikely to rescue her from anything more menacing than a bad case of the munchies. However, she thought, irritated with Nathan and his disappearing act, Seth was here. That had to count for something.

"So." She glanced at the station wagon and the step ladder strapped on top with multicolored ropes. "You do paint exteriors, right? I mean, that ladder, it's not an extension ladder."

Seth snorted. "Dude, that's a stepladder. We'd need a big ol' ladder to paint your house." He craned his neck to peer at her roof. "Like, it's tall."

"So, you have an extension ladder?" She wouldn't ask about insurance, just tools. Keep it straightforward. Seth was her last hope.

"Extension ladder." Seth shook his head, his eyes vacant. "No, we do not."

He didn't seem inclined to go on.

"So how will you do the job?" she prodded. "It's the second story that needs the paint."

"Well, like, we usually climb stuff. Or we go out a window and up lines. Rory, he's our line guy. Likes ropes. He's a rock climber." He lifted one limp arm and pointed at the forsythia. "Whoa. Big bush. You grow that yourself?"

Rhian felt like sticking her fingers in her ears and singing "lalalala." He wasn't stoned, he was *insane*.

"I really want the house painted. But I'm not sure about your system. Ropes? You use ropes?"

"Rory, dude. He climbs rocks. He can totally climb your house."

Rhian had a flash of her house being swarmed by college boys clutching paint cans in their mouths, brushes behind their ears, creeping and clinging to window ledges like mutant Spider-Man clones. *Nope.* She couldn't do it. Were all housepainters unstable dope fiends?

"Seth. Thanks very much for coming by, but I'm going to pass." She tried to keep her voice level, but she was mad that she'd gotten her hopes up only to have her time wasted again. Congress should regulate the housepainting industry. "I'll wait for someone who has a long enough ladder." *And isn't high during the interview.*

Seth shrugged his thin shoulders. "That is *so* a good decision."

He gave her a boneless wave and flip-flopped around the house to his car. Rhian kicked the side of the porch and stamped hard on a dandelion before she sank down on the steps. Her poor house—stuck looking like a three-year-old girl's princess birthday cake. It wasn't getting painted. Not this summer. Not by any of the weirdos or crooks who'd applied for the job.

BY THE EDGE of the driveway, Nathan stepped back to let the boy pass. He'd pulled in just after Rhian and Seth went around to the front of the house, and then he'd eavesdropped on their conversation. He'd have sent the kid packing after the first "dude," but she'd stuck it out through the ropes. She must be desperate.

He was a schmuck. If it weren't for him she wouldn't have had to talk to that stupid fool.

He watched the station wagon pull out and thought about following it. But he'd come here to see her again, even for a minute. And now he'd seen her and knew she was miserable and it was his fault. Hell.

Rounding the corner of the house, he was surprised to see her slumped on the steps of the front porch, head on her knees, fingers laced behind her neck. It shocked him that Rhian, who was so together, so sure of herself and confident in her world, was hurting. Whatever it was about the house and the paint was hitting her hard. He felt a surge of protective instinct: make better, fix, mine.

Screw it. Lindsey Hall wasn't going to find him this week. She'd want to drag this thing out to keep the suspense up. And the T-shirts Min's friends made were jokes. They weren't actually looking for Chris Senso, just piggybacking a joke on celebrity sensationalism. To him it had felt like a horror show. To them it was a funny cartoon.

So he'd stay. Long enough to paint the house and then he'd go. One week. Two tops. He'd help Rhian out. Then he'd move on.

RHIAN HEARD the footsteps and figured it was Seth. She'd have to be more clear. How could you say no so someone as thick as that kid could understand? She looked up.

It wasn't Seth. Nathan was standing on her sidewalk, movie-star handsome as usual in a navy T-shirt tucked into the waistband of perfectly worn-in Levi's. He was squinting into the sun and she thought she'd never seen blue eyes as dark as his.

It was ironic that he looked so perfect when he was an absolute nutcase.

"You left town," she said flatly.

"Turns out I didn't," he answered.

Was he throwing his unreliability in her face?

"'Turns out you didn't'?" she snapped. "Are you going for gold in the shiftless Olympics?"

"What?"

She stood up and approached him. Even though her chin barely came up to his chest, she was pleased to see him back up a step. After Seth, she wasn't feeling charitable toward housepainters. "Shiftless. I hired you even though your *one* reference was underwhelming at best and then you skipped out on me. Pretty much meets my definition of shiftless."

"I didn't skip anywhere," Nathan said, in a maddeningly reasonable tone. "I'm standing right here."

"You're nuts. You said you'd paint my house for free, which was crazy, and then the very next day you said you wouldn't paint it at all. Which was crazier because you *begged* me for the job in the first place. You're a flake!"

"I know it seems weird, Rhian, but if I can tell you—"

She interrupted him, really on a roll. "Is it the fumes? The lead dust? What? What is it that has your whole breed so messed up? The thing none of you—you painters understand is that this is my *home*. You think you can waltz in here and steal my money or break promises or taunt me with ropes and it won't matter. Well, I've got a newsflash for the Union of Brother Painters. I'm done. I'll paint this place myself before I let any of you near it again."

That hadn't come out as rational as it had sounded when it was in her head. But still. He didn't need to laugh. She watched him struggle not to. He held perfectly still, pressing his fist tightly to his mouth. If he laughed at her he'd better start saying his prayers. She glared at him.

"Ah, leaving aside the Union of Brother Painters and the ropes question." His mouth twitched but he held the laughter in. She gave him a grudging point for self-control. He continued, "I understand why you're angry, but I'd like to humbly ask that you let me paint your house."

"No," she snapped.

"No?"

She'd surprised him. Good. "No. Go away." She turned to go into the house.

"Rhian, wait. Please?"

"Why?"

"Because I…you're right about what I did. I was leaving. I almost did leave. In fact, if you turn me down, I *am* leaving. The truck is packed."

She rolled her eyes. Did he think she didn't know that? If there was one thing she understood it was being left.

He took two steps forward. He lifted his hand and ran it through his hair, messing the front, leaving it poking up. He was one of those beautiful people who really didn't understand how gorgeous they were, who truly didn't care. She wished she hadn't figured that out, because it chipped a piece off her anger. Much easier to be mad at a conceited gorgeous person.

"Here's the thing," he started, his voice matching the earnest look in his eyes. "My life is weird right now. I made a lot of changes recently. When I said I couldn't paint your house, I wasn't thinking clearly. But I don't want to be a guy who breaks promises. Help me out here? Let me keep my promise?"

If he'd tried to be bossy, she'd have said no. If he'd tried a flimsy excuse or a lie, she'd have said no. If he'd done any of a million other things, she'd have said no. But he asked so gently. He wasn't sure she would say yes. He wanted her to say yes, it mattered to him for some reason, but he was unsure. And that stripped the rest of her anger away. Whatever Nathan was, deep down he seemed like a good guy. The Bobalos were crooks and Seth was a stoner but Nathan might just be a guy who was what he'd said, going through some changes and feeling off balance.

"When you're talking about off balance and weird, you're not talking about drugs or something are you?"

"You mean like Super Stoner Seth?" He nodded toward the driveway.

"You heard that?" She had hoped he had come after she'd ended the humiliating interview but no such luck.

"Every word, dude," he drawled.

"Well?"

"No. It's nothing like that. Just personal stuff I need to work out." He put his hands in his front pockets and looked at her the way Jem did when he was mustering his charm to get her to bend a rule. "I have an extension ladder. I'll let you approve the color before I put a brush to the house. I promise I'll be here until the job is done. Want me to give you the keys to my truck as collateral?"

Now she was the one fighting a smile. She slapped her hands onto her hips. "Fine. I'll do you a favor and let you paint my house."

"Dude, you are so awesome," he said.

"Show up with a stepladder and you're fired," she threatened without any actual anger in her voice. Her house was going to get painted after all. She was happy. Totally happy about that. And well, yes, maybe also happy that Nathan hadn't left town yet. Because it was possible she'd been frustrated about her aborted chance at being a person who dates. If she could manage to keep her vibes from freaking him out again, maybe she'd have a chance to try a fling, too.

CHAPTER SIX

OF COURSE it rained the next day. It had been sweltering since April. Then Rhian decided to seduce her housepainter and it rained. Probably the universe was trying to tell her something but she didn't want to listen. She'd use this pre-fling time wisely, spending it on extra exfoliating and a mud mask.

Except she'd never exfoliated in her life and had had her fill of mud pies back when Jem was four. She wanted Nathan to show up so she could try to do whatever it was she was supposed to do to start a fling. Over a pitcher of beer last night Min had given her tips. Unfortunately, Rhian had forgotten most of them somewhere in the bottom of the pitcher.

She needed action. She got rain.

Well, if she couldn't start her fling, at least she could make some headway on her book. She scooped up her note cards and laptop and retreated to the kitchen. The yellow walls and cheerful dishes in the glass front cabinets helped make that room less dreary than her office. Plus she was closer to the snacks.

When the doorbell startled her out of the world of magic and princes she'd been creating, she glanced at the clock on the microwave and was shocked that three hours had gone by.

Pulling the heavy front door open, she was surprised to

see Nathan standing on the porch, rain dripping off the roof behind him and glistening in his hair. The man was actually better-looking wet. His perfect hair was finger-combed perfectly back. His eyes were clear navy under his rain-darkened lashes. The shoulders of his black T-shirt were wet and the fabric clung to his arms and chest, every muscle edged and defined. Her heart skipped. This was worse than being in high school.

"Nathan, I didn't think painters came out in the rain."

"I hate to waste a day, even a rainy one, and so I wondered if I could stow my stuff in your garage."

She stepped back to let him in and took him to the small entryway that led to the garage. They met in the narrow doorway as she paused to pull the door open and her breath caught when their hands touched briefly. There was no room to breathe. She'd never stood in this spot with someone who was taller than her, whose shoulders were so broad, who filled the space so completely. It was a relief and a disappointment when she got the door open.

She pointed to the half of the garage given over to sports equipment and toys. "I can move Jem's stuff and make some room," she said. She squinted at the garage, pretending to think about organization and storage, but really considering how she could turn this moment into the beginning of her fling. She was hopelessly out of practice—the past few years she'd been schooling herself in fling avoidance. God. What she wouldn't give for an instruction manual for the seduction of handymen. Handypersons, it would probably say. Instruction manuals were big on gender-neutral language.

She snapped out of her mental tangent when he said quietly behind her, "Great."

"Need help?" She went down a step to reach for the door opener. She had on her favorite blue shorts and a green tank top. Not exactly seductive, but passable, she supposed. Too bad she was wearing sneakers but it couldn't be helped. Should she start now?

His jeans gave her the answer. Or rather the way he filled his jeans to perfection when he went down the steps past her toward the truck.

If there was any chance she could get her hands on his ass today, now, well, 'no time like the present' had always been her motto. Should have always been her motto. It was definitely her motto from now on. She would write her own manual. "Seducing Your Handyperson in Eight Simple Steps." Actually, eight was a lot of steps. Maybe there was a way it could be condensed to three or even two.

He started to pull a ladder off the back of the truck and Rhian hurried over, taking hold of the other end. "I got it," he said but she didn't let go, wanting to be close to him. He backed up, sliding the ladder off the hooks, and she backed up, too, straight into a depression in the driveway overflowing with rain. Her sneakers filled with water. "Ugh," she said as she dropped her end of the ladder. He lost his grip and the front tipped down, landing hard on his toe.

"Ow." He winced as flushed with embarrassment, she muttered, "Sorry." In the seduction instruction manual, she'd include a Troubleshooting section, "Injury Occurs Before Seduction Commences."

He took the ladder to the garage alone while she regrouped. She hopped up in the back of the truck to find some way to be useful while she worked out her strategy. The last time she'd seduced someone she'd been in college and there'd been alcohol involved. This time around she was stone sober, wearing sneakers in a rainy driveway. Definitely a challenge.

She studied him while he carried empty buckets to the garage. After he stowed the buckets, he put his hands up and stretched, the length of lean muscle displayed in all its gloriousness under his soft, black T-shirt. Rhian was shocked by how erotic she found the sight of him. She hadn't been this turned on and excited and frustrated and confused since, well, since never.

He walked back to the truck and she hurried to look busy. "Are you taking the toolbox in?" she asked as she grasped the handle and pulled at it. The metal chest didn't budge. She tugged harder and her feet went out from under her. She sat down abruptly on the edge of a bucket full of brushes, which tipped and dumped her on the bed of the truck.

"Wow," she said, trying to laugh, "That's heavy."

"It's bolted in," he said quietly. "Are you all right?"

Her feet were soaked from the puddle and now her shorts had a big wet spot. At this rate the handyperson seduction manual would be all troubleshooting and no helpful hints. "I'm fine," she said.

He had his hands on his hips, looking at her with a frown. "You know you're paying me to be the painter, right? I can do this."

"I want to help," she said, wiping her hands down her shorts, leaving more wet streaks on the fabric.

He handed her a stack of drop cloths, which she promptly dropped on the floor of the garage when she swiveled to avoid Jem's skateboard. The top few stayed folded, but the bottom one came undone.

"Let me help," he said as they both reached for the same corner of cloth. He shied away, but not before their knuckles rubbed and fingers skimmed. She shivered and not because her shorts were wet and clammy.

They held the cloth taut and shook a careful fold down the middle. He advanced to her and joined his corners to hers. She curled her fingers over his, pressing gently, trying to send a signal. Her eyes met his, hoping to see something there that would tell her what to do. Was he interested? His eyes weren't as easy to read as she'd like. Or maybe they had nothing to say.

Maybe *she* needed to say something. "Nathan, I…"

He slid his fingers out from under hers. "Looks like you've got that then," he said, and went back to the truck.

Could he have realized what she was doing? Maybe there really was something wrong with her vibes. She shivered, this time from cold and shame. The green of her shirt was marked with grimy handprints and her shorts were a mess. Her shoes squelched water with every step and she was sure her hair, unlike his, did not look better wet. Flat and stringy were not good adjectives for a seduction manual.

"Uh, I'm going to change," she called, and then ran into the house. In her room, she closed the door, leaning back and letting the solid wood support her. How stupid was she? She should have waited for a better time, she should have made a plan, she should have…what did it matter? She'd wrecked any chance she might have with him and made a fool of herself in the process.

NATHAN HESITATED outside the door to the house. He'd cleared his truck, stacking the last load of paint neatly against the wall. Logically, he should leave. So of course he was hanging around outside her door. He wished he could figure out how to say something to her without hurting her feelings. He'd sensed her wanting as soon as he walked in. She was interested in him as more than a painter.

Which, if he weren't on the lam, would be fantastic. If he let his body decide, it would be a done deal anyway. But his mind wouldn't stop screaming that he had to stay undercover.

So he'd split the difference between body and mind. He'd go in, let her down gently, then flee. Leaning in, he knocked lightly on the door. "Rhian?" he called.

No answer.

He knocked louder but still no answer. She must have gone upstairs to change. He pushed the door open the rest of the way and stepped into the small, tiled hallway. To the left was the front door and the main hallway he'd seen on his way in. The brightly striped runner on the floor and a glass vase of wild flowers on the chest beside the door bravely combated the gloom of the day. Framed black-and-white photos hung on the walls showing Jem as a naked grinning baby all the way through to a recent shot of him lounging in the hammock.

He stretched his neck around the door, and to his right was the kitchen. He went that way.

The kitchen was exactly what he'd have drawn for Rhian if he'd been imagining it. Cheerful yellow walls, in a shade somewhere past lemonade and before outright lemon. The creamy white trim lent richness to the tone. A mix of glass-fronted and beadboard cabinets held dishes not matched but blended in a comfortable mix of cobalt-blue, lemon-yellow and emerald-green patterns and solids. A rectangular wooden table with three chairs was pushed against one wall under an oversize bulletin board covered in mementos from a fully lived family life. School papers, holiday photo cards, ticket stubs, drawings and notes were hung in an overlapping jumble that showed a dedication to memories and good times but not much organization. He recognized faces from the barbecue in some pictures, parts of the cobbled-together circle of friends and family he'd enjoyed.

His bare apartment depressed him more than ever. The New Hampshire house, even before Patricia had stripped it, had never felt as much like a home as this cheerful room. Patricia had spent more on decorating than normal people spend on their houses, but he'd never been able to shake the impression that he was living in a department store. Even the magazines on the coffee table had been staged—*Sports Illustrated* was relegated to a covered basket in the bedroom. If he'd had pictures on his wall of his friends and family it would be Matt and his mom and…well, only those two. This room, though, was what his childhood home had been like. He'd never imagined he would find it so difficult to replicate that warm, normal connected life.

Rhian and Min and Jem probably ate right there, at the wooden table, sharing stories about their days. He stepped closer to see the photographs tacked to the board.

The table in front of him was covered with stacks of note cards. He glanced down and couldn't help noticing that the top card in the pile closest to him was labeled Chapter 1.

Chapter 1?

He tilted his head to get a better look at the cards without touching anything. The cards were definitely an outline for a book. A novel. He scanned the table. He could only see the first card in each stack, but it seemed like a fantasy, princes and magic powers, a hidden secret.

She was writing a novel. How weird was it that the first person he'd had an actual conversation with since he'd left New Hampshire was a novelist? Or was it weird? Could she know about him? Was she using the painting as a way to get close to Chris Senso? The T-shirts flashed into his mind.

No. Not possible. Paranoid much?

She might be interested in finding Chris Senso but there was no way she knew it was him. No one did.

To prove to himself that this was just an innocent novel, that he wasn't scared to know she was writing a novel, he picked up the first pile. He'd thumb through them and then walk away. But he read the first card and then the next. He flipped back to the first and then went on. He was hooked. She wasn't just writing a novel, she was writing a damn good novel.

He continued picking up stacks and reading the cards, getting absorbed in the story of the prince with his hidden secret, impressed with the snippets of dialogue she'd sketched on some cards, the details of plot and scene jotted on others. He didn't hear Rhian come down the stairs until she came up behind him and let out a surprised "Oh!"

He guiltily dropped the cards he'd been reading. No way he should have done it. It was an unspeakable breach of writers' etiquette. One of the cards had fallen to the floor and he bent to pick it up. "Rhian, I'm so sorry. I shouldn't have looked at this." When he straightened with the card in his hand, he was met with fury. She snatched the card from him and slapped it onto the table.

"No. You shouldn't have. This is private."

"I know." He wished she could know how sincere he was. "I'm really sorry."

She gathered the cards into a sloppy pile and then

scooped the whole thing up, holding it tight to her chest. "I'm going to put these away. I'll see you tomorrow when you come back to paint."

He'd been dismissed. She spun to leave, but he reached out for her shoulder to stop her.

"Wait," he said. He felt the tension in her body through the thin cotton of the clean white shirt she'd put on. "You have every right to be angry. But I want you to know that your book is going to be amazing."

She half turned back to him, sparks of gold glinting in her hair where the sun, which had finally come out, slanted in through the windows. "What?"

"I read your notes. Which was wrong." He looked straight into her eyes. "But…you need to know, your story is amazing. Classic fantasy lines, obviously you've read Tolkien at some point. Then you moved out of that standard world and made this one your own. It's wonderful. The modern touches will bring it home to modern kids, but you left in enough fantasy that it will let them escape. The world you're building is familiar but fresh. The kid's voice in the dialogue is spot on. I'm in awe." He paused. "I had no idea you were a writer."

She shook her head and slid her shoulder out from under his hand, her jaw clenched tight. "I'm not. The door is through there."

She walked away, through the tiled hall and around the corner. He was left standing in her kitchen, too many thoughts and feelings swirling around him. Clearly his apology hadn't worked. He'd leave now before he made things worse.

He went out the front door and down the porch steps, cold drops of rain dripping off the leaves as he passed under one of the big oaks near the fence.

How had he managed to get into this mess? Painting a house for a woman who turned him on was bad enough. A woman who was following the hunt for Chris Senso. Who was writing a novel and doing it really well. The situation had so many potential pitfalls it was almost a joke.

Nathan put the truck in gear and backed out, his eyes on Rhian's house, the pink paint glowing even in the gloomy day. Despite everything, he was smiling. For the first time in months he felt alive, interested, excited. Rhian's anger hadn't quite been able to cover the hopeful pride in her eyes when he'd praised her book. He wanted to share the dream he saw shining in her eyes. He couldn't recall what it felt like to want to write a story the way she wanted hers, but he could recognize the feeling when he saw it. Rhian made him laugh and think and now, she'd made him remember what it looked like to dream. A smart man would be running for the hills, but how could he possibly leave all this behind?

WHEN HE GOT BACK to his apartment, he couldn't relax. He was full of jittery energy. It felt weird, uncomfortable. He walked to the kitchen and thought about making dinner but settled for a cold bottle of Harp instead. Tossing the cap into the garbage can, he lifted the bottle and took a long swallow. The beer on his tongue took him back to Rhian's barbecue and how much fun he'd had that night. The rain had stopped. Maybe he should go out and look for a park with a hoop, work off some of whatever was bugging him.

But he found himself in front of his worktable, staring down at the David Dale sketches he'd abandoned. He used his forearm to sweep everything aside, clearing a space in front. He put the beer down on the back corner of the table and switched on the light. *Paper*. He wanted paper. *And his markers*. That's what this feeling was. He wanted to draw. God, it had been so long he hadn't even recognized the urge for what it was.

He adjusted the light, grabbed a clean sheet of drawing paper and let the work flow.

Forty-five minutes later he threw his marker down, his energy spent. He picked up the now warm beer, his hand shaking slightly with relief, and took a drink while he examined the picture he'd done.

Different than David Dale, this was even less a cartoon than that work, but it was still stark, graphically clean and driven by the contrast of black and white. The young prince stood in a clearing in the woods, moonlight shining down through the bare branches of a winter forest, wonder and power shining from his upturned face and raised arms. It was Rhian's prince, the day he first tapped his magic. The picture was both triumphant and lonely, what he imagined a boy might feel when he touched the hidden talent that confirmed his unimaginable power and at the same time drew an uncrossable line between him and everyone he knew.

He took another swig of the beer and then pulled out a second sheet of paper. No hesitation. Putting the pencil to the paper, he started sketching in the scene when the prince is left on the doorstep of the village bakery. Without losing his focus, Nathan smiled. For the first time in a very long while, he was doing what he was meant to do and doing it well.

Matt had never believed him when he'd said Patricia stole his talent. He'd hinted that Nathan was one step away from believing in voodoo. Whether that was true or not, he knew this gift tonight had come from Rhian. He'd been able to use her dreams and somehow found his way back.

He'd committed to staying here until he finished her house—two weeks at the most. What if this, whatever it was about her, could, God…what? What did he want? He wanted to finish his book. He wanted to have his work back. He wanted to feel again. He wanted…Rhian. *He wanted Rhian.* He wanted her and her dream and her sneakers and her home and her life with people in it who cared about each other. Hell, if he was painting her house, taking that much of a chance, what would it hurt to do more? Go on a few dates, spend some time with her. Wasn't like it would last longer than the job.

MIN JOINED Rhian in the kitchen as she was pouring her second bowl of cereal the next morning.

"You and the Cap'n still close?" Min asked as she filled her own bowl.

"He's my main sugary cereal man," Rhian answered. "My only man, in fact."

Min paused with her spoon partway to her mouth. "What does that mean?"

"It means I'm such a loser, Min," she almost wailed. "The Cap'n is as close as I'll ever get to a man again."

Her friend's eyes filled in sympathy. "You're not a loser, buddy. Tell me what happened."

"I did what everybody said. I took a shot. Yesterday when Nathan was here. He was all wet and beautiful and— and here. So I went for it."

"And?"

"Nothing." Rhian put her head down, still humiliated.

"Nothing?" Min's voice was incredulous. "Absolutely nothing nothing, or a little something nothing?"

"Nothing, nothing, nothing."

They sat in silence for a moment and then Min huffed. "Men. What good is it to be that good-looking if there's going to be nothing?"

Rhian felt cheered by her friend's outrage. She pulled her bowl closer, determined to enjoy her breakfast. It didn't matter if she put on a few pounds—the Cap'n wouldn't mind.

"Well, what are you going to do now?" Min asked.

"Now?" Rhian was shocked. "Now I skulk inside the house, making absolutely sure not to run into him ever again."

"No second try?"

"You didn't see the nothing, Min. Besides I sucked at the whole thing. I don't remember how to do that stuff."

"Huh. I don't believe that. Out of practice maybe." Min dragged her spoon through the milk at the bottom of her bowl as she looked thoughtfully at Rhian. "I'm surprised. I thought he was into you. But I trust you to recognize a definitive nothing, so that's it, I guess."

"That's it," Rhian agreed.

The doorbell rang.

"Oh God," she groaned. "Tell me that's not him. What could he possibly want?"

"I'll get it," Min assured her.

Rhian stayed in the kitchen but could hear clearly when Nathan greeted Min and was met with an artic hello. He hesitated and then asked for her. Rhian closed her eyes. Min told him that Rhian was "unavailable." She held her breath until she heard him sigh and ask Min to open the garage door so he could get to his stuff.

When Min came back, she looked puzzled. "You're sure about yesterday? Because that did not look like 'nothing' to me. It looked like a flimsy excuse to knock on your door so he could see you."

Rhian shook her head. "No way," she said. *Right?*

THE WEIRD THING about being trapped inside her house because she was afraid of a housepainter was how full her day was. She set the margins and fixed the font and line spacing. Then she typed the words "Chapter 1" and started writing a novel. For a long time she didn't look away from the screen.

"PERFECT!" Nathan smacked his palm hard against the pink shingle in front of him. Another long curl of paint shredded off and fell into the bushes at the base of the ladder. Nathan wasn't much of a fighter, but right then he'd gladly have taken on all three of the Bobalo brothers. As angry as he was, they wouldn't have stood a chance.

The paint they'd used must have been old—was it possible they'd bought it at a flea market? Or maybe it had been lying in the back of their truck. For twenty years or so.

Whatever the reason, the paint was peeling off. No way he could slap a new color on top of it. This job, the one-to two-week favor he'd been doing for Rhian because he felt bad for her, had just expanded into a major project. Four weeks, even five. He really didn't know. He'd have to scrape and sand and then paint.

God.

He smacked the house again. Pink paint adhered to his palm and he wiped it on his jeans in disgust.

He had two choices. Go or stay.

Go and he could be free. Free to start hiding again. Free to crouch in some bare apartment waiting for Lindsey Hall to find him.

Stay and he could be with Rhian. Maybe. He could see if he could write again. Maybe. He could spend time in a town where he was getting to know people. He could feel normal. He could finish the job he'd promised to do and be square with his sense of honor.

Choice? What choice?

SOMETIME AROUND TEN he knocked on the front door. She held perfectly still until he went away. She was being juvenile, but she couldn't stand seeing him again.

Around one in the afternoon, her stomach complained enough that she had to stop for lunch. In the kitchen she sliced two tomatoes and some red onion for salsa. She boiled half a bag of frozen corn and mixed that in along with a generous share of olive oil, vinegar, lemon juice and salt. She mashed her avocado and seasoned it for guacamole.

Nacho chips, salsa, guacamole, lemonade, the first pages of her book fresh from the laser printer—she had everything she needed for a perfect picnic on the hammock. Except *he* was out there. Rats.

She settled at the kitchen table instead and read the pages she'd written. She made tons of notes and crossed out most of page four, but it was still an amazing experience. She was enjoying finding her voice for this work, finding her own way through instead of following a client's orders.

Nathan's words from yesterday echoed in the kitchen. He'd liked the mix of classic and modern, he said. Kids would respond to it. She'd found herself focusing on that duality as she wrote. He'd pinpointed a unique angle for her planned book. How had he seen that so quickly from her notes? She wished she had someone to share her pages with. Someone who'd offer insight and a fresh perspective.

Someone who'd…*oh!* Shirtless Nathan had appeared in the backyard. He was bending over, rinsing brushes in a bucket with the garden hose. She hitched her chair forward so her view was unimpeded.

Broad shoulders, sculpted back narrowing at the waist, and then tapering into his faded Levi's and…and…was that the hint of boxer shorts at the waistband of his jeans? The waistband of his jeans, mmm.

She was only staring, not drooling. Surely it was okay to stare when someone like Nathan was in your yard as long as it didn't devolve into drooling.

If only she hadn't messed things up yesterday. Maybe she'd have had a chance to find out what it felt like to be held by arms like his.

Yesterday. She'd been such an idiot. Why had she even tried to seduce him in the rain, wearing shorts and sneakers? She'd spent the best part of her adult life writing instruction manuals, for Pete's sake. She knew the value of gathering supplies and being prepared. Following proper procedures. If she did write a Seduction 101 Manual, it would never start with Step 1: Make sure your hair is limp and wet. Step 2: Cover yourself in grime.

Nathan turned off the water and walked around the corner of the house. She was left staring at the yellow wash bucket full of brushes. Could Min have been right this morning— had he wanted to talk to her? Was it possible she'd misinterpreted what happened yesterday? Could she handle the humiliation if she tried again and he turned her down? The world's most beautiful man was going to paint her house and then leave town. Was it so far out of the question that he would also date her before he split? One more try.

She circled the house and found him in the driveway,

with one foot up on the running board of his truck, tying his boot. He'd put his shirt back on and she felt a sharper stab of disappointment than she'd ever admit to about that.

"Hi, Nathan," she called. Did she sound nervous? She hoped she didn't sound nervous.

He pulled his jeans down over his boot and straightened up. "Hey. I was looking for you this morning."

"Oh," she feigned surprise. "You were?"

"Yeah." He used his forearm to wipe the sweat off his forehead, sweeping his hair back. She wanted to touch his hair. See how it felt to smooth it like that. "I have some bad news about the house."

"Bad news?" She was momentarily distracted from her fantasy.

"Yeah. The Bobalos didn't use the wrong color, they used the wrong paint. Or really old paint. It's starting to peel already on the southern exposure."

"How can that be? It's only been about five weeks."

"I know. But if the paint was old, well, it goes bad. I'm going to need to scrape before I can paint. If I put new stuff over that it's all going to come back off."

If a Bobalo or three had walked into her line of vision right then she'd have attacked them with her teeth, she was so angry. "Those crooks!"

"It's fixable though. It's going to take time. Four weeks, maybe."

"Oh. But you have to go?"

He hesitated before answering. "I do have to go. But my deadline is…flexible. I think it'll be okay if I stay."

Four weeks, she thought. Maybe longer. Did that change things? It was longer than two weeks, but Jem wouldn't be home. It didn't really change things, just added more time.

More time to experiment if he was interested but more time to be depressed if he wasn't.

He was speaking. She jerked her head. "What?"

"I said that wasn't the only thing I wanted to talk to you about. I need to apologize. I felt bad about yesterday. Reading your notes." He paused and met her eyes. "And stuff."

"Oh." *What stuff?* "Don't worry about it."

"I wanted to do something for you. Make it up to you. Maybe take you out for dinner?"

He was asking her to go to dinner? A date? Was that what this was? Or just an apology? Wouldn't a note have worked as well for an apology? Or a plant, a potted fern or something? Finally she stammered to life, "D…dinner sounds great. Without Jem I can use some company."

Ugh. Not the way to accept an invitation to a date. She really needed to work on her technique. Did anyone write dating manuals for the out-of-practice-woman? *101 Ways to Accept a Date without Mentioning Your Kid.*

He looked relieved and happy, though, his grin lighting up his face. "I've heard people talking about a place called Rosie's. Is it as good as they say?"

"Probably better." Rhian laughed.

"I'll come by around seven to get you?" he asked.

She jerked her head. No. She was so nervous she'd feel better if she drove herself. Having her car would give her an escape hatch, some control. "Actually, I have some things I need to pick up and work to finish, so why don't we meet there?" she asked, her words coming fast and jumbled.

Nathan shrugged. "You're the boss."

RHIAN DIDN'T HAVE any errands to do. That had been a lie. She didn't do any more work that afternoon, either. As soon as Nathan left she ran into the kitchen, poured herself a glass of lemonade and dug a handful of chocolate-chip cookies out of the jar on the counter. She'd made a batch for Jem to take on his trip and he'd insisted on leaving half for her.

She could have kissed him for his foresight.

The cookies would help settle her stomach and steady her nerves while she tried not to think about the fact that Nathan had asked her to dinner. Sort of. Maybe. Whatever.

She fled the kitchen and flew upstairs to the bathroom. She'd been given a second chance and this time she'd go by the book. Step 1: Make yourself gorgeous. (If not possible to achieve actual gorgeous, then use alternative Step 1: Make yourself as presentable as possible.)

She would go with the full treatment. She took a long steamy shower complete with shaving and conditioning and followed up with an apricot lotion. When she got out she towel-dried her hair, applied a dab of styling cream and then left it to air-dry while she thought about clothes.

She contemplated the contents of her closet. She was not wearing her sneakers. That was the only thing she knew for sure.

It took three tries to find the perfect thing.

She stepped into a short silky skirt in a luscious blueberry color and topped it with a short-sleeved tee with a silver crescent moon screen-printed at the base of the low scoop neck. She had a pair of sandals with a medium heel that were sexy but low enough for dancing. Not that she was planning on dancing.

SHE WAS EARLY of course. He'd think she was a nincompoop. Or worse yet, desperate. She hadn't done this in so long. When she went out with other moms they all stuck to the unwritten rule that time away from the kids is precious. Being prompt was a given. She'd forgotten that dates had different rules. Not that this was a date.

She should have hung around the parking lot. She should have stopped for gas. She should have stayed at home and eaten cereal by herself. The Cap'n would be lonely.

In desperation she turned to the bartender and ordered a beer. She drank it too quickly. And then Nathan came in and she almost dropped the beer. If he'd been handsome in a T-shirt, it was nothing compared to how he looked tonight. A summer sport coat, casual and elegant with a subtle check, emphasized the breadth of his shoulders. The crisply starched spring-blue shirt he wore with the collar open underneath revealed just enough of his tanned chest to make her heart race. He had changed out of his Levi's into different jeans, dark blue, looser, but still sexy as hell.

As he came across the vestibule to stand next to her at the bar, she was concentrating on acting cool and secretly hoping someone, preferably some playground mother, would see her with this fabulous man.

And then she saw the boots. Oh God, she thought, he's wearing the boots. The exact worn-in cowboy boots she'd always included in her fantasy of the perfect man. Why couldn't he make a misstep, maybe wear a pair of white loafers or gray walking sneakers?

"Sorry I'm late." He dropped onto the stool next to her and motioned for a beer with one hand. In his other hand he held a flat package wrapped in brown paper. "Got busy this afternoon and forgot to leave time to change."

"You look great."

"Right back at you." His grinned appreciatively as his

gaze slid from her ankles to her eyes, lingering on the scoop neck of her shirt. "You look different in a skirt."

"Taller?" she asked.

"I was thinking more along the lines of really hot."

She flushed. *As apologies went that was pretty good.*

"I like your boots."

"We aim to please."

You're doing a damn fine job. The hostess tapped Nathan on the shoulder to let them know their table was ready. He motioned for Rhian to go ahead of him, but she smiled and waved him on.

"I'll be right behind you," she said. Indeed.

She followed him down the two steps into the restaurant, soaking in the utterly sexy way he walked in those amazing boots. Of course this was lechery, pure and simple, and she wasn't proud of herself, but some things a woman couldn't help.

The hostess left them with the wine list, and Nathan asked Rhian to recommend something from one of the local wineries. When he'd placed their order and it was just the two of them at the table, she started to feel uncomfortable. What exactly were they doing? Was this an apology or a date? Friends or something more? The "really hot" comment made her think something more, but how sure was she? She wanted rules. She wanted someone to write down the steps she could follow in order to get this right.

Nathan pushed the paper-wrapped package across the table to her. "This is for you," he said. "Part of the apology."

Rhian blushed. She picked up the package nervously. He was watching her carefully, as if her liking the gift meant something to him. That was a lot of pressure.

She flipped the gift over to peel the tape off the back.
She had no idea what it could be—it was too thin to be a
book or note cards or just about anything she could think
of. She pulled the paper off and found two matted prints.
She turned them over and stared.

The top one was a pen-and-ink drawing, stark and
graphic, of a street in a small village. A basket rested on
the steps of a building marked Bakery and the light from
a full moon illuminated drifting snowflakes and rested on
the small hand of an infant extending up from the basket.
A shadow slipping away from the basket spoke of desperation, despair, regret and fear. She slid the second drawing
out and gasped, then looked quickly back at the first before
she looked at Nathan.

"It's my prince. How did you…?" She didn't know what
to ask. She didn't wait for his answer, but looked back at
the prints, eagerly devouring the details. It was the oddest
feeling to see her private world brought to life like this. It
made her imagined prince and his life real, vital.

"I don't understand," she said.

"To make up for my intrusion, I thought I could give
something back," he answered. "For your work."

"You did these? From my notes?"

He nodded. "I had to make some of it up, but what you
wrote…it was powerful. I couldn't *not* draw these."

She studied the sketches again, pausing longer over the
prince in the clearing. She looked back at Nathan, her eyes
wide and wondering. "Who are you?"

"That's not the response I was expecting, but since you
asked, Nathan Delaney." He glanced away from her as he
spoke, and the excitement that had been in his eyes faded.
Rhian was confused. She'd touched a nerve.

"I didn't mean your name. I meant, I don't know. You draw so beautifully, really amazing, so why are you—" She didn't want to insult him.

"Why am I painting houses?"

He didn't sound insulted. And he was looking at her again. That was good.

"Yeah."

He unfolded his napkin and put it on his lap. Then he picked up his spoon and tapped it on the table as he spoke. His voice was almost nonchalant and yet she had the feeling he was trying to tell her something. "Life is complicated. So we do what we have to do."

She knew about that. As much as she knew it had been right to leave, she still felt an emptiness when she thought about *Phases* and the things she'd planned to accomplish there.

Their eyes locked. There was more to his story and yet he was closed off again. He'd joke and pretend to share things, but there was something he was keeping to himself. He was definitely a man with secrets. Good thing he wasn't going to be around long enough for that to matter.

She smoothed one hand across the bottom of the forest scene. "Your apology is more than generous."

He touched the back of her hand with one finger. Shivers went up her arm. "I think I might still owe you something. Something special."

She held silent and still, unused to flirting, flustered by his tone. Wishing for a list of dos and don'ts.

Clearing her throat, she felt her cheeks heat. Time for clarity.

"Nathan." Getting the words out was harder than she'd imagined. "Yesterday, in the garage, I tried to…um. I mean, I wanted to…but then I thought you didn't want to, and I got mad. But now I…"

Oh, rats. She sounded like an idiot. Or a high school boy. An idiot high school boy.

Nathan rescued her. He covered her hand with his. Then he lifted it slowly and brushed his lips against the tips of her fingers. The kiss was gentle, but his fingers tightened on hers. She felt a rush of anticipation. She looked in his eyes and saw the blue smolder. *He was saying yes. Good Lord.*

"I know. Can my apology cover me being too stupid to say yes even though I wanted to very badly?" he asked softly.

She nodded. Then she swallowed hard and went on. "So. While you're here. Until you finish the house. We can…" She started to stammer again. He squeezed her hand and she realized he wanted to hear what she had to say. He was listening in that whole-attention way he had. She slowed down and collected her thoughts. "I don't date. Because of Jem. I like to keep his life simple and steady. So I don't date."

Nathan's eyes were serious and he nodded. So far so good.

"But he's away now. And you're here. And if you want to date, we can, I mean, I'd like to. Until you leave. Before he comes home. If you want to."

It was easily the most embarrassing speech she'd ever made to a man. But she did feel better after she'd said it. It clarified things, made them simple. Set up the rules. If he agreed.

NATHAN WISHED she'd stop talking about when he'd leave. He was going to leave when he finished the house. He had to. But that didn't mean he wanted to think about it all the time.

It was dangerous, staying, getting to know people. But he wanted it. Wanted Rhian. Wanted the way she made him feel.

And the amazing thing? For the first time in years he was going to spend time with someone without Chris Senso hanging over him, screwing everything up. With Rhian, he was Nathan Delaney. Period. Housepainter, basketball coach, date. All those things and nothing more. He was leaving before his other life could possibly matter. She knew he was leaving, he knew he was leaving. They'd do this and nothing more.

"Okay," he said.

She looked startled. And excited. "Okay?"

"Okay. You are offering me a fling, right? I'm agreeing." He grinned at her. "Should we order more wine? Seal the deal?"

And that was all it took. They poured more wine. They made a toast. And the evening moved on. Dinner was filled with casual conversation about everything and nothing.

One story followed the next and the waitress was clearing away the dessert plates before there was a lull in the conversation. Nathan was looking around the room with a satisfied smile on his face. He turned to look out the window. The dance floor was starting to fill up. The jazz trio was enticing people out and now that the rain had stopped, the night looked gorgeous.

"You come here much?"

Rhian sighed. "I wish," she laughed. "Jem doesn't leave a lot of room in my schedule for evenings out. And when I do go, it's with other moms or, worse, other moms and their *husbands*. Nothing like a pity dance or two to top off an evening of fun."

He laughed, she sounded so pathetic. "Pity dance?"

"You know, wife nudges husband and rolls her eyes at me. Husband sighs but asks me to dance. We cut the rug, talking about kids the whole time. Pity dance."

He couldn't imagine anyone complaining about dancing with Rhian. "Good thing we didn't bring any husbands or wives with us tonight." He held his hand out as he got up from the table. "Would you like a dance, Rhian, of the nonpity variety?"

She took his hand and he rubbed his thumb along her smooth skin. He put his other hand on the small of her back as they crossed the room, not because he wanted to guide her but because he couldn't wait to touch her.

When they stepped through the doors onto the deck, Nathan was pleased to hear the trio slow the tempo. He made his way to a space close to the edge of the deck and took Rhian into his arms. He'd been thinking about how she'd feel almost since he'd met her. Now under cover of the drifting strains of a waltz, he held her close. He smiled down into her face and lost himself in the deep, clear blue of her eyes. She put one hand on his shoulder and he held the other and they started to move to the music. It was better, if possible, than he'd imagined. She was light on her feet, graceful and fit perfectly in his arms. Her waist felt strong and supple under his hand and he stumbled when a vision of what she'd look like above him in bed distracted him.

"Sorry," he muttered.

Rhian smiled at him. Her smile was gorgeous, full of joy. "You're a wonderful dancer."

He squeezed the hand he held in his own. "You are, too."

He changed their direction and watched as she closed her eyes and surrendered to the music. She was so beautiful, he felt himself getting hard. He pulled her closer so he could brush her hair with his chin. So silky. The music came to a stop and he had to kiss her. He couldn't help himself and he didn't really want to anyway. They'd made their rules and now he was allowed to kiss her.

He gently lowered his mouth to hers. Feeling bloomed through him and he needed more. When he deepened the kiss he felt Rhian respond. She pressed her body against his and he knew she could feel how much he wanted her, wanted more. He rubbed one hand up her back, caressing the slender muscles.

She put one hand up tentatively and touched his hair where it curled over the back of his collar. She stretched the curl and smoothed it before letting it spring back. The shiver of her touch went down his spine and he moaned against her mouth. The deck at Rosie's was many things, but not the appropriate place to lose complete control. He pulled back with an effort.

"The music is starting again." He smiled at her and tightened his hold. "I'm feeling like another dance. Help me out?"

"A pity dance?"

"Something like that."

"I never get to hand out the pity dances." She took a tighter hold on his shoulder. "Come on, you poor thing."

She turned them back onto the dance floor for another song. "Pity dances don't seem so bad to me," he told her.

"I never had one like this," Rhian murmured from her position close to his chest.

Neither have I, he thought.

CHAPTER SEVEN

RHIAN AND NATHAN had stayed on the deck at Rosie's dancing until the musicians were packing up. Between dances, they'd stood and looked out over the lake and kissed and talked. Outside, the parking lot was almost empty. Rhian's head was spinning. She told herself it was from the wine, but she knew she hadn't drunk that much.

It was Nathan. He was holding her hand now and she couldn't imagine letting go. When the night started Nathan had been a fascinating stranger and now he was, what? What did you call someone you were planning to date for four weeks and no more? Someone who'd touched you and made you feel more than you had in years?

When they stopped next to her station wagon, Nathan wrapped her in his arms again. He rested his cheek on her hair and then he held her. He pulled in a deep, shuddering breath.

"I wish I'd picked you up at your place," he said softly.

"Why?" she asked.

"Because I'd be driving you home right now."

"I'm not drunk." Her laugh was false, even to her ears. "I can get home on my own."

"I don't mean I want to be your designated driver, Rhian." His voice was soft and serious, seasoned with desire. She was glad she'd brought her own car. Dancing and kissing and drinking wine were easy starting points. But she was having serious doubts about the rest— driving home, coming in—she needed to think again before she could take that step. What did it say about her that she was starting a relationship with him knowing it was going to end? What did it say about him that he wanted that, too? Did she need to be with a man so badly that she'd treat him so lightly and let him do the same? Was that okay with her?

She laughed again. Even more falsely this time.

"I'll see you tomorrow?" Nathan's eyes clouded with confusion and hurt. She couldn't look. Wouldn't care. "I need to go now."

"I didn't mean anything, Rhian," Nathan said. "I guess I hoped, but what I wanted was to be with you longer."

"It's fine. I'm fine. The night was fine. I'm just tired. Ready to go home."

He stepped back as she got in the car and closed the door. She saw him raise one hand in farewell as she reversed out of the space. He was still standing there when she left the parking lot and headed home.

NATHAN KICKED a rock hard and watched as it ricocheted through the empty parking lot. *Damn.* That wasn't what he'd been expecting. She'd essentially run away from him and he wasn't sure why. She'd said the night was fine. He was out of practice but he thought it had been more than *fine*.

He walked slowly to his truck. He was turned on and confused and lonely.

Still, at least he was living again, feeling things. Even this, he shifted in his seat uncomfortably, was better than the blankness he'd had before Rhian. She must be dealing with some crazy feelings, too, he supposed. If only he had more time to take things easy. But time wasn't a luxury he had.

THE NEXT MORNING Rhian felt like hell. She hadn't slept well, warring visions of the beginning of the night with Nathan, the way she'd left him at the end, her book, her life, had kept her up almost until dawn. If she was going to put an end date on her relationship with Nathan, why even start it? Why had he agreed? Was he that guy—the one who went from town to town, woman to woman, never setting down roots or getting involved?

Years of getting up with Jem had programmed her body so she couldn't stay in bed even when she wanted to. She found herself in the kitchen after too few hours of sleep.

Morning Lindsey! was on and Min's eyes were glued to the screen.

"I don't know why you're watching that garbage," Rhian muttered. Her voice was unkind, but Min didn't seem to notice. Rhian wanted her to notice.

"I promised Jem I'd keep up with the Chris Senso thing," Min said.

"Lindsey's an idiot," Rhian said.

Min turned completely around and leaned against the counter facing her friend.

"Whatever is bothering you isn't my fault, Rhian, and you know I hate to argue. But if it will help, I will."

Rhian held on to her anger. It made her feel strong.

"It's drivel. You're supposed to be highly educated and this show is…" She sputtered as she couldn't think of an insult damaging enough.

"Is not the reason you're angry." Min smiled gently. "Is it Nathan?"

How could Min *know* about that?

Rhian narrowed her eyes, prepared to lay down the law about inquiring into her love life when Min turned back to the TV and held up her hand saying, "Shush, we'll fight in a sec."

She wanted to make Min argue with her, but Lindsey Hall was sitting at her desk holding up a *David Dale* book and pointing at the author photo on the back.

"Exciting news! We have had a caller on our Senso Hotline who swears she knows this man," Lindsey Hall said. "Now I'm speaking directly to our mystery caller." The Hall Heads let out a collective "ooh." "I enjoyed our chat very much. Please, mystery woman, call us back with more news!" An 800 number and an e-mail address scrolled across the bottom of the screen as the Hall Heads started chanting, "Call us! Call us!"

Min shut off the TV. She tapped her finger on the table. "I think Lindsey's making the mystery caller up, but I do think she's got some info somehow."

"Don't be ridiculous. Who would call that hotline? Chris Senso's hairdresser?" Rhian practically snarled.

"Ah yes, the bad mood, I forgot." Min jumped on the counter and crossed her legs. "We were going to discuss Nathan, weren't we?"

"No, we were not." Rhian bit off each word.

"Did your date go badly?"

"It wasn't a date, it was an apology." Rhian stopped and stared at Min. "How did you know about that?"

"Well, you were seen on this 'apology' by Stephanie from the deli. When I walked down this morning for milk she asked me who your boyfriend was. I didn't know because you didn't see fit to share this news with me." Min put on an injured look. "But after she described him as a 'hottie' I guessed Nathan." She smiled sweetly.

"It wasn't a date and I don't want to discuss it. It's unfortunate that you and Stephanie and the rest of creation don't understand the concept of 'private life.' Next thing I know there'll be a Rhian MacGregor hotline number." Rhian grabbed a box of Pop-Tarts from the cupboard. "I'll be in my office." And she left the kitchen with very little of her dignity intact, but with her entire bad mood still heavy on her mind.

She sat staring at the notes she'd made for the book and the sketches Nathan had done. She couldn't stop looking at the drawing of the night the prince was left in his basket. The baby's delicate fist reaching up from the basket was heartachingly defenseless.

She kept seeing Jem when she was holding him as Mrs. Haver, James's mother, called to deliver the news about Christine and James and their deadly crash. She'd been watching Jem for two days while his parents went to Christine's college roommate's wedding. They'd agonized about leaving Jem but decided in the end to go. On the way home there'd been bad weather, an SUV had crossed the center divider and hit their car head-on.

James's mother had been hysterical when she'd called, but Rhian had felt a horrible shift out of reality. She had stared and stared at Jem's hands curled on the edge of his blanket. She'd held him and cried out her grief at the loss of the last home she'd had, the last of her family.

She'd rocked Jem and made him a million promises. She'd read and reread the letter Christine had written explaining how to care for him over the weekend they'd planned to be away. She'd stared at the second-to-last line where her sister had written she wouldn't worry because Jem was in good hands.

Rhian had tried to live up to that. To the idea of good hands. Now, with Jem away, her world was askew. She knew how to keep him safe and happy. But what about herself? She hadn't focused on herself in so long she couldn't understand her own feelings. Did she want Nathan if she could only have him for four weeks? Was it sex, friendship, the feel of a man's arms around her when for so long she'd been the strong one? Could it have been any man or was Nathan special?

How the hell was she supposed to shift from no dating to inconsequential fling? Would it be better if it did mean more? Better to forget changing anything, go back to technical writing and be alone, waiting for Jem?

Min knocked on the door and poked her head inside at the exact instant Rhian imagined spending the summer alone writing manuals for BinTech. She took one look at Min, blurted out, "My life is a mess!" and burst into tears.

Min flew into the room and put her arms around Rhian. Rhian tried to resist, but finally she put her head on Min's chest and sobbed. Min held her and rubbed her back until the storm of tears slowed. Rhian raised her head and said, "Everything is so confusing. I'm sorry. I was rude and awful before."

"Be glad I don't have a reactive personality. I can rise above your behavior."

"I am sorry, Min. Just because you understand doesn't mean I should be rude."

"Forget about that. What's confusing?"

"Nathan, Jem, me, writing, Mario from BinTech, life, sex. Everything."

"Okay, let me sort this out. First, I've met Mario and he's not confusing, he's a dead bore. Wrenches—that's what we talked about. What else did you mention? Jem? He's fine—talked to him this morning and things are great in the RV. Life, well, yes, it's often confusing. So that leaves sex and Nathan. Hmm. Should we address them together or separately, do you think?"

"You're impossible."

"What? I'm helping you sort out your life." Suddenly Min was looking not at Rhian but around the office. "Did you redecorate? Where are all your manuals and style guides and your box of gadgets?" With a sly smile she said, "You're doing it, aren't you? Writing your book."

"We did resolve, did we not?" Rhian stopped to wipe her face with the back of her hand. "I got you something." She opened the bottom drawer in her desk and took out a laminated card with the word *Change* in red letters on the front and Min's resolutions listed on the back. "It's to motivate you. I have one, too."

Min laughed. "Emphatic, isn't it?" She stood up and her eye was caught by the sketch of the infant prince. "Whoa, Rhian. That's Kit. Who did this?"

"Nathan."

"The housepainter, Nathan? Your Nathan? Sex and Nathan, Nathan?"

"Yes, I mean no, but yes, that Nathan."

Min whistled. She put down the first sketch and picked up the second. "These are amazing. What's he doing painting houses?"

"I'm not sure."

"You're going to find out, right?" Min's voice was full of meaning, but Rhian shook her head.

"It's complicated."

"He's hot."

"I'm confused."

Min brushed the hair back from Rhian's forehead, her gentle touch spreading warmth.

"You said 'confused,' but I think you meant 'scared.'" It was a statement of fact, not a question, so Rhian didn't answer. She didn't need to because they both knew it was true.

"Rhian, honey, this is intimidating." She held up the sign with *Change* written on the front. "Look at how big you made these letters. And they're red, for crying out loud. I don't need a degree in psychology to guess how you're feeling. But you can do it. Write your book, live your life, have some Nathan." Min placed the sketch she'd been holding on the desk. "By which I mean some sex."

Rhian felt that tingle again. Why did her body *do* that?

"I'll do the writing. Stick to my resolutions. Which don't say anything about sex."

Min scrutinized her *Change* card. "Hey, mine either. Can I submit revisions?" She curled one arm around Rhian's neck in a quick hug. "Don't worry so much, honey. Redo your sign but this time use pink. Lavender. Lime-green is the most emphatic you're allowed to be."

"It's already laminated."

Min chuckled. "For someone who's holding a sign that says *Change* you're awfully set in your ways."

"I don't know how that happened. I used to be a person who had dates, who knew how to do this. But now it's more trouble than it's worth. If he's leaving, why start?"

Her friend leaned down. "You've been away from the game for a while, so let me lay it all out. Sex with a guy who looks like Nathan? Highly unlikely to be more trouble than it's worth. Also, that unsettled feeling? You want him. Take care of that and you'll feel much better." Min winked.

"Goodbye, Min," Rhian said.

"I'm off! Last thought—sex is good for the creative process."

Min shut the door before she could reply. Rhian sat and listened to Min's car head down the driveway.

TWENTY MINUTES LATER Rhian slammed her hand on the desk and yelled, "*Thinking* about sex is definitely not good for the creative process!" She pushed back from the desk and ran upstairs for her sneakers. Basketball! She'd get out there and practice so she could impress Jem when he returned.

NATHAN HAD STOPPED at the paint store on his way to Rhian's house that morning. He stowed the drop cloths he'd bought in the bed of his truck. When his cell phone rang his hand twitched. He needed to settle down before he got to her house. She was nervous enough for both of them.

"Hello."

"If I ask how you're doing are you going to bite my head off?"

Nathan sat on the bumper of the truck and ran a hand through his hair. Matt.

"The book had me pissed off."

"Things have improved since then?" Matt sounded hopeful and Nathan couldn't blame him. It couldn't be easy being the agent responsible for what was on the track to becoming a public relations disaster. He decided to throw his friend a piece of good news for a change.

"I did some new work."

Nathan held the phone away from his ear to avoid being deafened by Matt's whoop of joy.

"Not much, and not David Dale. It's just—"

Matt interrupted. "I'm sorry. Did you say not David Dale? What else could you possibly work on?"

"It's complicated. I wouldn't have told you, but I wanted to let you know I did some drawings that didn't have a single dismembered body part or lava flow."

Matt was silent. Nathan could almost hear his friend trying to figure out how to be positive about what was surely, from his point of view, not that positive a development.

"I always want to see new stuff from you. No need to be a one-trick pony. After you finish David Dale we can look at this new stuff and see what's going on."

"I heard that 'after David Dale' comment loud and clear." Nathan sighed. "It's not my story anyway—just illustrations."

"Not your story?" Matt's voice held carefully controlled hysteria. Nathan started to think it hadn't helped to share this.

"Rhian, the woman you spoke to, had a story and I did illustrations for that."

"So you got a house painting job, too?" The brittle edge was still there.

"No thanks to you."

"Sorry about that. You guys are getting close?"

"Come on, Matt. It's business."

"What? Is she married? An alien? Patricia's evil twin— no wait, can there be eviler twins?"

Nathan's jaw clenched. "Leave it alone. She's a client. That's all you need to know."

"Might be all I *need* to know, but I *want* to know more."

There was a hint, just a hint, of lechery in Matt's voice. A tiny twinge of leer. Nathan contemplated hanging up the phone and turning it off for the day. But there was no need for both of them to behave like children so he banged the phone off the bumper of the truck a few times, savoring the metallic clang it made with each knock.

He put his ear back to the phone and heard Matt say, with scorn in his voice, "I've heard all I need to on that subject."

"Matt?" Nathan knew his friend deserved the truth, but since he wasn't sure what that was he'd have to make do with less. "I need time. I'll finish the book as soon as I can. And I promise I'll let you know about the other stuff."

Matt sighed but Nathan heard a smile in it. "A couple days when we're this far behind shouldn't matter. Hey, speaking of killing people, did you know Lindsey Hall has some mystery caller who said she knows you?"

"Mystery caller?"

"On her Senso Hotline."

"Patricia," Nathan spat her name.

"You want to kill her or should I?" Matt's voice was flat. He would joke, but Nathan knew his friend absolutely had his back. "The call's got the whole thing stirred up to epic levels. The Hall Heads went nuts."

"Good God, this is insane! Why does anyone care?"

"Chris Senso's a media sensation. People love him."

"Chris Senso is made up, Matt. You made up his name."

"Maybe I should call the Senso Hotline. There's a reward. I like those T-shirts."

"She has no right." He meant Lindsey Hall but could easily expand his rage to cover Patricia.

Matt spoke soothingly. "She doesn't have a moral right, that's for sure. You want to be private for your own reasons."

Nathan cut him off.

"You know damn well what those reasons are. You were

there when it all went to hell at school. People get nuts about fame."

"That's the whole problem. People *are* nuts about fame. Chris Senso's famous and Lindsey Hall wants him on her show and what you think doesn't matter."

"It's definitely Patricia?"

"Could be a hoax. If it's legitimate, it's Patricia. Nobody else knows except me."

"I told her I'd send her more money." Nathan shook his head slowly. "How can she be so stupid? So heartless?"

"Try not to worry. I'll do what I can on my end. I'm not sure the call is legit. Could be a prank or could be Lindsey trying to flush you out."

"Thanks, Matt." Nathan hung up and wondered how much luck he'd need to finish Rhian's house before Patricia decided to screw him over again.

BY THE TIME she missed her twenty-third shot in a row, she was sweaty, frustrated and angry. She ran hard for the rebound and stomped back to the spot she'd picked in front of the basket. She whipped the ball as hard as she could at the backboard and ducked as it ricocheted back at her.

"Someone needs a lesson," Nathan called as he walked up the driveway toward her.

Rhian flinched. She hadn't heard him pull in. "This is all your fault," she ground out as she advanced toward him. She scooped the ball up and glared at him.

He took a step backward, looking intimidated. "Um, what?"

"You made this look easy. You put this hoop up to torture me. I can't make the ball go in!" *You agreed to my stupid deadline without a protest. You make me think about things*

I'd rather ignore. You're amazing. I'm frustrated. And that's your fault, too. Rhian threw the ball at Nathan hard, but he caught it and tucked it behind his back.

"Pupils shouldn't throw things at their teachers." He shook his finger in mock correction.

"Show me. What can I be doing so wrong?" She wasn't just talking about basketball.

"Sometimes it's trying too hard." He handed the ball to her but kept his hands on it for a second. "You're not going to throw this at me again, are you?"

"Not if you teach me how to do it." She smiled as she wrenched the ball away from him. "Now. Instruct." *Unconfuse me.*

"Yes, ma'am." Nathan stepped behind her. "Aim for the front of the rim. Be with the ball."

Rhian nodded. Her every nerve was strained backward toward him, but she locked her eyes on the basket. Be with the ball.

"Your stance is good, but you're tense—"

"Obviously."

"—which makes it hard to shoot. Relax."

Tightening her grip on the ball, she ground her teeth. He sounded like Min—next thing he'd be telling her she needed a pink ball.

"Maybe more relaxing."

Rhian whipped her head around, "Move on!"

"Right. After relaxing…" he muttered with a definite undertone of laughter.

"Don't push me, pal."

He put his hands on hers and lifted them to mime shooting. "Get the ball up in a nice arc. Push it with your fingertips. Follow through with your other hand after you release." It was magic. She did relax, into his touch, his steadiness, his strength. She was sick of being in charge and sick of planning. Sick of worrying. She liked to color inside the lines, not draw freehand. Nathan pressed her hands on the ball with his and then murmured, "You're ready, Rhian. Go for it."

She tossed it up. When it went in, relief and something more rushed through her. She reached for Nathan, remembered how sweaty she was and let him go. He stepped forward and put his arms around her. She spoke into his chest. "I shot eight thousand times and not one went in. Everything sucked until you showed up."

"You want a gold star from the teacher?"

She stiffened. *Sex.* He might as well have just said, *Do you want to have sex?* Her good feelings drained away and confusion swamped back over her.

She stepped back. "It's not the wanting part, Nathan. I hope you know that much. It's the knowing if I should say yes. That's where I'm having trouble."

He stood, hands at his sides, too good to be true in her driveway. "I didn't mean…" he started but she stopped him.

"You did mean it. I meant it. But I need time."

"Time is the one thing we don't have," he reminded her.

She didn't look at him again as she walked quickly around the side of the house and in the front door. She went to her office and made a sign with her writing goals for the week on it. She wouldn't think about him, outside, working alone, maybe with his shirt off. She pounded her desk, then took some calming breaths. She needed to focus. On something besides sex.

CHAPTER EIGHT

RHIAN'S SLEEPLESS NIGHT caught up with her finally. She'd worked hard and gotten a lot done. Chapter two was taking shape. With Nathan's sketch in front of her, she'd gone back to the first chapter and filled in more details. His drawing had shown her ways to make the town come alive. She was making progress on the book. Things were good.

If only she didn't feel like such a jerk.

She'd avoided thinking about Nathan while she was writing but a wave of humiliation at the way she'd treated him came over her now. Every time they got anywhere close to moving forward she ran away. It was time to make up her mind.

But there wasn't a decision to make. She could no more have him around painting the house, laughing with her, being kind, and not get involved than she could fly to the moon. She was already involved. It wasn't the idea of sex, either. It was everything from the way he'd treated Jem, to the drawings he'd done for her book, to the way she'd felt when he held her hands that morning.

If it was going to end when Nathan left town (and it *was* going to end) then at least she'd have this much. Something to think about while she went back to her ordinary life. If this summer was for a fantasy career then it could be for a fantasy man, too. She'd go for whatever she could get from Nathan and not worry about who he was.

She went on a circuit of the house, peeking out the windows to spot him before he saw her, but she didn't find him. He'd set up ladders and spread drop cloths over the plantings at the back of the house, but Nathan and his truck were nowhere to be seen.

Typical. He'd probably left for the day and she'd be stuck with this craving for him until he decided to show up again.

NATHAN CAME BACK to her house with a six-pack of beer, a sack of sandwiches, French fries and two pieces of decadent chocolate cake. Something was holding Rhian back. So he needed to be more aggressive. She needed to make up her mind and he was the man to help her with that. In his experience, takeout always helped the decision-making process.

He rang the doorbell but there was no answer. *Good Lord. When would he catch a break with this woman?* He shifted the bag on his hip. Where could she have gone?

What the hell was he going to do with all this food? Maybe he should forget Rhian and get a dog. He'd wanted a dog but Patricia wouldn't agree. Was Rhian a dog person? Probably. Maybe if he couldn't persuade her with takeout, he'd get her a puppy. At his truck he balanced the bag in one hand while he fumbled in his pocket to find the key.

He got in and started to back out but the glare of the sun hit him in the face and he stopped to find his sunglasses. Which were not there, of course. He had left them behind on a windowsill. He'd put them down when clouds rolled in briefly after lunch. This was not his day.

Wearily he opened the door of the truck and started back

to get the glasses. Rounding the corner of the house he saw Rhian sleeping in the hammock and was shocked at the hard, bright burst of emotion he felt. All the frustration he'd felt just seconds ago was gone, replaced by desire. What should he do? He'd brought the dinner and it was his excuse to make her talk to him. Should he stick with the original plan and go get the food or go without it, trusting to fate?

Screw fate. He trusted chocolate cake and beer. He told himself to take it slow but he was definitely jogging on his way back to the truck.

She was still sleeping when he got back. He put the food down and sat gently on the edge of the hammock, careful not to startle her.

She looked beautiful. Her hair curled around her face from the heat of the day and her arms were curved to make a cradle for her head. He wanted to stroke that shining hair but settled instead for a featherlight touch on her shoulder.

SHE WAS AWARE of him when he sat down on the edge of the hammock. All her senses jumped to life as if they had been waiting for him. She couldn't be sure she hadn't dreamed about him. She was thrilled. And scared.

"Rhian, I brought sandwiches and beer. Can we call a truce?"

His voice is so sexy, she thought. *I could lie here all day and listen to him talk.*

"Rhian."

His voice was a caress she felt down to her bones. *If he says my name again that'll be the sign and I'll wake up.*

"Rhian, you still asleep?"

She opened her eyes and stretched from head to toe, hoping she didn't look too awful.

Nathan was leaning over. His eyes were so blue, fanned by those dark, thick lashes; she could keep looking into them and never find their end. She sighed.

Then with a determined breath, she reached up to put her arms around his neck. This time she wasn't going anywhere until she'd had everything he was willing to give.

He slid one arm over her and bent his head to meet her lips as she rose to him. She watched as his eyes deepened with rising passion and then she let herself go. It wasn't about *letting* him kiss her or deciding what to do anymore. She was with him; he would take her where she was dying to go.

With a ragged breath he pulled back from her. She reached for him, but he pulled away. "Rhian, I have to know if this is okay. I won't want to stop this time. I just came to talk or to eat dinner and I don't want—"

She tightened her arms on the back of his neck to pull him closer. "This is what I want," she murmured as she dragged her hands through the curls at the back of his neck. "And this." She nipped at his bottom lip and then plunged into a deep kiss.

He rolled onto the hammock with her and they were touching and learning, exploring and tasting together. He leaned on his elbows to unbutton the light cotton blouse she wore and when he revealed her breasts, straining against the satin cups of her bra, she arched toward him. She wanted to feel him on her skin. He filled his hands and then his mouth with her as he unhooked her bra. She was on fire.

Even as she arched her back and moaned with pleasure, she was tugging at his T-shirt and the waistband of his jeans, trying to get to him. She wanted to drive him as he was driving her. But the hammock was rocking and she couldn't get a purchase and finally she pushed both hands hard against his chest.

He looked up, blue eyes glazed with passion. "What?"

"We can't do this here. Get up and we'll go inside."

"Oh Lord," he moaned, but he stood up and pulled her hand to drag her up, too. She caught her breath as he picked her up and settled her, straddling his hips, and continued to kiss and taste as he moved toward the house.

"You can't carry me, you'll kill yourself." She loved this feeling. She was going to die from the strength of him.

"Shut up and tell me where."

"The couch, anywhere." She heard the moan in her voice but couldn't stop. The heat of his erection was driving her mad and she had to get inside and get him undressed. She hadn't ever needed like this.

She kissed his neck, just under his ear. It was so intimate and so private she kept her mouth on him, licking and biting gently while she let his scent wash through her. She shuddered in pleasure as she tasted his skin.

He opened the door with one hand and stepped inside, kicking it shut with his foot, his every move an agony as her breasts brushed his chest and his erection prodded her shorts. He put her down long enough to tug at the waistband of her shorts and pull them down. She shimmied out of her underpants as her hands fumbled with his jeans and then he was free.

"Do you—" She started to ask and he jerked his head and kicked through the tangle of his jeans for his wallet and a condom. Then finally, finally, he picked her up again and she was sliding down slowly, so slowly onto him, taking him inside her, deeper inside her until she was filled and she thought she might die with the sweet, sweet feeling of completion.

"Oh Rhian," he panted. "I don't think I can go slow. Tell

me what you want." In answer she pumped her hips, eyes closed, head thrown back, throat and breasts bare.

He lowered his head and they moved together, taking both of them to a climax faster and harder than any she'd ever had. He held her still against him and she savored the broad strength of his smooth chest against her skin. She didn't want to move ever again. Finally, though, he shifted under her.

"I have to put you down," he said into her ear. Her head was still buried in his chest when she felt tears start in her eyes. She'd never been a post-sex weeper, but this had been more than sex. She'd wanted to devour him with her hands, and her mouth, and her body. The way he'd carried her and held her had made her feel so safe, she stopped thinking, let go and let the feelings overtake her. When it was over and he'd still held her, she'd taken those precious seconds to hide her joy. She'd never had sex like this, wild and urgent, and sure. Had she been waiting her whole life to experience something this intense and true?

"Thank you," she murmured.

"That was mutual," he answered. His eyes were concerned when he touched her chin gently with one finger. "Are you okay?"

She started to wrap her shirt closed and then met his eyes and dropped her hands. "I'm fine." She smiled at him. "But you do know we're in the hall, not on the couch, right?"

"You said anywhere." He shrugged. "This was close."

"I did say anywhere, you're right." She paused, considering. "But I think I misspoke." She shrugged out of her shirt, loving her own daring, and wanting to have more of what he had to give if she could. "I really meant the couch."

He folded her in his arms, running his hands down the

smooth curves of her back and cupping her bottom. "So the hall was a mistake?"

"Nooo. Not a mistake exactly. Nothing that can't be corrected at any rate." She put her hands between them and smoothed the planes of his chest and stomach and then down farther. She saw his eyes widen and heard his gasp when she gave an exploratory squeeze. "Want to try again?"

His answer was to bury his face in her neck and breasts, tasting and touching as they moved down the hall toward the living room.

In the end it took them quite a while to actually make it to the couch. And when they'd finally got there, they lay together, him collapsed on top of her, Rhian too exhausted to push him off.

"You're smothering me," she managed.

He groaned but rolled to one side and slid his arm under her neck to cradle her on his chest.

"Mustn't smother you. I want to keep you around."

She was too tired to answer and he was too tired to hear if she did.

When they woke up later they were ravenous.

"Didn't you say you brought me dinner?" She opened one eye as she traced a light line around his nipple.

"If you stop touching me I might be able to remember where I left it," he mumbled into her hair.

She sighed, but stopped her hand. "Feed me?"

"Outside, I left it outside."

They both lifted their heads to gauge the distance to the door and then sank back down.

"You'll have to go, I'm naked." She giggled and then slapped him lightly on the shoulder.

He lifted himself on one elbow and surveyed the length

of her. "You are naked." He grinned. "Hmm." He let his fingers trail down her side, dipping into the curve at her hip. "I can't remember if I kissed this part of you, right here."

As he was moving in, she shifted slightly and then shoved. She leaned over the edge of the couch to grin at him as he lay on the floor. "Now that you're up, you really have to get the food."

His arm shot out and captured her wrist and yanked her down on top of him. "Looks like we're both up. Let's eat outside."

She kissed him again through her laughter and it was several more minutes before they untangled themselves and got to their feet. Neither of them could find all of their clothes, but they put on the bits they could find, grabbed two cold beers from the fridge and headed outside to look for dinner.

Deli sandwiches had never tasted so good. They ate the French fries cold, since neither of them could face the long walk inside to the microwave and they were both too hungry to leave a scrap uneaten. When they were full and licking the last few crumbs of chocolate cake from their fingers, they settled down in the hammock again, arms and legs twined, her head on his chest.

"I still think we could have managed here," Nathan said.

"Didn't want to take a chance of spilling at a critical moment," she answered.

"They were all critical as far as I'm concerned."

He couldn't see it, but her mouth stretched in a satisfied smile. "On that we agree," she said.

He put one leg down and started the hammock swinging gently. She closed her eyes and sighed. He was amazing. This was amazing.

"Do you have to go home?"

"Nope." His tone was lazy and, she thought, as satisfied as hers. She hoped so anyway. "No one's waiting up."

"It's been years since I've lived alone. Min left this morning. The house doesn't feel the same."

"Have you heard from Jem?" He put his hand on her hair where it lay under his chin and stroked it gently.

"We talk on the phone every night. He's having a terrific time and doesn't seem to miss me, but it's hard."

"You two seem so close." He hesitated. "Is it rude to ask how long…"

"His parents, Christine and James, died when Jem was seven months old. A car accident. I was twenty-five. I was watching him for the weekend. First time I had him alone."

"I'm so sorry, Rhian."

"He's my family now." Rhian's voice was tight. "My dad left my mom before I was born, and he died when I was two. My mom had heart disease. She died when I was in college but by then we weren't that close." She paused and then went on. "Christine and James got together in high school and married straight out of college. They were my real family, the only ones who counted."

"I don't know what to say, Rhian." His hand kept smoothing her hair and she thought he didn't have to say anything. Holding her when she hadn't been held in so long was enough for now.

"Tell me about *your* family, where are they?" she asked.

"My mom died a couple years back. She was an artist, had a studio and sold her stuff in a gallery on Cape Cod."

"So you come by your drawing talent honestly?"

"She always encouraged me, never passed judgment."

"What about your dad?" she prompted.

"He died my freshman year of college." He shifted under her. "He's the reason I played basketball, why I went to Maryland where it's big-time ball. He loved watching me play and I loved making him proud. The trouble was, I was really good. That wrecked everything."

He sounded so sad. She'd seen how much he enjoyed playing basketball. It was weird to hear this tone when he was talking about it.

"When my dad was dying, it all went to hell. He'd been sick for a while, colon cancer. Maryland was ranked high in the NCAA tournament and I was a freshman star. It was a perfect storm for the sports writers. The media went nuts. I was in *Sports Illustrated* in one of those human-interest stories. *People* did a big article about us. My mom was in *Family Circle*. We were so stupid we didn't know enough to say no." He shrugged a shoulder and his mouth turned down as if to disavow the importance of what he said. "All of a sudden it wasn't about how well I could play. It was about me and my life. My private life." His muscles were tensing under her and Rhian thought about telling him to stop. Some things were too hard to talk about. Maybe this was his.

He went on, his voice sarcastic now. "My girlfriend gave an interview to *Cosmopolitan* all about our sex life and her future life as the wife of a pro player. I broke up with her, but that meant other girls trying to get a piece of me. It was all about what I could do for these people because I was good at the game and famous."

She shifted so she could see him. He looked older, his face hard, with lines drawn around his mouth. She wanted to kiss him, tell him it would be okay. But she knew from experience memories like this didn't fade. You could bury them under the surface, but when they bobbed up again they were as harsh as the first time.

"The night we clinched a spot in the Final Four, my mom called me to tell me I should come home. My dad was going and it was time to say goodbye. I told the coach what she said and..." Nathan's voice broke and he smiled a horrible, wry smile that was so painful Rhian reached for him. "He said I had to stay. Said my dad would understand."

"Nathan." She breathed his name and all of her outrage and sorrow were in the one word.

"I called my dad and he...he agreed. He'd never played in a big game like that. 'Make me proud,' he told me. I was on autopilot, but every single thing went right. I don't remember the last two games. The only thing I remember is the final shot when we won the championship, watching the ball go through the hoop and feeling nothing."

He pulled in a deep breath to steady himself. "I ran to the hotel still in my uniform. I called my mom, all I could think about was getting home to see him. But he was dead. Died before the game started. He had made them promise not to call me. He never even saw it." He put his forearm up over his eyes. "I swore that was it. I'd never play another game. Fame would never have the chance to screw with me."

She pulled out of her comfortable position and sat up so she could see him better. He dragged his arm off his eyes and gave her a half smile. "I don't usually tell people that story."

"It's a horrible story. You must have felt so alone."

"I promised myself I'd never let the world into my private life again." He laughed, but it was bitter and brittle.

She lay her head back down on his chest and smoothed

and stroked, trying to ease the tension from his muscles. "At least you've managed that."

Was that why he was painting houses when he had such an artistic gift? Maybe he was afraid to try again where he'd been hurt before.

"Seems like it." He didn't sound happy about that. "It's part of why I left the night of the barbecue. You had those shirts."

She was lost. How had he gotten from basketball to the barbecue. Shirts? What shirts?

"Oh, God. The Chris Senso shirts?" She felt her face flush. The shirts had been a *joke*. But from his perspective, knowing what it was like to have your privacy invaded, she could understand him thinking they were horrible. The hunt for Chris Senso seemed in very bad taste. "I'm so sorry. I never thought."

"I know. I had a bad reaction but it was about me, not you."

"Still. We should leave the poor guy alone." She shook her head. "Maybe he's a recluse like Salinger and this thing is messing him up so he can't write."

He spoke softly, his deep voice gentle, almost a whisper. "Or maybe he's just a guy who wants to be normal."

Rhian closed her eyes. Lying like this and talking to him was as amazing as the sex had been. It had been so long since she'd had this kind of comfort with a man. She let her mind drift as his hand smoothed over her hair. While she was relaxed now, she didn't feel much like sleeping. She shifted positions and slid her pelvis closer to Nathan. Now she felt very much awake and if she was not mistaken, Nathan wasn't interested in a nap, either. She slid a hand down into the waistband of his jeans and was pleased to feel him suck in a sharp breath. Nope, not bedtime yet. They would please each other and wash away some of the bitterness.

THE MOON WAS OUT and the stars were peeking down on them. They'd proved that the hammock wasn't quite as hard to manage as Rhian had thought.

"I haven't been this tired in years," she mumbled.

"I should go," Nathan said.

She wanted him to stay, but she needed him to go. There was too much happening for her to handle right now. She hoped it wasn't the wrong thing to do, but she was going to let him go home.

"You need to be up and painting bright and early tomorrow."

He poked her gently in the side. "Why? Is the boss going to get mad at me?"

"You never know what the boss might do," she chuckled.

She walked barefoot next to him, carrying the one sneaker she could find, to the gate. He took her in his arms, rubbing his cheek on her hair.

"Sleep well, boss," he murmured.

She put her arms around him and soaked in one last hug. "You too, hired man." She stepped back first.

He drove away, lifting one hand in farewell as he had done the night before. He was still an unknown. Hadn't told her anything about what he'd done between college and the last four months or so. He hadn't mentioned a recent friend or lover, or any personal relationship except his mother, Matt and that horrible girl in college. As far as she could tell, he was rootless. Which was what she wanted, right?

No strings. No ties. No emotional breakup. Her heart tugged then. She hoped she was doing the right thing.

WHEN NATHAN GOT to his apartment, his fatigue had evaporated. He wouldn't sleep if he lay down, so he didn't even try. He flipped on the desk lamp and picked up his pen.

As the night deepened, Nathan was more absorbed in his work. Words flowed as they hadn't in months. He wasn't sure he'd use the stuff he was putting down, not for the current David Dale book. But he needed to keep going, to write it through.

When he put his pen down, he closed his notebook without reading over the pages. It felt good to have worked—that was enough for now.

Soon he was going to have to start facing things. Lindsey Hall, Patricia, his unfinished book, Rhian. He'd almost come clean to Rhian. But he'd lost his nerve. The only person besides Matt and his mom that he'd ever told was Patricia and she had been a colossal mistake. Matt had tried to talk him out of it, but Nathan had been convinced Patricia understood him. He'd imagined them with children, summering on the Cape. Thanksgiving with Matt, living the life Rhian had with Jem. What he hadn't know was that Patricia had been with him in the first place because he had a lot of money and looked good in a tux. Finding out that he was Chris Senso had made him infinitely more attractive to her, cementing their relationship. Until she realized he was never going public.

CHAPTER NINE

IN NATHAN'S EXPERIENCE few people were able to resist warm cinnamon rolls. Add gooey icing and only true psychos would say no. He felt no twinge of conscience as he prepared to exploit this weakness of human nature to have his way, again, with Rhian. He rang her doorbell.

When she didn't answer he thought about coming back later, but there were the cinnamon rolls to consider. They wouldn't be as effective when they had cooled. He didn't want to squander any advantage now that Rhian had finally stopped running away. Besides, her car was in the garage— he'd checked.

He rang the bell again. Still no sound from inside the house. He went around the corner and checked the hammock to be sure but all he found was one sneaker and her lacy bra. He picked both up and carried them back to the porch. This time he didn't so much ring the bell as lean on it.

A few seconds later a door slammed inside and feet pounded down the stairs. Rhian ripped the door open and glared at him. "Touch that doorbell again and you're dead," she said.

"Sleeping Beauty is in a royal bad mood?"

She tugged him into the house, and he thrilled at the touch of her hand on his arm. "She'll be in a much better mood if the handsome prince hands over his treasure. Please tell me you've brought me cinnamon rolls."

"Look what else I found." He held the bra up, hooked over one finger.

"You are a modern hero—this morning's breakfast and last night's underwear," she said, leading him into the kitchen.

"I actually read this move in a book, *The Housepainter's Guide to Heroic Mornings*," he said, following happily.

She grabbed two mugs and poured orange juice into them and then slid a plate across the table toward him while she sank into a chair.

She bit into a cinnamon roll and closed her eyes. "Perfect."

Oh, he loved the way her face looked, blissful and content. He loved that he had done that to her. It made him think of other things he could do to make her face look blissful. There was a drip of icing on her bottom lip, and he used one finger to scoop it away. Her lips were so full and the thought of what they'd done to his body yesterday made him want more. He gently pressed his finger against the slight indentation in the middle of her bottom lip and when she opened them, he slid his icing-covered finger inside.

Her eyes widened with surprise. Then her lids swept down as she slowly and seductively licked the icing from his finger. When she was finished with that finger she held his wrist and with exquisite delicacy licked and sucked her way through every finger of his hand.

She looked up briefly and murmured, "I've wanted to do this since the day we met. I've dreamed about your hands."

That was it. He shoved his chair back to get to her. He knelt in front of her and pushed her shirt up over her stomach, reveling in the just-awakened taste of her skin.

She put her hands in his hair and held his head close as she arched against him.

Standing quickly, he bent and scooped her up. "At least I know where I'm going this time," he said as he carried her toward the living room.

Her hands were busy roaming and caressing first the muscles of his chest, then down his arms. Her mouth followed where her hands had been, and he was panting hard with desire before he put her down on the soft rug. He held her gaze while he pulled his T-shirt up and over his head. Her breath hitched and he almost came just knowing how much she wanted him.

He nudged his knee between her legs and then wedged it firmly against her as he deliberately undid his belt and his jeans. He kept a firm, steady pressure, and she tilted her hips to get more. He shifted to take off his jeans and boxers and then his knee was right back in place and she arched even farther. She was asking for more.

He leaned over and pulled the hem of her shirt up, an inch at a time, chasing it up with his other hand, rubbing and sending shivers through her. When he got to her breasts, he pulled the shirt over her head in a quick move and then, still using his knee to keep her on the edge, he cupped one breast, testing the hardened nipple with his thumb until she pushed off the floor toward him with a sharp cry. She reached for the waistband of her own jeans, but he captured her wrists in his hands and pulled them up, over her head. He pinned them there with one hand while with the other he undid her pants and shoved them down and off. He looked at her stretched beneath him, skin flushed with pleasure and passion, and he knew he couldn't wait any longer.

But he had to. He had more he wanted to do.

He moved his knee so he could kneel over her and then started to rub, making sweet circles and then slipping one finger inside, and he knew she was almost gone. When he lowered his mouth and tasted her breast as he continued moving his finger in and out, she did lose herself.

He tugged a condom out of his pocket one-handed. Then he pressed Rhian's hands into the rug firmly and murmured, "Don't move an inch." He put the condom on and rolled back to capture her hands again.

She closed her eyes, but opened them as she reached to pull him onto her and into her. While he stroked slowly she watched his face, eyes growing darker, passion growing, and she moved with him to climax and then followed.

He collapsed onto the ground next to her, one hand still holding her breast, the other flung over his head. "God, Rhian, you're amazing."

She propped herself on one elbow as she looked him over. "Mr. Delaney, so are you."

"I am disappointed, though."

She looked bewildered. "I'm at a loss."

"I went to a lot of trouble to bring you *warm* cinnamon rolls. And now, thanks to your lack of control, they're cold."

Laughter started to bubble up in both of them. "*I* can't control myself?" she asked. She reached down and gave him a squeeze.

"Right. You can't." He shook his head even as his eyes widened with desire.

"You're quite sure it's me who's at fault?"

His breath was coming faster, but he managed to smile at her before shifting onto his side so he could reach her more easily. "Quite, quite sure," he growled. "I'll show you."

She wrapped her legs around him and rolled so he was under her. Just after he slid inside her, she paused. "I can put the rolls in the oven later, if you want."

He carefully, gently tucked her hair behind her ear. She turned her head into his hand to hold the contact longer. He spoke so softly he wasn't sure she'd hear him. "I want whatever you want, Rhian MacGregor."

SHE STOOD at the front door and waved as he went outside to start work on the house. "I have to work," she said. "So don't you dare ring this doorbell before quitting time."

"Writing your book?"

She ducked her head, still feeling shy about admitting it. "Trying to."

"How much have you gotten done?"

"Most of two chapters. Your pictures were an inspiration." His eyes searched her face as if he wanted something more from her. She shrugged. "I guess we better get to work."

"Yes, ma'am." He bowed slightly and then grinned at her as he went down the steps. His grin was so sinful she almost followed him just to see what would happen, but she really had to get to work. She'd vowed to write her book and she couldn't let anything, not even amazing sex get in the way.

Late that afternoon Rhian decided she'd done as much as she could. She'd finished her second chapter and was doing a timeline to be sure the events she had planned made sense logically and chronologically before she got any deeper into the writing. But the details were swimming in her blurry brain and so she called it a day.

She went out the front door and around to the side of the house where she'd heard Nathan scraping the paint. He saw her and came down the ladder to greet her with a quick, firm kiss.

"Okay, that's nice." She nodded her head appreciatively and then kissed him back. "Very nice. But I have to eat. Right now." She backed up a step and watched as he considered reaching for her again.

"Don't even think about it, pal. I might not be any good at basketball, but I'm fast and slippery. You couldn't catch me."

His eyes sparkled and his hands tensed at his sides. He was going to try.

She couldn't resist a dare.

He feinted left and then when she dodged right he was close behind her. But she was fast, faster than he'd thought, and it was a close race around the house and back to the front door. If she hadn't had to fumble with the screen door she would have made it safely inside, but he grabbed her waist and held tight.

"Now we'll see who's making the rules," he growled as he pulled her closer. They were both out of breath and laughing too hard for him to put much effort into his seduction. After they kissed each other thoroughly she pulled away again and slipped into the house, closing the screen door between them.

"You've fed me so many times. I want to take you out. Are you up for dinner?" she asked.

"I think we've already established that I'm up for about anything." He winked and gave the screen door a tug, but she held the inside handle firmly.

"I'll take a second to change and then we can swing by your place so you can change, okay?"

He started to nod and then stopped. "I'll run home now and then I'll come back and pick you up?"

"Okay. But it really will just take a second."

"I want to shower, so we'll split up—it'll be faster anyway." He flashed a bright, insincere smile and it hit her that he was hiding something

"Okay," she agreed. She watched him thoughtfully as he walked to his truck. What was he hiding? Was he married? Homeless? Did he have some weird fetish—leather and whips all over?

Maybe she was making an enormous mistake. Even if Jem wasn't going to get hurt when Nathan left, she still would be. She couldn't deny that her emotions were already engaged and she also couldn't deny that she didn't know much more about Nathan than she had when he first showed up.

She sat down on her bed and dialed Min, but all she got was voice mail. How was she supposed to sort out what she was doing without talking to her best friend? She couldn't do this alone.

She left a slightly desperate message and hung up. Min didn't call back in the next five minutes even though Rhian stared at the phone and willed her to. So she called back and left a *thoroughly* desperate message. When that still didn't work, she gave up. She wouldn't be able to figure this out now, certainly not before Nathan got back, so she would just go with it, at least for one more night.

CHAPTER TEN

RHIAN DIRECTED him from her house to an unimposing bar and pizza place in the center of town. As they parked down the street she said, "It isn't Rosie's, but Chet's has the greatest fries and the music is good."

Nathan took her hand and grinned. "You think fries and rock and roll are the way to seduce me, huh?"

She led him inside. "I'm counting on it."

Chet's unassuming exterior was upscale compared to the interior. The lighting was dim. Red leather booths lined the walls and a few tables were set up in front of a small dance floor. The bar looked wonderfully well used, though, with a wide wooden surface scarred by cigarette burns and who knows what else. A few people were seated at tables and in the booths and the bar stools were all taken.

Rhian waved to the bartender. "Hey, Sharon!"

The dark-haired woman waved back.

They chose a booth well away from the stage where the band would play. "It tends to get noisy later," Rhian explained.

A tall blonde wearing too much eye makeup approached to take their order. "Hi, Rhian, who's your friend?" she asked with a clear look of appreciation for Nathan. He glanced away—he didn't enjoy that kind of attention. But Rhian jumped in with introductions.

"Diane Miller, Nathan Delaney. He's painting my house. He's keeping me company me since I'm all alone now."

Diane's face softened and Nathan thought maybe she wasn't so bad when she said, "I can't believe your little guy is old enough to go off by himself. I remember the day the two of you moved in."

Rhian nodded her head. "Trust me, I'm outlawing birthdays. There'll be no more growing up if I can help it."

"Oh, growing up's not so bad. Wait till you see Rachel tonight."

Diane brought them two beers and a basket of fries. Behind her the band—several teenagers of indeterminate sex—started to appear with their equipment.

Rhian leaned closer and pointed with her elbow at the only remotely feminine member of the band who was putting together a drum kit. "That's Diane's youngest, Rachel. Her band is really great—you're in for a treat."

Nathan lifted a dubious eyebrow. "This band?"

"They don't look like much but they're really good. Wait till you hear them cover 'Born to Run.'"

"Which one of them's a boy?"

"Jordan—the one in the shiny shirt. But Rachel is the one who channels Bruce. She's amazing."

He wasn't convinced, but he kept his doubts to himself. Besides, he thought, she'd been right about the fries, so maybe the band would surprise him.

Rhian waved to Rachel. Another teenager wearing a velvet sport coat waved and shouted hello from behind the keyboards.

"You know all these people," he said. Ever since he'd started writing and hiding his name, his circle of friends had shrunk. Rhian lived the life he dreamed about, at home in her neighborhood and in the business of her neighbors' lives.

Rhian dunked a fry in gravy before replying. "When we moved here I had to make it home. I picked it because it was close to the city and I still had—" she paused "—friends there. James and Christine's home had always been my base. I spent holidays and everything at their house. Back then I thought—" She paused again.

She took a swallow of beer and smiled sheepishly, "I'm going to come clean since I sound incoherent. I was engaged. To this jerk named Len. Min calls him Stupid Len, like that's his legal name. We dated in college and then when we got out we were living together. We started this literary magazine called *Phases*, together and got engaged. We weren't going to get married right away, but…. He was the one, I thought. The only guy I'd ever dated seriously."

He knew enough of the chronology of her life to know what was coming next. Her jaw was tense and she took a deep breath. He realized she did that when she was trying not to cry.

"So then the crash and I had Jem. The first couple weeks were, well, they were nothing I want to ever live again. It was a sick joke. I wanted it to end but it wouldn't."

He took her hand and held it. It was the most he could do now, besides wishing he'd known her then.

"Things sort of settled down. I pulled back from the magazine because I was so over my head with Jem. Len stepped up. Everything was going great. We felt like a family. Jem even slept in our bed. We were holding it together."

"Right before Jem turned three, I thought we should get out of the city. I found the house here in Richwoods. Len and I packed, that's the really pathetic part of this whole thing—we packed. *All* of our stuff. The movers came and then he didn't come. He moved his boxes out of the pile and the movers were looking at him like he was crazy and he said he wasn't going to come with me. With us."

Nathan's temper flared hot and sharp. He tightened his hold on her hand. Maybe it was a good thing he hadn't known her then, because he didn't think he'd have been able to resist beating the crap out of the jerk who'd let her go.

"In a way it was good he bailed in that supremely idiotic way, because the mess with the movers and sorting the furniture on the spot made me so mad I couldn't cry. I ended up leaving a lot of my stuff with Len."

She laughed the self-conscious laugh of a person who's trying to deflect pity. "My friends told me he unpacked his things, our things, and stayed right in that apartment, living the life we used to live together, publishing our magazine, until he met this girl named Melanie and she moved in. They got married last year and good luck to her is all I can say."

"If I were you I'd have a lot more to say." Nathan's anger was still simmering.

"Well, I did say one more thing." She shot him her lopsided grin. "I sent them a wedding card and signed it 'your ex-fiancée.' I told them I was skipping the gift since they already had my blender. That felt pretty good."

He laughed. She was amazing, the way she took what life gave her and continued on. He sat back and stretched his legs out. Even though she'd ended with a joke, he knew it had cost her something to share with him and he wanted to be as open as she was. She deserved that. If he couldn't tell her everything, well, this much wouldn't hurt.

"My ex-fiancée took everything when she left except the bed. Too many memories, I guess."

Rhian burst out laughing. "I can't believe it. You have an ex-fiancée, too? We should start a club." She stopped laughing quickly and touched his arm gently, solicitously. "I'm sorry, I shouldn't laugh. Were you hurt?"

"Stunned, I suppose. Glad I found out who she really was. At least I didn't get stuck with her."

"Why did you come to Richwoods? If it's okay to ask?"

He hesitated and then told her the truth. "I was driving. Leaving memories behind. I wanted to go somewhere new. I didn't care where. But my alternator blew right outside Richwoods. It took a couple of days to fix and I decided to stay."

"You live here because your car broke down?" She was staring at him with something like resentment.

"Basically." Actually, he'd taken one look at the town and recognized that it was the kind of place he'd always dreamed about living. He didn't tell her that because it would bring up questions about why he was leaving.

"But what about your stuff? Did you bring everything with you?"

"Patricia took everything with her. I still have a house in New Hampshire. That's part of why I have to leave. But I've been happy here." He looked at her and lowered his voice. "I like the people."

She stared at him, looking baffled.

The band started the first song, a cover of "Layla" and he held out his hand. "Come dancing, Ms. Left at the Altar?"

She stood up and put her arm around his waist. "I guess so Mr. Left at the Altar."

As they spun into a slow dance, Nathan realized she'd been right, the band was good. And he was right, too; he definitely liked the people here. A lot.

WHEN THEY PULLED into her driveway that night, he turned off the truck but left the interior lights on. He drummed his thumbs on the steering wheel and glanced sideways at her.

"I have a confession. I Googled you yesterday." He said it almost casually but she tensed.

"What?"

"Looked you up on the Internet."

"I know what Google means. What's your point?"

"There are archives from *Phases* with your stories. You're good, Rhian. You said you're not a writer, but that's a lie."

She pulled back toward the door. "I didn't mean to lie. I don't think of myself that way anymore."

"What way?"

"As a writer."

"But you are." He pushed a strand of hair back behind her ear. "I hope you don't go back to technical writing. You have a gift."

She moved her head away from his hand, her eyes flashing resentment. "What about you? Look at those sketches you did and then tell me what you're doing on a ladder outside my house every day."

"It's complicated," he argued.

"So is my life, Nathan."

He reached for her again and she let him pull her closer. When she looked up at him, his face was tight and tired. He was still beautiful to her and she was sorry she'd brought up things she already knew he didn't want to discuss. It shouldn't matter to her if he squandered his talent in the long run because their relationship was destined for the short-term only.

"I'm sorry I bugged you about your work," he murmured. She sighed and closed her eyes.

"Did you really like the pieces from *Phases?*"

He had his lips on her forehead and spoke against her skin. "Amazing."

"I loved that magazine."

"It was better when you were there. The best word for it now is 'stupid.' I wonder why?"

He was so good at that. Taking a hurt and gentling it with a joke or a whisper or touch. She tipped her face and caught his lips on her own, lingering over the firm, fantastic feeling of his kiss on her mouth. Her hands went to his arms. The muscles gave her hope; she drew strength from their solidity. He put his hands in her hair and tugged gently to separate the strands and smooth them against her neck. Then he bent to taste her neck at the spot behind her ear where the hair fell away, licking the intimate span of skin, making her shudder.

Her pulse quickened and she inched closer, molding herself to him. If this was a fling, she'd take it. Escape couldn't be wrong all the time, she thought as she stroked his back, his arms, his hair.

She wanted him again, but not how they'd been before. She wanted him properly, in her bed, and she wanted to wake up next to him in the morning. He would breathe next to her and fill her bed, her bedroom, her heart.

Oh Lord, please don't let me love him. But she was afraid it might be too late.

Breaking her kiss, she framed his face with her hands and took a deep breath. "Come inside?"

He nodded quickly and moved to kiss her again but she stopped him. "Will you stay?"

He nodded and put his own hand on her cheek. "Show me the way, Rhian."

And she did.

In her bedroom, she pulled back the antique quilt, exposing cool cotton sheets. He had lingered in the doorway but he took one step inside. He was tall and his broad shoulders filled the space, changing the very air of the room. She beckoned him closer and sat him down on the edge of the bed to unbutton his shirt. Her fingers felt amazingly alive as they brushed his chest, glancing off the taut, muscled skin, advancing down over his stomach. She hadn't done this in so many years, undressed a man, knowing he was submitting to her touch and desires. She knelt between his knees to finish the last three buttons and then pulled the two sides of his shirt aside. She left it hanging open around his beautifully sculpted chest. Leaning down, she reached for his right boot. He toed his foot out of it and she slid it off, feeling the weight of it drop into her hand. When she'd removed his left boot, she moved closer and slid her fingers into his waistband to unbutton his jeans. The zipper went down, each silver tooth loosening one by one, sending her blood boiling hotter.

She'd never had a man in this room before. It was so intimate she was overwhelmed. She had invited him in and asked him to stay and she wanted to be sure she had something wonderful to remember if he left. When he left.

"Would you mind closing your eyes for a minute?" she asked, a little shy.

"Are you going to tie me up?" he asked, a little hopeful.

"That is an excellent thought and one you should hold on to for later."

Obediently he lay back on the pillows. He was so tall

he stretched almost to the bottom of the bed. His skin glowed in the light of the bedside lamp and she was reminded of what she'd thought when she first saw him: he was a god. Absolutely perfect.

She stripped off her clothes and then opened her closet and took out the silky, utterly flimsy negligee she'd bought for herself a year or two ago. She'd never worn it although she'd tried it on several times. She'd never had anything so perfectly gorgeous or explicitly sexy and she hoped he wouldn't think she was ridiculous when he saw her in it.

She went to the bed and knelt next to him, touching him softly, and whispered, "You can open your eyes now."

"Oh, Rhian." His eyes widened and his body came to total attention. He reached for her and then there was no more room for words as they fell over and into each other. If she'd been able to think, Rhian might have been amazed at the way she took command, but she was too intent on taking her pleasure and satisfying him.

When she straddled him, satin sliding over his chest and puddling around her thighs, she saw that he was close to losing control. She put one hand on her own breast and teased the nipple, pulling and tugging until it stood hard and desperate against the sheer lace.

"What are you doing?" His voice was tight with desire as he watched her and she knew he wanted more. She lifted her arms high and arched her back, throwing her breasts into relief. Then she licked one finger and circled her nipple, wetting the satin and lace until it clung tight. She cupped both breasts and leaned forward, close, almost touching him before arching back again. She couldn't believe how wet she was just from watching him watch her.

He reached for her breasts but she grabbed his wrists and moved his hands to her hips instead. He cupped her bottom and lifted her to settle on him. She kept teasing and caressing her own breasts as she rode him hard. She moved forward slightly and the pressure was so exquisite, so exactly right that she climaxed. His eyes widened and he gasped once before pulling her down as he followed her.

She was sated and thoroughly exhausted, but also reveling in the aftershocks of the most amazing sex she'd ever had.

"Good Lord, you might want to warn me before you do that again." His voice held all the satisfaction he felt, and a sharp stir of pride burst in her. She'd done that to him.

"It might be a while," she sighed.

He pulled her close and buried his face in the lace at her breast. "I don't think so, Rhian. In fact, I hope you started a trend."

Rhian smiled to herself and counted every cent her outrageous negligee had cost to have been money well spent. Before long he was asleep beside her, one arm still wrapped around her.

He filled her bed so perfectly she didn't see how it would be possible to sleep there alone again. She lay awake, watching him sleep, wondering at the beauty of his face. The laugh lines around his eyes reminded her of the fun she'd had when he taught her to play basketball. Even though his eyes were closed, she had memorized the intent, watchful way he looked when she was talking to him. He had so much to offer. Was, in so many ways, an amazing man.

But before she drifted to sleep, she reminded herself of how little she knew about him, how little he was willing to let her know. He was living in Richwoods because his car broke down. He was leaving as soon as he finished the house for reasons he refused to share. Keeping this as a summer romance, far away from her life with Jem, was the right thing.

CHAPTER ELEVEN

THEY SPENT every minute they could together for the next four weeks, falling into what Rhian found to be a satisfying pattern. They'd work, stopping for lunch midday, then call a halt in the late afternoon. He never failed to ask about her book and she never failed to take something away from their conversations. He had such insight, not just into the storytelling but also the technical aspects of plot and character motivation and theme. His interest kept her writing when several times she thought it would be best to quit.

Sometimes they played basketball. Sometimes they talked about her book. Sometimes they had mind-blowing sex. They listened to Rachel's band and ate cheese fries. They went dancing twice. They had dinner with Cindy and Ned, and afterward spent hours by the lake talking. Rhian told him about the Thursday night band concerts in the park downtown and was surprised when he leaped at the chance to sit on lawn chairs with her neighbors listening to show tunes.

Her house was gradually reemerging from its coat of garish pink and this time the color was exactly right.

Then there was the sex. She'd called Min and confessed that she had been right. Now that she'd "gotten some" as her friend so delicately put it, she felt Satisfied and Smug.

Nathan brought her out of herself in ways she'd never felt, showing her how to release and hold on, take and share, and be. She was alert and sexy and alive.

She dialed Min and listened to the phone ring as she kept one eye on the TV. The promos had promised big news today. Nathan had gone to his apartment to pick up a change of clothes. He'd be back later that morning.

"Hello?"

Rhian smiled to hear Min's familiar voice. "Hey, it's me."

"Why are you calling now? I'm watching *Morning Lindsey!*"

"Me, too. Let's multitask."

The theme song came on and Lindsey was pacing the front of the stage and waving to the Hall Heads in their bright wigs.

"How's the project? Any leads about the provenance of the paintings?"

"Hints. The details are there waiting to be found."

Rhian held the phone with her shoulder as she got out a yellow cereal bowl and poured Cap'n Crunch. She cocked an eye at the TV and saw Lindsey behind the desk with a photo of an auburn-haired man on the screen behind her. The Senso Sightings map was lit up and the cardboard silhouette was in place in the chair next to her.

"Who's the guy?" she asked Min.

"Chris Senso's agent, Matt Callahan. Aren't you watching?"

"I turned the sound down so I could talk to you."

"She says since they can't find Chris Senso, they're going to stake out the agent. He works in Boston, outside the mainstream publishing world, so she figures Chris Senso comes to his office on the sly."

"She's getting desperate, huh?" Rhian said. She imagined Jem would be sad if Chris Senso was found when he wasn't watching the show. Maybe Lindsey would stretch it out a few more days.

"How are things with you? Writing coming along?"

"Chapter seven has been put to bed."

"And Nathan, you putting him to bed also?"

This was why she'd called Min—to talk about Nathan. "He's about finished with the house. I don't think we have more than one or two more days left before he packs up."

"Has he said anything?"

"No."

"How do you feel about it?"

"I went into this thinking it was best to use him as a starter guy. But Min. He's—" she paused "—not a starter guy. I wish we had more time."

"Oh dear."

"Damn right."

"Well." Min sighed. Rhian could almost feel Min's concern despite their separation. "What do you want?"

"I go back and forth between wishing I never met him to wanting to kidnap him and tie him up to get one more day with him."

"That's a big spread."

"I know." She put her spoon down, not hungry anymore. "What I want doesn't matter anyway. The ball's in his court. Actually he owns the ball *and* the court."

"My fingers are crossed."

Rhian figured she could use all the help she could get.

"DAMN IT, Matt. Why can't we stop her?" Nathan sank down on the edge of his mattress.

"Because she's a psycho bitch?"

"Hasn't she broken any laws yet?"

"No." Matt's voice dropped. "But if she puts one toe outside the line, we're going after her with both barrels."

"And if she doesn't?"

"We keep our fingers crossed."

"Matt! That's not a plan." Standing up, Nathan paced to the front door and looked out the window. How long would it be before he looked out and saw someone waiting with a camera to stalk him.

"It's not like you were actually planning to visit me."

"She's pulling out the stops. We've got to end this."

"You deserve that, I get it."

Nathan turned and leaned back against the wall. "It's more serious now. There's someone else involved. Someone I like."

"Rhian MacGregor?"

"You'd like her, too."

"She doesn't know?"

"Of course not. But the more important thing is no one can know about her. She's got a kid. A normal life. She wouldn't want the crap that comes with the cameras." Wouldn't want him if he brought that. Rhian fit perfectly into the small town of Richwoods. Fame would wreck the balance, destroy relationships that mattered to her, steal any chance he had of spending more time with her.

Remembering that this was what Matt was going through, he said, "How are you doing?"

"Phone's been ringing all morning. I think I'm famous. Can't get out the door and Jerry, my intern, told me they practically ripped his shirt off when he was coming in."

"Damn it!" Nathan felt like punching something. "You shouldn't be mixed up in this. I'm sorry."

"First, I'm fine, Nathan. They don't care about me. My life isn't interesting enough to hold *my* attention, let alone Lindsey Hall's." Matt's voice was calm, reassuring. "And second, I wouldn't have traded this ride with you for anything."

Nathan's breathing slowed. Matt was unflappable. The call waiting on his cell phone beeped. He glanced at the caller ID.

"Patricia's on the other line. This can't be good."

"Good luck."

He clicked over. "Hello?"

No one answered. She had hung up. Just what he needed. One crazy person stalking him on TV and one crazy person stalking him by phone.

AT ONE THAT AFTERNOON, he finished painting the house. Friday. Perfect day to finish a job, finish his time here, finish his relationship. Except he wasn't ready.

He knew Rhian wanted him gone before Jem came home. She didn't want to complicate her life. But for him it had been the opposite. He'd agreed to the deadline because he wanted to have this life. Now that it was time to go, he didn't want to give it up. He'd promised himself and Rhian he'd stay long enough to finish the house. He would keep that promise.

CHAPTER TWELVE

SHE SQUINTED UP at the patch under the bathroom window.

"What do you mean the paint wouldn't adhere?"

"Adhere, it means stick or stay on."

She shot him an irritated glance. "I know what it means. Why is it happening?"

He lifted his shoulders in an elaborate shrug. He was enjoying himself. He'd bought a small can of paint called "Shriek" which was close to the color the Bobalos had used. When he got back he painted a two-by-two foot section of the house and then brought Rhian out.

"This doesn't make sense. Does it have to do with the bathroom? Are the shingles damp?"

He rubbed his chin, parodying deep thought. "I may have to study this problem. Gather theories."

"Theories?" she asked him with her hands on her hips, obviously starting to catch on. "About paint?"

"Maybe Seth is available for consultation."

She stepped back and crossed her arms. "Now I know there's something going on. What are you up to?"

"I told you. The paint won't adhere." He put his hands on her shoulders and leaned his forehead against hers. "Might take a few days to figure out. I'll have to stick around a while longer."

Her eyes widened. She rolled her head, still keeping contact with him, to look at the house and then, carefully, rolled back. "Right. Adhesion problems can be…"

"Sticky," he offered helpfully.

"Could take a few days."

"Could."

"What'll we do in the meantime?"

He squeezed her shoulders gently and then slid his hands down her back, gathering her carefully, gratefully to him, as he tilted his head and met her lips with his own. "Hang out."

A WEEK HAD PASSED since he thought of the not-finished-with-the-house loophole. Nathan was in a bubble. That's how he thought about it. Like the Astrodome. Everything inside was fine and green and the weather was always perfect.

Outside the bubble, things were going to hell. On Monday, Lindsey Hall's mystery caller confided that Chris Senso had already had fifteen minutes of fame. The remainder of the week's shows were devoted to the formerly famous. Tuesday was one-hit wonders, Wednesday was heroes from small-town disasters, Thursday former child stars and Friday was a mixed bag of lottery winners, medical miracles, tech whiz kids, and white-collar criminals. The country watched in fascination as she grilled them on David Dale trivia. It was bad. Very bad.

Matt had moved into his office so he wouldn't have to run the camera gauntlet every morning. He said the takeout was better than it was near his house. Bad again.

Patricia called twice and hung up. He got pissed off and called her, but she wouldn't answer. Annoying and bad. Also confusing.

That was outside the bubble.

Inside the bubble he had Rhian and his writing.

Now that he wasn't painting—still waiting to solve the "adhesion" problem—he had plenty of time for both. He'd never felt more alive. Rhian was his good-luck charm, his muse, his once-in-a-lifetime woman. When he wrote, the story flowed as it hadn't in years.

"You're insane, Nathan—a woman can't cause you to write." Matt said, during their Friday morning phone call. "However, if this particular insanity gets the book done, then I'm all for it."

"I want you to meet her."

"Can't risk it. The press is like my house-arrest bracelet. Alarms go off when I move outside my defined periphery. Two days ago I went for a round of golf with some buddies. Some guy was hiding in the bushes with a camera on number seven. He must have thought the great Chris Senso was there. Guy jumps out right when I'm cranked back for my drive. Scared the shit out of me. I shanked it so bad my ball ended up in Connecticut."

"I can't believe this is happening to you."

Matt sighed. Nathan sighed. Nathan promised himself that the second Lindsey Hall said she had another big announcement, he'd hit the road. Until then, well, call him Bubble Boy.

"DO YOU EVER WONDER if he was in jail," Min asked Rhian. Rhian was dusting her bedroom as they talked on the phone about, as usual, Nathan.

"It's crossed my mind that he could be a murderer or a bank robber. But he seems too normal and, well, nice." For all his strength and skill with athletics, he was a gentle person. She didn't think it had been jail. At least not for anything violent.

She finished the bedside table and shifted to the top of her dresser, moving the collection of framed pictures, her jewelry box and her small silver-backed mirror onto the bed so she could dust properly.

"What else could it be?" Min wondered.

"I've ruled out bigamy and witness protection." She ran a hand over a black-and-white photo of Jem as a one-year-old. He'd been learning to walk but he was still so pudgy and helpless. In some ways he still needed her to protect him. When he came back he deserved to find that his life was as he'd left it, not mucked up with a stranger who might or might not stick around.

The paint-adhering thing was cute but confusing. Far from a commitment, it might mean he was still having car trouble. Or he wanted more sex. Or he couldn't think of where to go next.

"What about prostitution?" Min snickered.

"Not that he wouldn't be qualified." Rhian sighed. *Heck, he'd be worth every penny.* She sat on the edge of the bed and the memory of the first night he'd spent there with her swept over her. He'd filled her room so completely she hadn't known how she'd go back to sleeping alone. She still didn't know. "But I don't think that's it."

"Have you tried asking him?"

Rhian sighed. "Not in so many words, no. He shuts down completely anytime I get close to what he's been doing since college or why he doesn't do more with his art. The other day I asked him what his ex-fiancée was doing now and he couldn't answer me. I hate to spoil our time with questions he doesn't want to answer."

"Or you're afraid of what he'll say. Maybe you'll find out there's nothing wrong with him and then you'll have to think about keeping him."

"Keeping him? He's not a puppy, for God's sake." But Rhian felt her face flush. Could Min be right? "I'm not keeping him. That was clear from the start."

"But what if the truth is he's a good guy having some trouble? Would you try?"

Rhian got up from the bed and started dusting again. She needed to keep moving so she could keep her thoughts from following where Min was trying to lead. "Listen, Min, I better go."

"Can I advocate for a face-to-face with your man? You owe him honest questions before you cut him loose."

"He owes me honest answers is more like it."

"Make the first step," Min went on gently. "Even if it's scaring you, you need to know before you make your decision."

Rhian protested as she put the last picture back in place. "I made my decision. He's got to be gone before Jem comes back."

"But if you have the facts maybe you'll rethink that."

"What answers could he possibly give that would change a rootless, shady man into a person I'd have in Jem's life?" *In my heart*, Rhian's brain whispered.

"Okay. But do it anyway," Min said. "See you soon."

Soon. There was that word again. Rhian hung the phone up and let it hang in her slack hand.

She had to figure this out now. She could keep on the way she'd been with Nathan, stick to her original plan, let him go when he finally decided to wander off. Or she could somehow scrape together the courage to face her desire to try for more.

Damn. There it was. She wanted more. She wanted everything she could get and then more. She'd had her beautiful time with Nathan and it was ending and it wasn't enough.

But if she forced Nathan to come clean and what she found wasn't bad or scary, that changed everything. A summer fling was one thing. A long-term relationship scared her cold. Min was leaving sometime this year. What if Nathan stuck around long enough for them to get attached before he left, too?

When she was a kid and her mother had brought so many new men into their lives she'd given up getting to know them. But it hadn't been easy. She'd had to put a wall around part of her heart and she couldn't bear seeing Jem do the same thing.

But what if, somehow, this guy stayed? Her heart soared at the idea of spending a lifetime with Nathan. She wanted a chance at that even if it did leave her dangling outside her safety zone.

He couldn't want that, though. He'd agreed to end the relationship back at the beginning. He'd made up that adhesion problem but it was the flimsiest of excuses. All it would take was him deciding to paint that last patch and the house would be finished and he would go. If he was really thinking of staying, he'd have discussed it with her normally, not faked a paint problem. He'd decided to linger, but he hadn't decided to stay.

She shivered.

She owed it to herself to find out the truth. She'd ask him Min's questions and give him his chance to stay. Tonight. She couldn't stand to let this go on anymore. The thing to do would be to seduce him, properly this time. Get him in the right mood, blow his mind and then when he was off guard, go for the truth. It was slightly dirty pool to purposely plan a seduction and then probe into this place he was obviously trying to protect. Sometimes a girl had to play dirty pool, though, if she wanted to get a shot at something better.

But what if he doesn't go? Nathan not going was way more scary than Nathan going.

RHIAN WASN'T a wall punching kind of person but, as she eyed the pale yellow wall next to the kitchen phone, boy, was she ever tempted. Chet had screwed up her perfect night. Now she was stuck.

What did she *want* to be doing? Preparing for her night of wonder with her man. What was she *actually* doing? Answering distress calls from Chet who was calling in the bet she'd lost at Jem's going-away barbecue. She'd said she would waitress. Chet was short-handed and, apparently, unable to understand the words 'please don't make me, I'm planning a night of amazing sex.' Actually, she hadn't said exactly that, but he wouldn't take no for an answer. Maybe she'd punch Chet's wall.

Two hours later, she pulled her station wagon to a stop outside a three-story Victorian on Front Street. It had been converted to apartments but was nicely maintained with trim bushes and flower-filled planters in front. It was... pleasant. She double-checked the sheet on the seat next to her. Yep, this building matched the address printed on the quote he'd given her what felt like years ago.

She'd decided she would give him her book to read. Nathan's would be the first eyes that saw the pages. When she'd first thought of it, she'd backed away. But then she saw that it was what she needed. She'd give him the book to read and that would seal her commitment to their relationship. He wouldn't know that, but she would. It would close one back door and make her take a chance.

Grabbing the thick envelope off the floor of the passenger side, she got out and smoothed her skirt down self-consciously. The skirt was the short, silky one she'd worn the first time Nathan had taken her out. On top she had a scoop-neck T-shirt that fit more snugly than her norm. It made her feel obvious in a way she didn't ordinarily enjoy. She took a step, wobbled on the unfamiliar height of high-heeled sandals she'd swiped from Min's closet and then found her stride. It was ludicrous to waitress in an outfit like this.

But she wanted this night to be special. Waiting tables would delay the moment when she could be with Nathan and she figured why waste the time completely? She'd imagined how it would feel to have Nathan watch her all night, knowing she'd dressed up for him, and teasing both of them with the anticipation of later.

For once in her life she was going with style over logic—the *Guide to a Practical Waitress Wardrobe* losing out to the *Handbook for Seducing Your Man in Public*. She sincerely hoped she wasn't making a mistake. Her arches already hurt.

This was her first visit to his place. He'd never invited her and she'd stopped hinting, partly because she'd been afraid of what she might find.

This quiet, charming, respectable building was not what she'd expected. Trailing lobelia and pale peach daylilies alleviated some of her dread. In fact, the outside of the apartment was solidly reassuring. It was no fleabag motel or room-by-the-week flophouse.

She rang the doorbell of his ground-floor apartment

once, quickly, before she lost her nerve. Was it possible that Min was right? Maybe all his talk about leaving had a reasonable explanation—she could help him problem-solve, figure the solution out.

She heard him moving around inside and then he cracked the door, keeping the security chain on. The one eye she could see widened with surprise. "Rhian! What are you doing here?"

He didn't open the door. She couldn't have felt more stupid.

"I wanted to see you for a minute." *Open the door and look at my outfit, dummy.*

He glanced over his shoulder, away from her skirt. Away from Min's supersexy shoes. *Was he blind?* "Okay."

If she could have sunk through the boards of the porch she would have. Why wasn't he opening the door? Was it possible he had a wife inside there? A girlfriend? A boyfriend? "Could you maybe open the door?" she managed to say.

He jerked back, rattling the security chain. "Give me a second? I need to put on pants."

He closed the door. *Pants?* He needed to put on pants after everything they'd done together? After all the times she'd taken his pants off? She heard hustling, muffled thumps and drawers slamming. Was he having to hunt and subdue the pants before putting them on? Should she leave? Forget about the last fantasy night? Forget about the lunatic she'd been spending time with? No. She shifted her feet inside the illogical shoes. She was here. There were day-lilies and lobelia. It was still possible this would be okay.

Nathan opened the door, all the way this time, his breath coming fast. He was, in fact, wearing pants. Khaki-colored work pants with a blue canvas belt. A dark green T-shirt was tucked neatly in and his work boots were laced and tied. Not a hastily pulled on ensemble. "Come in," he said. "Unless you'd rather talk outside, because we can." He started to slide out through the opened door, backing her up onto the porch.

She stepped forward just as firmly, forcing him back inside. "No." Rhian was determined to see the place now that he'd gone to such pains to destroy the evidence of…whatever. "I'll come in."

She stepped inside and her first impression was that Nathan's apartment was charming. The high ceilings were graceful and the afternoon light streamed in through the tall front window. The room had a wide doorway, obviously formerly part of a dignified foyer, leading into another room with the same high ceilings and a corner fireplace. She almost let herself relax, reassured by the classically elegant space.

Her second impression was…not so great.

There wasn't much evidence that the apartment was occupied. A basketball lay in one corner of the entryway next to a pair of sneakers and a baseball cap. No pictures, no knickknacks, no clutter of years or even months of accumulated living. No TV, no stereo, no CDs. The table near the window was absolutely bare except for a lamp and Nathan's brown leather wallet and silver key ring. The window had white curtains in a tone-on-tone stripe but they looked about fifty years old and Rhian would have bet her last dollar they'd come with the place. The apartment was as impersonal as it could be without being empty.

She gestured to the Adirondack chair that was pulled up close to a picnic bench. "Family heirlooms?" she asked, unable to keep the disappointment out of her voice. She'd allowed herself to hope. Stupid.

He shrugged. "Temporary. You want a beer?"

Her heart sank further. He didn't even apologize. He knew what this must look like and he didn't care. She gripped her book tighter. Min's questions suddenly seemed like the most futile spit-in-the-wind gesture.

He walked through the wide doorway and made a right turn through a narrower one. She followed him, seeing— and wishing she hadn't—the mattress on the floor, stack of books next to it, striped comforter pulled up neatly. But no amount of hospital corners could make up for the fact that he was a grown man sleeping on a mattress on the floor like a college student. Like someone with no intention of staying very long.

Coming here had been a bad idea. She wished desperately for her sneakers and jeans. Confronting this disheartening place in her sexy outfit was like being arrested in a Halloween costume—undignified. Sighing, she continued on to the short back hallway. She was surprised to see the refrigerator in the hall, the open door blocking her way.

She managed to keep her disappointment out of her voice this time. "This is…different."

"Yeah, this building used to be one house and the apartments are kind of chopped up. The kitchen is minuscule so the fridge is out here." He straightened and closed the door, handing her a Harp. "It's convenient for midnight snacks."

His dimple winked at her and she remembered how his grin had started to break down her defenses the first time she saw it. She had loved the way it made him look so devil-may-care. She hadn't known how much she'd come to resent that attitude.

She half turned back to the bedroom but he leaned against the wall behind him, propping his shoulders and stretching his legs out, crossed at the ankles. Apparently they were going to talk right here. She wanted to be the smart, logical, self-aware person who walked away from him before he walked away from her. Because he wasn't staying. If his lack of verbal commitment to her hadn't made that clear, his lack of physical commitment to this place certainly should have.

But who could be smart or logical when Nathan Delaney was *leaning* against the wall two feet away? His athletic grace, so much a part of him when he was in motion, was no less evident when he was still. It was in the way he held his shoulders, the slant of his hip and waist, even the ripple in the muscles of his forearm when he lifted his bottle. Would it be bad to make love on a mattress on the floor? Was she bad to want one more night before she started facing reality? Hadn't she had enough reality in her life? Wasn't she owed some fantasy?

A final seduction, one last night of absolute animal gratification. But she wouldn't give him the book. She'd already given him her heart and she was pretty sure she was going to have it handed back to her in pieces. Her book wouldn't get caught in that.

"So why the surprise visit?" he asked.

"I had this plan, for tonight," she said, gripping her envelope tighter as she sipped from her bottle. "I wanted to have a special night with you. I was going to dress up and ply you with champagne and then take you to bed and have my way with you."

He turned toward her, one shoulder still propped on the wall, the other arm stretched across to rest on the opposite wall. He licked his lips and desire shot straight through her. "All of our nights are special, but that one sounds perfect," he murmured. "And you started the dressing-up part already." His eyes traveled down her skirt to the high-heeled shoes and back up again. Her toes curled with the intensity of his examination.

"Yes." She swallowed, trying to calm her breathing. "Except instead I'm waitressing at Chet's."

"Waitressing?" He blinked.

"I lost a bet." She pushed her bottle against his arm. "Which actually was your fault. But anyway, I told Chet I'd work for him and he's calling in the debt tonight."

Nathan moved closer, pressing his body against hers, thighs, hips, stomachs meeting with gentle but firm pressure that made her want to press back. He leaned in, both forearms against the wall on either side of her head. She loved feeling him surround her. Why was she doing this? Why wasn't she walking out? Because he was looking at her like he wanted to consume her and she didn't want to think.

If she were writing a manual called *How To Date But Not Get Involved* her first piece of advice would be find someone who didn't turn you on. It was impossible to be rational and turned on at the same time. And rational, Rhian thought, as Nathan stroked a hand under the sleeve of her shirt, was overrated.

Raising one eyebrow, he grinned wickedly as his eyes skimmed down her body. "Will you wear an apron? A very little apron to go with this," he said, leering, "very little skirt?"

"I'm a waitress, not a French maid." She blushed. She'd wanted him wanting her, but it felt uncomfortable.

He kissed her firmly and then pulled back and said matter-of-factly. "Any apron will do. I have a good imagination."

She punched him in the arm, but it had no effect on his grin. She wanted to punch him harder. Where the hell was his telephone? Why couldn't he have a family photo. Even a picture of his old fiancée would have been better than nothing! He didn't even have a magnet from the pizza-delivery place.

Holding his beer in his right hand above her head, he reached out with his left and hooked one finger in the neck of her shirt. "How about some pregame, Rhian? Set the scene?"

Oh. She couldn't. Sliding sideways, she turned her head away from his and gently disengaged his hand. "Nathan, we can't."

"But we already are," he protested, putting his hand back.

She pushed against him impatiently and dropped the envelope. As she watched, horrified, the pages of her book slid out of the flap. Bending quickly, she reached for it, but Nathan was there before her. Her forehead met his with a sharp crack.

"Ow." Rocking back on his heels, he pressed his beer to his temple. He squinted at her with one eye, the other closed in pain. "You okay?"

No. She was *this* close to crying and mad at herself for it. No, no, no, she wasn't okay and would never be okay. she clamped her lips shut and stuffed the pages back into the envelope before he saw them. "I'm fine."

He put one hand out, trapping the pages on the floor. "Is this your book?"

A lie was on the tip of her tongue, but it wouldn't have helped. His dark blue eyes were on hers. "It's your book." This time it wasn't a question.

Why couldn't she speak? She needed a lie, something to get her book and herself out the door.

"Rhian?" His deep, gentle voice had been such a comfort

to her, so familiar from late nights in her bed, early mornings in her kitchen, afternoons on the hammock. Now it killed her. Put a hole, the beginning of a break in her heart.

She pushed at his wrist, but he didn't move his hand. "I have to go," she muttered.

"So go," he said. "But I'm keeping the book."

He caught her hand with his other one, gently holding her still, keeping her with him. One finger stroked up her wrist over the pulse point. "Come on, Rhian. Let me read it. Please?"

She closed her eyes, feeling the already uncomfortable high heels on her feet, her legs bare under the skirt, her heart pounding.

"No," she whispered.

With a swift jerk he yanked the stack of paper and the envelope out from under her hand. He straightened and held it over his head. "I'm holding it hostage. I'll give it back later when you hand over that tiny skirt."

She stood up, too, looking at her book held high over his head. No way she could reach it. No way she would humiliate herself by trying. "Nathan, give it back."

The harshness of her voice must have startled him. He lowered the book and held it out, his eyes puzzled. "Sorry. Bad joke."

Which was not what she wanted. She hadn't intended to hurt him and yet she had.

"Fine. Keep it," she said. "I have to go."

She wobbled again on the heels as she turned away.

"Wait, Rhian. I don't have to if you don't want me to." He caught up to her at the front door. Held the book out. "Here. I'm sorry I teased you."

She looked from him to the book. She was pathetic. She

had looked forward to sharing it with him and stupidly she couldn't force herself to stop wanting that. Sighing, she pushed the envelope back to him. "I'm sorry, too." She squinted at the early-evening sunshine in the pretty courtyard. "See you later."

CHAPTER THIRTEEN

SEVEN MINUTES INTO her shift she dropped an empty glass, shattering it on the kitchen floor, and remembered why she had quit waitressing. She wasn't good at it.

Ten minutes after that she mixed up the orders for two hungry families. Both moms sent her death glares while plying their children with packages of Saltines, and Chet threatened to fire her. He took it back when he saw how close she was to walking out on her own.

She went back to drop off another basket of bread for the hungry families and the dad at table nine, a stocky guy with a thick mustache, brushed his arm against her thigh as he stretched to get a peek down her shirt.

If she'd been holding a menu she'd have whapped him over the head and told him her outfit had nothing to do with him. Instead she had to settle for a very mean look to convey her thoughts, namely *yuck* and *ew* and *you're a dad* and *stop*. Unfortunately, the man's wife had also noticed the thigh brush and the look she shot at Rhian definitely meant *get your trashy high-heeled self away from the father of my children.*

Rhian took the hint.

She fled to the restroom to regroup. The one stall was unoccupied and she locked herself in, leaning against the wall and trying to calm down. Okay, she'd always been a bad waitress, but not this bad. The truth was, this mess was all about Nathan.

She'd let herself care.

She'd let herself get tangled.

She'd let herself fall in love.

She was so screwed. And not in a good way.

She followed the instructions for everything from her toaster to the lights on her Christmas tree. She knew better than to ignore the rules and yet, somehow, she'd lost track of that with this relationship that could no longer technically be called a fling.

Even that afternoon she'd lost her nerve and handed him her book. She'd been standing in an apartment that couldn't have been more clearly temporary if it had been a bed in a hostel and she'd still grasped at a moment of hope. Dumb. And now he had her book. She wanted it back with a physical longing.

She heard someone come in the bathroom and she let herself back out of the stall. A harried-looking woman was leading her daughter to the sink. The girl, who looked to be about three was covered in ketchup, both hands, her chin and all down her shirt. A big blob was caught on the toe of one light-up Barbie sneaker.

"Uh-oh," Rhian said. "Looks like a ketchup attack." She was trying to get a smile out of the kid, whose face was pinched, but instead she got a venomous glare from the mother. *Oops. Leering dad's wife.*

She was a *mom*, she wanted to tell the woman. She didn't dress like this normally. The skirt hadn't been intended to ensnare any man except one shiftless house-painter. The shoes were killing her and she would never,

ever wear them again. They weren't even hers. However, she couldn't say any of those things. Saying them would mean acknowledging that this poor woman's husband had indeed tried to peek down her shirt.

"Do you want me to get a cloth from the kitchen?" she asked instead.

"No," the woman said shortly as she jerked her daughter closer to the sink. "Put your hands under the water, Kerri. We'll get you cleaned up in no time."

Rhian stood helplessly. She was being ostracized from her tribe. The woman saw a hussy. She had no idea who Rhian really was, that she knew how to deal with ketchup messes and crying three-year-olds. That she understood too-long waits in restaurants and flaring tempers. That she was on the mom team.

What was she doing in this getup? In this life?

Closer to tears than she'd been all night, Rhian left. At least she'd make sure the woman's food was out by the time she got her daughter cleaned up.

As she rushed back to the kitchen, she scanned the crowd. He wasn't here yet, which meant he was there, in his bare, pathetic apartment, reading her book. *Her book.*

She was trapped. Trapped in these clothes, knowing Nathan was reading her book. Trapped in a nonrelationship with parameters she'd created that ruled out the possibility of them caring for each other.

Rhian took a deep breath. Just get through it, she thought. Plunging into the bustle of the Friday-dinner rush, she covered her unease better, joking with her friends and people she knew from Jem's sports teams, smiling at strangers, but not really seeing any of them.

She didn't notice Nathan when he came in. He was

suddenly there behind her, his breath warm on her neck as he spoke in her ear.

"You look awful damn sexy in that apron." He tugged on the strings knotted at the back of her apron and she almost dropped her tray, shocked by the surge of desire that shot through her, and immediately irritated with both of them.

He was wearing a dusty-blue shirt with white piping on the collar and yokes and white mother-of-pearl snaps. It was a cowboy shirt from a very upscale cowboy store. Where did a housepainter get the money to buy the clothes this guy wore, anyway? The square silver buckle on the leather belt in his dark brown jeans was practically begging to be undone. His height set him apart from most of the men in Chet's and the way he moved, confident and athletic, pushed him above the rest. He was so sexy he looked like an ad for…well, for sex.

Which had always turned her on before, but tonight it made her angry. How could she have thought it would be okay to date someone just for sex? How could he? When he left that square of her house undone, why hadn't she said enough's enough and sent him on his way?

"I have to work," she said, struggling to control her breathing.

"If you got fired, you'd come live with me and be my kept woman," he said.

Her heart beat hard. Who was he kidding? Kept with what? For how long?

"Sit anywhere along the wall—that's my section."

He looked puzzled but stepped back. "Rhian," he started to ask, but she turned away and picked up two empty bottles from the table behind her. She bobbled one and dropped the other, which luckily didn't break. She crouched down to pick it up and noticed him admiring her legs when she did. That had been the point of the short skirt when she'd planned it, but she found she didn't enjoy now.

"It's really busy, Nathan," she said as she stood up.

He stuck his hands in his front pockets and shrugged. "Okay. But before you go, can I say…" He leaned in to whisper in her ear again. "I loved your book. Thank you."

She ducked her head and walked away. She had never in her life been more irritated than she was by that "thank you." What game was he playing? They were supposed to have been about fun, sex, a summer fling. He was still leaving. So why did he put any energy into the rest of it?

Hell, the man had bought her a flower basket for her front porch, hanging the cascade of blue and purple flowers last Tuesday when she was napping. He should have been spending his money on sex toys, vibrators and lingerie and…and handcuffs, not home improvements.

Thank you, Nathan Delaney. Thank you very much for nothing.

She walked blindly back to the kitchen, ignoring the tourists at table six who were waiting not so patiently for their check. Setting her tray on the prep table, she caught Chet's concerned eye. "I'm exhausted."

"Least you stopped breaking stuff."

"For now," she said.

Back in the bar she refilled pitchers of Bud for a table of college boys and dropped menus off for her friend Denise's family. She brought Nathan a Corona and a menu but didn't stay to talk. She took an order from a table of kids who'd come to listen to the band and had to go back three times to clarify details. If she owned Chet's, she'd have fired herself. As she left the table the third time, she glanced at Nathan. He raised his eyebrows and mouthed, *You okay?*

She nodded and went back into the kitchen, conscious of her short skirt and high heels, but not in a good way.

When she went past him next, Nathan caught her wrist. "Did something happen?"

"Nothing happened, Nathan. Nothing changed." Which was the whole problem.

She pulled away and went back to the kitchen.

Once the band started to play, the food orders slowed down. She swung past Nathan's table every once in while. He asked her to sit down, but she said she wouldn't have a break until nine. She didn't want to talk to him.

The next time she looked for him, he wasn't at his table. She glanced around the dance floor but didn't see him. Diane came by and jerked her head toward the door.

"He went out. Looked like he had a call."

WHEN HIS CELL PHONE RANG, Nathan pulled it out and glanced at the caller ID. Patricia. "Hello," he said, half expecting her to hang up again. When she answered him, he stuck a hand over his left ear to block the noise and made his way through the tables to the door.

"You've been crank-calling me," he said, once he was outside and could hear.

"I have bad news and I didn't know how to tell you," she answered.

The door of Chet's opened as a family came out and Rachel's voice crooning "Back Streets" reached him. "You in trouble?"

"No. Actually it's good news for me. It's bad news for…" She didn't finish.

Nathan felt like she'd punched him in the gut. "Me."

"Except it doesn't have to be," she hurried to say.

He cut her off. "Quit screwing around, Patricia."

"I knew you'd take this badly. I was afraid to call."

He waited.

"Actually there is part of it that's good for you. See, I met this agent, Gary. We hit it off and he put together a deal for me and so the good thing is that you don't have to send me money anymore."

Nathan stood with his back against the building. The bricks were warm from the collected heat of the day. He leaned his head back and closed his eyes. This was the end. No matter what Patricia said next, his life was done. The bass beat thumped behind him.

"The deal is great. A book and interview and I'm getting a reality show. I'll be the host, like Ryan Seacrest." Her voice rose in excitement. Nathan didn't know who the hell Ryan Seacrest was, but he was sure it wasn't someone he'd ever want to be.

He was watching a train jump the tracks and barrel right at him. Which was close to the way he'd felt when he met Patricia. She'd been so vibrant. She'd pulled him out of his increasingly isolated life and made him feel engaged again. If only he'd known that Patricia wanted to be the center of the whole world, not just his.

"Who would ever have imagined that I'd have my own show!"

"You would. What does it have to do with me?"

"Nathan, Lindsey Hall has you. Someone else, not me, turned you in already. She was going to break the story on their information anyway."

He closed his eyes. That was it then.

"So what's your thinking, better you than someone else?"

She didn't hear the sarcasm, answering honestly. "Right."

"Damn it, Patricia! This is wrong. I gave you everything you ever wanted when we were together. We broke up. I moved on. You should move on, too."

"You moved on?" There was naked curiosity in Patricia's tone.

"Moved on to a new place, I meant."

"This *is* me moving on. I'm moving on to my own TV show. The first thing is the interview on Lindsey Hall. We're going to discuss my show *Hide and Chic*. The idea is that I'll go around looking for celebrities and we'll sneak up and film them. It'll be like 'E' meets one of those Discovery Channel shows where they track wild animals."

If he didn't know better, he'd think he was high. "That's the most ridiculous pile of shit I ever heard," he said.

"Well, get used to it, Nate, because you're going to be the first guest on my pile of shit." Was it possible she was insulted?

"Guest?"

"Game? Quarry? We haven't really finalized all the concepts."

"Victim, Patricia," he spit. "Don't kid yourself. You know I want to be left alone."

"Oh please. You don't want to be left alone. People who want to be left alone become garbage men or tech-support phone center geeks. They don't write bestselling novels and auction the movie rights to Hollywood!"

"I didn't write the books to get famous!" he shouted, and then added more quietly. "I wrote them 'cause I liked the kid, David Dale. I thought he was funny."

"And that sweetness is why America is going to love you."

"Please don't do this."

"Honey, it's already done. Lindsey Hall already had you from someone else. She's only going with me because of the whole ex-fiancée thing. I'm telling you the truth, Nathan. Someone already turned you in. So now you need to let me know where you are so I can come there."

So she hadn't found him yet. "Tell you where I am?"

"Wouldn't you rather set this up rationally instead of always looking over your shoulder and having me surprise you someday?"

"You won't find me."

"The only reason I haven't yet is because I haven't tried. Honey, I know your social security number. I have a copy of the registration for the truck. I know where you and your cousins go on that dumb trip every year. I've been to Matt's vacation place in Tahoe. Are you never going home again? Never paying taxes? Never having a bank account? Please." Now she was impatient.

Of course she was right. He'd been fooling himself. He wasn't some Abby Hoffman revolutionary who'd live underground for the cause. More than anything he wanted to be normal.

His hands were shaking and his breath was coming short. He was so deeply angry he had trouble pushing air through his lungs. "I never thought I'd say this, but I hate you, Patricia. You don't get anything else from me. Not now. Not in the future. And sure as hell not on national TV."

He hung up. His stomach pitched and he bent over, elbows on his knees, and waited to see if he was going to throw up. How had it all come apart so fast? Hell. It wasn't fast. He'd stolen this time with Rhian. No way he should have been able to keep Patricia and Lindsey Hall and the rest of the psycho celebrity-stalkers at bay this long. He'd gotten something he never should have been able to have. Now it was over.

He straightened up. Another group of people came out of Chet's and the lights and music washed over him before the door whisked shut and left him in darkness again. Rhian, he thought.

No. He couldn't think about her. She wasn't interested in the long haul anyway. She'd wanted a summer fling and she got it. The fling was over and he didn't have time to look back. From now on he was going to think about himself first because he couldn't afford not to.

He stuffed his phone back into his pocket and went inside.

RHIAN WAS WIPING a table when he came back in. He cut directly through the crowd to her. His face was set. Almost blank. She'd never seen him like his. The phone call must have been bad news. She dropped her cloth and met him near the dance floor.

"What happened? Was it bad news?" she asked.

"What?" He looked surprised.

"Your phone call?" she prompted as someone bumped her from behind, jostling her forward against Nathan. He put a hand out and steadied her.

"News I should have been expecting." He ran his hands back and forth through his hair. "I'm leaving. Now. Tonight."

"What?" The band had started again behind her and she was having trouble hearing. Surely he hadn't said…

A pit opened in her stomach. He wasn't allowed to say that. Not tonight. All of her earlier anger and irritation fled. She would have to drive home alone. Sleep in her bed alone. Wake up alone and spend her day alone. What had been her life five weeks ago was now utterly unimaginable.

She knew without a doubt that she wanted him to stay. She wanted to ask him Min's questions and find out he was a good guy and they could make this work and then he would stay. The music throbbed behind her and another dancing couple bumped her.

"Can we go outside?" she asked.

He stepped back and let her go ahead of him. She needed to think, to make a plan before they reached the door and stepped outside. He pushed the door open from behind her. Goose bumps rose on her arms when the cool air hit her.

She tried to read his face, but it was tight and closed. She'd never seen him like this.

"I couldn't hear…what did you say?"

"I'm leaving." His voice was flat.

No denying it that time.

"But, when? I mean…"

"Now. Tonight. Look, Rhian, I'm sorry about this." But his voice didn't sound sorry. He didn't sound like he felt anything.

"You're sorry! What the hell does sorry matter when you tell me you're leaving just like that with no warning? Why would I care if you're *sorry?*"

She hated the sarcasm in her voice, but she couldn't stop it. She was so mad she wanted to throw things. She ripped off her apron and threw that.

He caught the apron before it hit him in the chest. His eyes opened wider. "You're mad?"

"Shut up."

The door opened behind them and a pair of men came out, leaning against the wall on the other side of the door to smoke.

Nathan dropped the apron on the ground. "You don't get to be mad, Rhian." He leaned in, his voice low and furious. "You're the one who put the time limit on us in the first place. You're the one who made the rules. This was fun and sex and it was never supposed to be forever. That's how you wanted it."

"You agreed to it pretty damn fast," she snapped back.

"Which is exactly my point. You knew what you were getting. Me. Me until the house was finished and then I was out of here. *We* agreed to that."

I was scared, she wanted to protest. *I didn't know you. Didn't know myself. Didn't know I'd want you in my life so badly it would feel like the worst horror show in the world when you decided to leave.* But she wouldn't tell him any of those things. Not when he was throwing her rules in her face and *leaving*.

"Shut up," she said again. She couldn't believe she'd said that—it was worse than a curse in her mind. But she couldn't hear him throw her own words back at her to justify this nightmare. She couldn't stand knowing she'd made this happen.

"You know what, Rhian?" Nathan's mouth twisted as if he'd made an unpleasant discovery. "You had me for the past five weeks. I was in your house, in your bed, in your life. Like I promised. Like we agreed. Now I'm leaving. Also what you wanted. I was never supposed to be part of your 'real life.' Sex and dates and dancing and everything else you could take from me, but only until Jem came back and reality kicked in."

"That's not how it was," Rhian protested.

"Oh yeah? What about today? You came over to make sure I'd be all hot for you later tonight, but when I asked to read your book, you said no. I had to *beg,* Rhian. Inside the bedroom, I'm fine. Outside the bedroom—or, God forbid, when your real life starts up again—no thank you, Nathan. You wanted what you wanted and I gave it to you. That was fun. Now I'm going. I'm done."

Could you actually be pierced by words? It was true, every word of it. At the same time none of it was true. She'd set it up to seem like what he thought, but somewhere along the way she'd lost her heart, given it to him. Except she'd never told him and now it was too late. He was leaving. For real this time, and she didn't mean enough to him to make him change his mind. Which hurt so much she couldn't think about it. She wrapped herself in her anger to protect what was left of her heart.

"Fine. You should go because that's what you do, isn't it? You run. You were running when you showed up in Richwoods. You were running the night of Jem's party. The whole time we've been together you've been ready to run. So get started. I'm sure there's a town fifty miles down the road that needs a painter or whoever you decide to be next."

"What does that mean?" He was more in control now, focused on her.

"It means exactly that. You and I both know you've been lying about who you are since the minute I met you."

"Yeah? Who am I?"

"Oh please, Nathan," she said. "There's no point. You're going. Pack your secret identity and go."

He took a step toward her. "What secret identity?"

"No." Rhian was tired of this argument. She might have been brave enough to confront him when she thought there was a hope he might stay. But now it was a waste of time. Her heart was sore. "I've said enough. See you around."

She spun on Min's shoes and walked away. She didn't know where she got the strength, but somehow she made it to the door and into the bar without looking back.

She had no idea what had just happened. All she knew was that she'd finally allowed her heart to open to someone after so many years alone and now he was gone and she was left again. Alone. Again.

She held it together until she got home. Her house was waiting, the pale pink Nathan had layered on softly luminous in the moonlight. She unlocked the front door and closed it, flipping the dead bolt. Then she couldn't force herself to take another step. She slid down the door and knelt on the cool wooden floor, resting her forehead in front of her. The hard wood was at once painful and comforting.

It all came out in a torrent. The uncertainty that had been an undercurrent to her time with Nathan. The hurt and anger she felt at the way he'd treated her. And the pain of having her heart broken again. Just like Christine and James and her mother and Len and everyone she'd ever loved. They'd all left her and now Nathan was gone, too, and she was mourning before she'd even had a chance to find out if she had the courage to ask him to stay. Before she'd had the chance to convince herself that she wanted him to go.

NATHAN DIDN'T GO BACK to his apartment. He pulled into the traffic in front of Chet's and made a right on Main Street. The signal at the corner was red. He eased the truck to a stop, knowing this was the last time he'd stop at the corner of Main and River, in the town of Richwoods, New York. When the light changed, Nathan pulled forward, took the next left that led to Route 79 and drove.

He clenched his jaw and gripped the steering wheel so hard his hands hurt. He'd been shocked when he saw her at the door. He'd had to hide away all his David Dale work. But once she was in, all he could think about was her skirt and getting her out of it. He'd liked that she was at his place. He wanted her there.

But it had all been part of her act, a tease. His glance fell on her book, lying on the passenger seat of the truck. He'd wanted her to want to share that with him. But she hadn't. He didn't know why she'd given in, but he was sure she wouldn't have if he hadn't begged.

Why had he ever thought that stupid relationship with her stupid rules was a good idea?

Hell.

And what exactly had she meant about his secret identity? It wasn't possible she knew, was it? Patricia had said Lindsey Hall already had information from someone else. Was it Rhian?

He remembered how nervous she'd been. She'd shown up at his house unannounced. She was dressed up, not in her normal clothes. Could she have been expecting Lindsey Hall? Could she have set up some sting, but then Patricia sneaked in and scooped her? Rhian had certainly been off center about something.

Shit.

He'd been wrong about a woman again. How was it possible for one person to be so thick?

Three hours of hard driving later, lights swam up at him out of the darkness, a neon sign advertising Budweiser, another flashing Air-conditioned Rooms. A motel, a bar and a minimart at the crossroads of Route 17 and nowhere. Three hours from Richwoods wasn't nearly far enough, but he needed to stop thinking. Nathan swung the truck into the parking lot.

A neon sign outlined the name, the Windsor Tavern, in hazy purple. Perfect. He needed a beer and the straightforward surroundings of a bar. No one would try to trap him or use him, and as long as he paid his tab no one would bother him.

He pulled open the door, relishing the smoky, family-unfriendly interior. No more women for him. No more anything. Screw his supposed talent. All he'd ever gotten from being good at things was trouble and heartache.

He signaled for a beer and put a stack of money in front of him on the bar. He wasn't going anywhere for a good long while.

CHAPTER FOURTEEN

RHIAN TRIED TO stay asleep. If she pulled the covers over her head and stayed there for the whole day she wouldn't have to think about Nathan or her ruined night or her ruined heart. But she couldn't do it. Outside her window the birds were singing, the sun was shining, and the air had that freshly washed sheets smell. Mother Nature wanted to kill her. Finally she threw back the covers and went downstairs.

She flipped on the TV, hoping the noise would keep her company. Lindsey Hall was seated at her desk next to the cardboard silhouette, which was now wearing dark glasses over the pasted-on author photo and holding a map of the United States in its hand.

"Oh please," Rhian muttered. But she paused when she heard what the woman was saying.

"I repeat, we are very close to Chris Senso!"

The Hall Heads in their bright wigs howled madly and Lindsey beamed broadly at them and her TV audience. "There are a few details we still have to work out, but it's only a matter of days now before we will unveil the secret identity of the superhero author himself."

Rhian was surprised she didn't feel excited at all. Disappointed and sad. Of course that could be because she'd wrecked her life. But she still would have thought she'd be interested after all the time she and Jem and Min had spent on this topic. Instead she just felt sorry for Chris Senso. Soon his life, whatever it was, would be overrun with Lindsey and her Hall Heads.

Lindsey turned to a board behind her. "To whet your appetite, I've worked with our mystery caller, who by the way, we'll also unveil in a few days, to provide details about our elusive prey."

She pulled a cord and a strip of paper slid down, revealing a sentence. "Chris Senso is thirty-three."

She pulled the string again, revealing a second fact. "He's single."

Lindsey pumped her fist in the air and winked suggestively. "But for how long?"

Another tug of the string showed "Boxers not briefs."

"Good grief," Rhian muttered. "Underwear?"

She had had enough of Lindsey Hall's theatrics. The phone rang and she reached for it. On the TV Lindsey pulled the string a final time revealing a close-up shot of a man's behind in worn Levi's. Rhian appreciated a good ass as much as the next woman and this one was definitely fine, but really. Chris Senso had gone to a lot of trouble to be anonymous and now his behind was blown up to ten times normal size and beamed across the country. She clicked off the TV as she pressed the phone to her ear.

"Rhian, I want to kiss you!" Min's voice was charged with excitement. "If you hadn't made me write those resolutions with you I never would have done this. I have an interview with Danielle Matcliffe! I might be getting a job!"

Rhian's heart sank. What she wouldn't give to be discussing Chris Senso's butt instead of this. Real life. Min was leaving. She was really leaving. She managed to sound normal when she answered, "Min, I'm so glad for you. Who is Danielle Matcliffe?"

Min laughed. "I'll forgive you for not recognizing her name only because you are a peon without an advanced degree in art history. But she's this amazing writer and researcher and her department—at Princeton, no less—has a tenure-track opening. She wants to see me as soon as possible. Amazing."

"I'm so happy for you," Rhian choked out the words and then, oh rats, she started to cry. "I'm sorry, this is rude. You're happy and I'm—" She couldn't finish.

"Are you okay? It's not Jem?"

Rhian sniffled a reassurance that everyone was fine.

"Nathan." Min said his name in a flat tone, leaving no doubt that she knew the reason for the tears and was placing blame starting now. "You had your talk and he's gone."

Rhian sucked in a breath and managed to hiccup her way through an explanation. "We didn't even get to the questions. We had this, this fight, and there was no point."

Min was quiet for a moment while Rhian worked to gather her thoughts and emotions.

"I don't know what to say, Rhian. I feel awful. I thought he was a keeper." Min's voice was full of compassion.

"I knew it was going to be over. It's ridiculous to cry when I was going to let him go anyway. But I wanted to try and he, we, argued… Excuse me." Rhian put the phone down while she blew her nose. Then she went on. "The pathetic thing, Min, is that I think I love him." Tears threatened to engulf her again, but she swallowed them down. She was finished making an emotional wreck of herself. "I didn't mean to love him, but I think I do."

"You. Love. Him." Min didn't say anything else for a second. "Okay. You said you argued, what was it about?"

Rhian told her, all her hurt and bewilderment coming out. "I decided I'd ask him those questions. But I wanted to have a fantasy night first. Then Chet made me waitress so I got dressed in this sexy skirt and an apron and your high heels—"

"Heels? To work at Chet's?" Min's voice rose in surprise.

"Exactly. I was going to, you know, tease him while I worked, and I went to his apartment to set it up. I had it all planned." Or almost all planned. She hadn't expected the part where he left. "The outside of his place was nice, but he doesn't have any stuff. Less than you'd have in a hotel room. But I still thought… Oh it was so stupid… He was going to read my book…" She trailed off.

"Oh honey, you fell hard." Min's words were low and rich with emotion, reaching through the phone like a hug.

"But then he got a phone call at Chet's and he told me he was leaving. Leaving right then and not coming back. He stood there at Chet's and said goodbye for good."

"I don't understand."

"Yeah. Your confusion is nothing compared to mine." Rhian slumped against the wall and let herself slide to the floor. She put her head down on her knees and shut her eyes.

"You were teasing him in a short skirt and heels and planning hot sex later. And he got some phone call and had to leave right then? Before the sex?" Min's voice was baffled.

"Exactly."

"Maybe he won't talk about his past because he spent it in a monastery."

Rhian couldn't help snorting. Miserable as she was,

talking to Min and sharing a joke was comforting. "I wish this had happened before I started to love him."

"Oh, Rhian." The caring wrapped up in that simple phrase almost brought her tears back again.

"I know. Stupid, stupid, stupid." Rhian clenched her fists.

"Honey, it's not stupid to love people. Don't think that, just because of this one lunatic. Or even because of this lunatic and that other one you were engaged to. There's someone out there for you to love."

"It's not worth it, Min. I have Jem and you." For a few years, she thought. "And my book is going great. I don't need some stupid man to complicate things and make me feel like this. I'll stick to what I'm good at from now on."

She could almost hear Min shaking her head when she said, "We both know that's an extreme position, but I'll let it go under the circumstances. Are you going to be okay?"

"I am okay. I mean, I suck right now actually, but I will be okay." She'd have to be for Jem so she would make sure that she was. "I'm sick of thinking about Nathan. Give me something good to keep my mind off him."

There was a short silence. And then Min said brightly, "Road trip!"

Rhian smiled as her spirits lifted with those two ridiculously juvenile words.

"You're working," she protested.

"I can take four days off." Min said dismissively. "That is what Jem has left on his trip, right?"

"Yes," Rhian said slowly.

"Well, what's more fun than an RV? Let's meet them. Where are they?

"Philadelphia."

"Cheese steaks? Yes!" Min's enthusiasm was starting to

perk Rhian up. "Can we do that Rocky thing—run up the steps of the art museum?"

"You're an idiot."

"But you're almost smiling, aren't you?"

"Okay. Road trip. I'll find out where the RV is parked and hop a flight."

"See you tonight, my friend."

"Min." Rhian swallowed hard to keep her voice steady. "Thanks."

"Don't thank me until the road trip's over. We might end up in jail or like, broken down on the Pennsylvania turnpike."

"Right. You're very wise."

After they hung up, Rhian was smiling. Her heart was still broken and she was just as confused as she'd been. She wished she'd never met Nathan in equal measure with wishing for him back. But she was going to see her boy and her best friend that night. *This* was how people cared for each other—by coming together, not by leaving. Thank God for Min reminding her of how life should be.

Tonight her life would get back to normal, cleared of all complications, and her heart… Well, she'd have to take care of that when she could.

NATHAN DRAGGED the dusty brown curtain across the windows of the motel room before he collapsed back in bed with his eyes closed. Drowning anger was never a good idea. It took too much beer and left him feeling like roadkill the next day. He'd rather still be angry.

That wasn't exactly true. He'd *rather* still be "not angry" and enjoying himself with Rhian in their pathetic pretend relationship. Shit. If a time machine was ever invented, he'd pay any amount of money to go back to the day he met Patricia and start over by staying in bed. Or strapping himself to an anthill. Or doing one of those cage fights against a platoon of Navy Seals. Anything if it meant he'd never met the woman who had ruined his life.

Now he was angry *and* hungover. Bad combination. He closed his eyes and tried to clear his mind. The bed was lumpy and not very clean, but he couldn't make himself move. If he could get to sleep, maybe he could waste this entire day. He'd worry about how to waste tomorrow and next week and the rest of his life when the time came. Right now he needed to waste today.

Eventually sleep carried him away.

WHEN HER TAXI pulled up in front of the Philadelphia Elks club where the RV was parked, Rhian almost missed seeing the small figure in a sky-blue T-shirt standing on the steps to the front door. Her eyes were focused on the RV looming over the cars in the parking lot, motor humming in the evening air. But when Jem jumped and started waving, she caught the motion from the corner of her eye. She threw a crumpled twenty at the driver and shouted, "Keep the change," as she leaped out the back door.

In less than a second she was across the sidewalk, on her knees, gathering her boy to her chest. His skin smelled like summer and boy and everything familiar and sweet. His hair was warm and silky and hanging long down his neck in the back. He was both bigger and smaller than she expected and she held him tight to give herself a chance to remember who he was. Jem. Her boy. She might be on her knees on a strange street in downtown Philadelphia but, in all the ways that mattered, she was home.

"I missed you, Rhian." His voice was muffled and his thin arms were wrapped hard around her.

"Oh, honey, I missed you, too." A few tears slipped out of her eyes and down her cheeks. She rubbed them off in Jem's hair and reveled in the love they shared. Each of them had lost so much that day Christine and James died. But they'd built something good, something true for each other. How could she have thought, even for a second, of letting someone unreliable into her life— into Jem's life? Now she knew Nathan had been a terrible mistake and the only good part was that Jem hadn't been around to see it.

NATHAN FACED UP to what he wanted. He answered the phone, which had been ringing every hour on the hour since he'd checked in to the motel four days ago.

"Where are you, Nathan!" Matt shouted. Which surprised the hell out of him because Matt never shouted. Cajole, tease, joke, yes. Shout? No. Nathan rolled onto his back.

"Lindsey Hall knows who you are. Someone turned you in and they've plastered your ass, literally your ASS, all over the airwaves." Matt moved from shouting to bellowing. "And you decided to what? Go on a quest, take a vow of silence, get a new agent? Where *are* you?"

"It's Patricia," Nathan said, answering a question Matt hadn't asked, ignoring the one he had. "She says someone else gave me up but her information was better so they went with it."

"I knew it." Nathan thought he heard a fist slamming something on Matt's end of the line. "God. Why didn't you listen to me in the beginning. People who don't like the Red Sox cannot be trusted."

Nathan managed a smile. This was territory familiar since second grade. "I don't like the Red Sox."

"Right. Which is a problem, but we have bigger issues." Matt's voice had calmed but now it rose again. "Like where are you?"

"I…don't know." Nathan wasn't sure where he was. Was Windsor the name of the town or just of the bar? "Here's the deal. I quit." He'd planned this. He knew it was the right thing. So why did he feel there was a goddamn hole in his stomach? "I'm not turning this book in. I'm done."

"What? Nathan, stop. Tell me where you are and I'll come there."

"No need. I don't want it anymore. I never wanted it if it was this way."

"You don't mean that."

"It's the way it has to be."

"You have a contract, Nathan. For this book and two more." Matt was talking in his business voice now—the one he used with publishers and movie people. Anyone on the other team. It was new to hear it directed at him.

"Listen, you're my agent. So agent. Buy the book back. Let them hire a ghostwriter. Sell them the Senso name— that was never me anyway."

"Are you drunk?"

"Not at the moment, no."

"I'm not letting you throw your career away."

"If I keep my career, I lose my life. I want my life, a real life, and I won't get it if I'm still Chris Senso."

"Which life exactly are you talking about?" There was a burst of static and Nathan imagined that Matt was up and moving around his office now. His friend thought better on his feet. "The life where you live like a hermit in New

Hampshire, afraid to let anyone get close? The life where you live like a gypsy, begging for painting jobs and squatting in some crappy rental? The life where you crash someplace you don't even know the name of and do nothing, not even answer the phone?"

And that hurt, Nathan thought. The words, the tone, the whole package. "Matt," Nathan said.

"No. Don't 'Matt' me." His friend took a deep breath. "You don't know how to have a life. What happened in college has twisted everything you've done since. You think if you can give up enough stuff—basketball, friends, your name, writing—that somehow you'll be happy. That's not the way life works. Life is more than breathing."

"Chris Senso's life isn't what I want. If I keep writing that's what I get. They'll have Chris Senso coffee mugs and Christmas ornaments."

"Pinup calendar is more likely, based on reaction to the ass shot," Matt muttered.

Nathan ignored that comment. He didn't know what Matt was talking about, but he was pretty sure it wasn't good.

"My point is if that's the life I have because I'm writing, then I don't want to write."

"But that crap you're talking about wouldn't be your *life*." Matt said. "God, Nathan. Grow up. That's Lindsey Hall and Patricia and the crazy people like them. Your life is you. Nathan Delaney. Doing the thing you love that you're best at in the world. People don't love your books because Chris Senso wrote them. They love your books because they're great books. David Dale is a kid people want to think about, spend time with, share with their own kids. Doesn't that matter?"

Nathan closed his eyes. It couldn't matter. That was all.

"Not anymore." He put his forearm over his eyes, trying to block out the light. If he could be silent and alone in the dark he could stop thinking about this. Stop hearing Matt's voice saying things that were so true they hurt. Especially because he wasn't going to listen. "I'm going back to my apartment to get the book and I'm going to burn it."

"Don't. Just don't."

"It's as good as done."

"Nathan," Matt's voice snapped with anger. "Burning your book, dropping out, it's not going to change the fact that Lindsey Hall has you in her sights. Quitting might make her story better. You go from hero to tragic hero. What's your plan to deal with her?"

"My plan is she doesn't find me."

"Which is why you're the author and not the agent. Lindsey not finding you is a wish, not a plan." The agent voice was back.

Nathan stood and paced to the window. His truck was right there in the parking lot. Was it unreasonable to think he could keep driving until Lindsey Hall and Patricia and everyone else forgot about him?

"So?"

"So here's what plans sound like. Plan A, you do Lindsey Hall and we rake in the royalties from the butt-shot calendar."

"Why do you keep talking about my butt?" Nathan jerked the curtain closed again.

"Better you don't know. Plan B—we steal their thunder. Use another outlet to tell the story. On our terms. In our words." This gift Matt had for rapid-fire planning had been legendary in their circle in high school because it had invariably led to the kind of ridiculously perfect mischief that is irresistible to boys of a certain age. When they'd first come up with Chris Senso, he'd spent innumerable hours listening to his friend do this, pick at a problem from every angle until every obstacle was removed and the road was smooth ahead. Things had changed, though. What Matt the agent wanted wasn't what Nathan wanted anymore.

"No."

"Come on, Nathan!" Matt shouted. Two times in one day Nathan had made him shout. And there had been that punching sound. Maybe Matt was going to join him here in his current position off the deep end.

"I can get *Vanity Fair* and they can do a profile—it's good writing and you control the environment. We can do Terry Gross—she'll let you talk about the books not personal stuff. I have people at *People*, but that's as bad as Lindsey Hall."

"Stop it."

"Pick one."

"No," Nathan barked. "I stay me. I keep my life the way it is. Those are the key points you need to keep in mind for any new strategies. You're my agent—I don't pay you to do what you want. You do what I want."

As soon as it came out, Nathan felt bad. He and Matt never talked about money. It was true that Matt had made a lot of money from Nathan and the David Dale jugger-naut, and also true that technically Matt did work for him. But they'd never been that—employer and employee.

Matt was quiet for a long beat. "Okay, boss. I'll send you a memo when I work out the exact parameters for how to turn you into a ghost and keep you that way."

The phone clicked off. Matt had hung up on him. *That* never happened. Matt was…well, Matt. Scary smart, innately polite, deeply loyal and, above all easy going.

The guy was so mellow people in college frequently accused him of being stoned when he was just Matt. Unruffled and happy. Until now. *Crap.* The sinkhole of his life sucked everyone in. Quitting was the right decision. He needed to end this before anyone lost anything else.

"THAT'S CHEATING," Rhian panted as Jem jumped around, pumping his arms in triumph.

"It is not!" he protested.

"It should be."

He grabbed the ball and tossed it up in a lazy arc, watching as it hit the backboard and then came down. "I won. And I didn't have a famous guy teaching me how to shoot." Jem's Uncle Kevin had connected Nathan to his college hoops career after seeing him play at the barbecue. The boy had been disappointed when he got home and discovered he'd missed his chance for a repeat game with a legend.

"You took advantage of me. You faked a *head injury* to win a game of one-on-one." She was moving toward him, her motions nonchalant. She'd show him sneaky.

"Not my fault you're a sucker." He attempted to spin the ball on his finger. It made two revolutions before falling off. He grabbed it and held it in his left hand, poised for another attempt.

Rhian darted forward and slapped the ball away. She grabbed it, raced back to the line they'd painted to mark half court, and made a clean jump shot. "Who's the sucker now?" she taunted.

Jem lunged for the ball. Game on.

A champagne-colored Cadillac Escalade pulled into the driveway. Rhian paused, waiting for it to back out. She assumed it was someone turning around. But the SUV came forward, halting on the half-court line, right in front of Rhian. Jem moved up beside her, holding the ball cocked under his right arm.

A woman got out of the driver's side and looked from them to the house. Salesperson? Realtor? Extra from a movie set who'd taken a wrong turn three thousand miles away on Ventura Boulevard?

Long, dark hair bounced on her shoulders in a way Rhian had only ever seen in shampoo commercials. She was a good three inches taller than Rhian and wearing a short, sleeveless dress printed with red poppies and paired with high red sandals. The combination should have been slutty at two o'clock in the afternoon, but on this woman with mile-long legs and pouty lips, it was flat-out sexy. *Who was she?*

"Rhian MacGregor?" the stranger came forward, holding one perfectly manicured hand out to shake. "I'm sorry to barge in, but I wondered if I could ask a favor?"

Was it more rude to wipe your hand on your shorts before shaking hands or to let the grime from an afternoon of sweaty basketball pollute the skin of a person like this? She went with a quick swipe on the shorts. She glanced at Jem and then back to the woman. No way this woman was selling something but, if not that, then why was she here?

"Um, okay."

"Wonderful. I'm Patty. We're new in town. We bought this old house on the west side and it desperately needs to be painted." Her perfect mouth pouted perfectly and Rhian was back to the stray-actress theory.

Jem lost interest and went back to practicing foul shots. Thank God, he was eight and not fifteen.

Patty kept it just this side of gushing as she went on, "I

love the color of your house. Do you mind giving me your painter's name?"

"Oh," Rhian said, feeling ambushed. Would this punch-in-the-gut longing for Nathan happen every time someone said the words "house" and "paint"? Rhian resisted the temptation to walk away. The woman was giving off a weird vibe, too friendly, but if she was new maybe she was just trying too hard. Rhian forced her voice to be normal, "Nathan Delaney."

"Nathan," Patty repeated the name softly, and smiled. Then she seemed to remember what she was doing and pursed her lips. She took a Blackberry out of her red leather bag and waited with the stylus poised. "You have his number?"

Rhian rattled off Nathan's number.

The woman punched the keypad and then raised her eyes and asked casually, "You two are friends?"

"No," Rhian choked on the word.

"Oh. It's just you had his number memorized." Patty looked at the house again. "Is it too much bother for me to use the little-girls' room?" She grimaced in mock shame. "Errands all morning…"

Actually, it *was* too much trouble, Rhian thought. She didn't like this person—and not just because she moved as easily in high heels as Rhian did in her bedroom slippers. But good manners won out.

"Sure," she said. She glanced to Jem and said, "We're going inside. Come in if you want a drink."

Inside Patty looked around as eagerly as if she were considering buying the place. "Your home is so cute, Rhian. I love these photos of your son."

"The bathroom is through here," Rhian answered, leading Patty to her office. The door to the powder room in the corner was open slightly.

Rhian retreated to the kitchen, wanting to allow the other woman some privacy but remaining close enough to escort her out as soon as she finished. How did Pretty Patty know her name, anyway, Rhian wondered. And why would a woman who looked like her, drove a car like hers, and had a *Blackberry*, for Pete's sake, buy a home in Richwoods? "Richwoods: An Absolute Backwater" wasn't the chamber of commerce slogan, but it might as well have been.

Jem came in. "Is there any lemonade?" he asked as he flopped into a chair at the kitchen table. He must have just pushed his hair back off his face because it was sticking up in sweaty spikes.

Rhian opened the fridge and pulled out the glass pitcher of lemonade. Patty popped into the room from the hallway, appearing so suddenly she startled Rhian.

"Rhian, I have to ask—who did those drawings over your desk?"

Enough with the weird prying. She put the pitcher on the counter and faced the other woman. "You didn't mention how you know my name," she asked. She kept her voice civil but with an edge—she wanted an answer.

Patty flipped her hand in a who-knows? gesture near her head. "I asked someone at the deli."

Rhian supposed that could be true. Still, she was finished sharing. "All right." She moved toward the other woman, herding her out the door. "Good luck with your house."

"You didn't say. Who did those drawings?"

And she had no intention of saying who did them, either, but unfortunately Jem spoke up from behind her.

"Same guy—Nathan the painter." Jem had asked about the drawings when he came home and saw them. She almost regretted being honest now.

Patty turned to her. "Is that true?"

Rhian shrugged, hoping to get the woman moving again but she was craning her neck toward the kitchen. Thinking Jem would spill more information, maybe.

"Are they from a book? Did he say what his inspiration was?"

Rhian turned back to Jem and gave him a subtle head shake. "We have somewhere to be in a few minutes, Patty. Like I said, good luck." She spread her hands slightly, hoping to appear more intimidating because she was *not* discussing Nathan with this woman.

"I'm sorry for intruding," Patty said, her eyes open wide and pouting prettily again. Which, if Rhian had been a man, might have had the desired effect, but all it did was make her want to roll her own eyes and give Patty a punch.

"Would you consider selling them?"

"No," Rhian answered. Her ingrained politeness almost had her tacking "sorry" on the end, but she stopped herself.

Finally. Patty was on the porch. Good. Next, she needed to be down the steps and moving on down the road in her gas guzzler. Rhian gave her a wave and shut the screen door. Then she shut the heavy inside door. That should be a big enough hint.

The doorbell rang.

"You have to be kidding me," she muttered.

Yanking the door open, Rhian glared at Pretty Patty, all pretense of civility gone.

"Do you have Nathan's address? I might swing by instead of calling—I'm eager to get my project going."

"Two thirty-eight Front Street," Rhian said.

She shut the door again, but this time she watched through the peephole to make sure the woman walked away. *What a crackpot!*

Offering to buy her drawings? Did her house look like eBay?

Rhian slouched into her office. She closed the door behind her and crossed the room to lean her hands on her desk.

She remembered the night Nathan had given her the drawings. She'd been falling for him before that, but his art bringing her words to life had been the most wonderful gift. She thought he was someone special. Someone she could trust.

Looking at the drawings reminded her of how much she'd shared with him. She hated that she'd never found out what he thought of her book. That she'd never told him how much she loved playing basketball or that she couldn't listen to Bruce Springsteen without thinking of him.

The smart thing to do was to take the drawings down. Step one for getting on with your life after the world's most confusing breakup: "Cleanse your life of all crap that makes you think thoughts better left unthunk."

But somehow, she couldn't put the drawings away. She liked them. She loved them. She loved Nathan, too. She had been trying very hard not to, but it wasn't working.

Was she really ready to let everything they'd had drift away without even knowing why?

She picked up her phone and dialed Min's number. After the road trip, her friend had returned to Virginia to finish the last few days of work on her project.

"Min, I made a horrible mistake," she said, her voice shaking.

"Okay."

"I should have asked him those questions. I shouldn't have made him temporary. I should have found out why he went crazy, and tried to help."

"Um, we're talking about Nathan, right?"

"Can you come home and lock me in the house until I remember why I don't want to see him again?"

Min laughed. "You know I'd do anything for you, dear, but I'm here for a few more days."

"Rats." Rhian crossed her arms over her stomach. "Can I handcuff myself to my bed? Jem can bring me meals."

"That would make you crazier than Nathan."

"He is crazy. So why do I want to see him again?"

"Maybe you weren't quite ready for it to end. Maybe you want another chance."

No, Rhian thought, that's idiotic. But the words "another chance" echoed in her head. Did she?

Rhian let out an impatient huff. "I had this all decided weeks ago. Before I started anything, I made the plan. Jem comes home, Nathan goes away. Simple. Clear. Which is how it happened. Just not in the right order." She laughed ruefully, "Still, it doesn't feel right. Can you believe I'm complaining because a plan went right?"

"You going to do anything about it?"

"I don't know. I mean, he left. I could call his cell. But that's stupid. I mean, what would we have? A long-distance relationship?"

"Maybe it's time to stop thinking things to death and do what you feel."

"No plan?"

"How well did that work out last time?"

"That was an anomaly."

"Or maybe it was a sign from the universe that Rhian

MacGregor needs to take a chance and do what her heart says without an eighty-seven-point plan."

Rhian laughed. "Eighty-seven points is an awful complicated plan."

"Not for you."

Rhian hung up and looked back at the pictures. The man who'd drawn these was obviously capable of so much insight, so much love and emotion. So why had he taken off in the middle of the night without an explanation? She sighed. Maybe knowing why he'd left would be enough. She touched the picture again. Maybe not.

CHAPTER FIFTEEN

RHIAN'S HOUSE WAS not on the way to his apartment. He wouldn't lie to himself about what he was doing. Or not doing. What was he not doing? He was not being smart, safe or logical. He was not sticking to his plan. But what the hell? He could drive past the woman's house—just to see.

See what? his mind asked.

Shut up, he answered.

See Rhian and Jem playing basketball, that's what, his eyes reported.

They looked happy. Rhian put a shot up from three-point range—nothing but net all the way. The first day he taught her to shoot she'd been so tense under his hands. He'd wanted to do much more than show her how to shoot a foul shot, but right then that was all she was ready for. Later there'd been her and them and the too-few days of time together.

He stepped on the gas, and now he did lie to himself. He told himself he was better off. He was glad Rhian had said he had to be gone before Jem came home. Jem was back; Nathan was gone. End of story.

His apartment was dry and hot and, even though it had only been five days, it felt abandoned. He walked through the rooms, cataloging the things he'd need to do before he could leave. Depressingly little.

He dropped into the chair at his worktable and stared at the pages of the newest David Dale book. The one no one would ever read. He lifted the pages and imagined touching a lighter to the edge of the pile. He pulled his hands carefully away.

He'd finally worked out the ending. David Dale didn't die, Silvertip didn't die. Emma, David's friend, found a power of her own right before the book ended. He'd planned to keep her around.

Now Emma would never see the light of day. He picked up a pencil and pulled a pad of paper closer. He was curious to see what could have happened to Emma if she'd been allowed a full story arc, a full life with David Dale.

The art took him the way it sometimes did to a place he hadn't expected. Two minutes into the thing, he wasn't drawing Emma, but himself and Rhian. It started with a sketch of them in the driveway, the day he taught her to shoot the basketball.

She was sheltered in the curve of his arms and his hands gently supported hers on the ball. Her eyes were focused on the basket and her mouth was a determined line. His eyes caressed her profile while his lips whispered encouragement. And words of love.

Love?

God damn.

He tacked the drawing up on the wall and took a new sheet of paper from the pad. This time the sketch was his fantasy of what might have been.

He and Rhian were on the roof of her house where they'd stood that day when he put up the hoop for her. In the picture the sky was dark, but they were lit from behind by a window.

She was in front of him, leaning back into him, letting him support her. Letting him love her. His arms were twined around to clasp over her chest. The pose said, *We belong together.* In the picture he was leaning his chin on her hair and soaking in her scent. He loved the way she smelled, fresh and clean like a spring day. He loved the silk of her hair. He loved the way she moved, so sure and free.

Putting down his pencil, Nathan stared at the two pictures side by side.

He loved Rhian Macgregor.

He looked around the apartment again, at the crappy furniture and the bare walls and no evidence of who lived here. Matt was right. This wasn't a life. He never should have agreed to the terms of that stupid deal with Rhian. He never should have lied to her about who he was. He never should have left.

His heart started beating faster, pumping hope through his body. If he quit David Dale, could he be the kind of man Rhian would want in her life and Jem's? If he could be normal, an ordinary man with an ordinary job, maybe he could find a way to convince her to take a chance on him.

He jumped up and went to the fridge, hungry for the first time in days. Wooing a reluctant, likely still pissed-off Rhian called for planning. It called for gifts. Food and gifts. He would bring food and gifts and then he'd grovel.

Knowing that Jem was home complicated things. He respected the way she protected him. He wouldn't mess with that for the world, but he needed to see Rhian. He'd do it on her terms, respecting and protecting Jem as much as he could.

Three hours later, Nathan walked up the sidewalk to

Rhian's house balancing several brightly wrapped packages, one pizza half pepperoni half plain, a six-pack of beer, one of soda and a bag of still-warm chocolate-chip cookies. His mouth was dry and he tried to focus on not dropping anything to keep his mind off how nervous he was.

She looked great when she opened the door. Shocked and appalled, but so exactly right. He'd missed her.

She stared at him.

His arms were starting to shake. "Can I come in?"

"I don't know."

"That's fair." He had no idea what to say next. When he'd imagined this scene, talking to her, the screen door had not been between them.

"You left," she said, her voice quiet and sad.

"I know. I never should have. I have stuff to tell you—"

He shifted uncomfortably, aware that she hadn't made a move to open the screen. Aware that she hadn't said anything.

"I've been here, Nathan. You could have called."

"It's not the kind of thing you can tell over the phone."

The six-pack carriers were cutting into his hand and he shifted to try to resettle the stack of packages. But he thought her eyes had softened. He'd hoped it would help him get in the door.

He tried again. "I had to see you. I brought Jem some things and dinner so he wouldn't think it was about us. I don't want to break our deal about him. If you want me to go without seeing him, I respect that. Just tell me when we can see each other. Please." He had planned to grovel. He'd continue if he needed to.

"Jem's at Brandon's house."

Nathan slumped against the wall, the air gone out of his lungs. "That changes things then."

"Maybe."

"Rhian, let me in? Please?"

SHE WANTED TO SAY YES. She'd dreamed about seeing him again and now here he was at her door. But she was scared. What if she let him in and let herself hope and he…well, what? What could he do that he hadn't already done? *Stay,* her heart offered. *He might stay.*

"You can come in. We should talk." She held the screen door open for him and took the beer out of his hand.

He followed her wordlessly into the kitchen and piled his packages on the table as she opened two bottles of beer and handed one to him.

Rhian felt him looking at her and turned away to take a piece of pizza. He filled her kitchen in such a wonderfully welcome way. She wanted him. She wasn't surprised by that since it seemed she'd wanted him every minute since she'd first laid eyes on him.

"Rhian, I owe you an apology," he started. "Maybe a couple. That last night I was in bad shape. I said things I never should have said. I thought I had to leave, and maybe part of me thought if I wrecked things between us it would be easier to go."

"I just wanted to know why."

"When I tell you everything, you'll understand. I hope." His clear blue eyes looked into hers and she saw there his sincerity and his desire. Her pulse leaped. Jem was at Brandon's for a sleepover. He wouldn't be home until the morning. She was aware of the empty house in an almost uncomfortable way.

To distract herself, she turned to the packages and let out a low whistle. "Is this all for Jem?"

Nathan moved to stand behind her. She had trouble swallowing her last bite of pizza. She was achingly aware of him so close to her. His height and his strength might have made him intimidating but to her they were thrilling. He put one hand on her shoulder as he reached around and pulled a box out of the stack.

"This one's for you," he whispered.

"I missed you," she admitted. "I wasn't supposed to, but I did."

"Rhian," he breathed her name, and she got scared of what he might say next. She needed more time to think.

So she focused on the gift. The box and wrappings fell to the floor as she shook out the present.

"It's a Knicks game day jersey," he said. It was safe to look at him again because he'd moved back from that intense moment also. Was he scared, too? She turned to him and saw him starting to smile, the irresistible smile that had hooked her from that first day when he'd rescued her from the roof. God, she loved his face when he was happy.

She slid the too-long jersey on over her head and mimed shooting a jump shot. "How does it look?"

"Perfect." His voice was husky and his eyes glowed as he stepped closer and put his arms around her. He was hard before he pulled her against him. She could feel it. He bent his head and nibbled her neck.

She should stop him. She knew he would if she asked. But she didn't want him to stop. She loved him, and God help her, he'd been gone but he was back.

She spread her hands on the broad muscles of his chest and stroked his hard stomach to the front of his jeans.

"Oh Rhian." He took a deep breath and then pushed the neck of the jersey and her shirt aside to slide a finger under the lace of her bra. He slid his left hand down over the curve of her hip.

She needed time to think. But she couldn't think, not with him pressing and kneading and licking and rubbing her every nerve into a frenzy.

Oh Lord she'd take this for now.

She fisted her hands in the smooth linen of his green shirt, tugged it free from his jeans and unbuttoned it, eager to find his skin and to press herself against it. To wrap herself in him. When his shirt was loose and swinging from his shoulders, she thought she might lose herself right then. He was so beautiful.

"Let's go upstairs," she whispered. It was no worse than what she'd done all summer. Who could blame her for wanting one more night of this?

"We need to talk." His voice was low and insistent.

"We will. Promise." She combed her hands in his hair and twisted her head to kiss his neck. "Please?"

"I'm serious. There are things you need to know."

"Jem's gone for the night. Please?"

He held her face, gently cradling her cheeks, fingers splayed along her jawbone. He searched her face. What did he want to see, she wondered.

Finally, he bent his forehead to touch hers. When he lifted his head up again, his lips were pressed in a firm line and he nodded, once, businesslike, decision made. He took her hand.

In her room, she lay on the bed and he stood over her, the soft light from the bedside lamp throwing his eyes into shadow and making his dark hair even darker. The play of muscles in his arms and chest mesmerized her as he leaned over and toed off his boots and then dragged off his jeans and shrugged out of his shirt.

Their loving was slow and deep. They were savoring, stretching each touch, each moment. Making it last.

Afterward, lying together, Nathan put his hand up to stroke her hair. "I didn't come here for this."

"Shh." She put her hand up to cover his. "Isn't this good?"

He raised himself on one elbow. "Of course this is good. But you haven't seen me in days and I walk in the door and we have sex. We need to talk."

She bit her lip and tried to slow her breathing. Of course they had to talk, but it didn't have to be now. "Tomorrow."

"I have to explain. About my life. So we can think."

She closed her eyes and took a deep breath. "All summer I waited for you to tell me about yourself. But you never did. Can't we do this one more time, be Rhian and Nathan from the summer?"

His hands moved to her shoulders, his grip tense. "I don't want to lie to you anymore."

"I'm not sure I'm ready for the truth." She knew he needed to talk, but his need made her nervous. He must have something big to tell her and the bigger the secret the more likely it was to be something she couldn't live with.

She had an inspiration. "What if I ask you three questions, three possible things that would be deal breakers? If we're still okay, you spend the night and we talk tomorrow?"

"It's not like that—" He started to protest.

"Were you in jail or is the law in pursuit of you?"

He was so startled his laugh was more of a bark. "What? Why would you think that?"

She shook her head. "We're not talking right now. You're answering questions and then it's back to business."

"If your first guess is jail, you're going to need more than three questions," he said with some impatience.

She cut him off again. "Guessing right isn't the point. I'm ruling out the horrid possibilities, and then if it's none of those, this night is safe. Answer my first question."

"I'll do this now, but tomorrow the conversation goes my way."

"Agreed. Jail?"

"I got caught drinking senior year of high school and my dad had to bail me out."

"Recently?"

"No. No jail time. No officers in pursuit."

"You'd look good in one of those jumpsuits, though. I'd make you leave it unzipped right to here." She pointed to a spot halfway down his chest and then bent her head and licked him.

"You're not allowed to do that in the visitor's room."

"I'd be the warden."

"Ooh, a kinky mind." He rolled her onto her back and pinned her arms before he lowered his mouth inches above hers. "I like that in a warden."

She squirmed and he let her go. "Number two. Secret family? You know, wife and kids in Hackensack, waiting for Daddy to come back from his business trip?"

"Where do you get this stuff, *the National Enquirer?*"

"Answer the question."

"I have one very ex-fiancée in California, I think."

"You think she's in California or you think she's your ex?"

"I know she's my ex. I'm not sure exactly where she is, but I'm hoping like hell it's California. Or Chechnya. Is that farther away than Uzbekistan?"

She raised an eyebrow and he shrugged, saying, "Rather not see her again for a while."

She had one question left. *If I let you back in will you*

turn around and leave me and Jem? seemed too obvious and pathetic. What else could be really awful? Are you a drifter with no roots? Could you walk away with no explanation? Do you scare me down to my bones? But she already knew the answer to those.

"One left."

"I'm sifting through the sordid possibilities." She shrugged and gave in. After all, she'd already decided she would have this night and so it didn't matter what he answered or didn't answer. "Are you in the CIA?"

He rolled his eyes. "I can't believe you saw through my cover. Yes, I'm assigned to the suburban-mom division. I paint houses, peek in windows and report back on the state of wading pools in yards across America."

"Well, it's not a jumpsuit, but CIA could be kinky. I'm good."

"You're nuts." But the warmth in his voice took any sting out of the words as he kissed her gently. "Feel better?"

"I wasn't feeling that bad before." She sighed and put her hands on either side of his face. She'd done her best to forget him, but it hadn't worked. She knew him and loved him and couldn't erase him. She kissed him softly on the forehead and then longer and lingering on his lips. "What would make you feel good?"

"You know what I'd really like?" Nathan's eyes sparkled as he grinned wickedly at her.

She rested her hands on his chest and grinned back. "I can't imagine. Spies probably have all sorts of twisted desires."

He leaned away and scooped up the Knicks jersey from the floor. Tossing it to her, he said, "It's not exactly a cheer-leader fantasy, but would you put that back on?"

She held the shirt up and then slid it over her head.

Rhian blushed when she saw the way he was looking at her, appreciative and possessive and hungry.

"You're blushing."

"You're staring."

"Planning."

"Good things?"

"Really good things." His answer was a hum she could feel in her chest. "I have an active imagination."

Much later they were lying back on the pillows, his arm around her shoulders, her head cradled on his chest. She was hovering on the edge of exhaustion, both from all the things they'd been doing and all the thoughts she was purposely keeping from thinking. It was a weird way to feel—worn-out and too keyed up to sleep.

"What's in those other boxes downstairs?" she asked idly. "You didn't bring any other useful shirts, did you?"

"You wicked woman. How many do you need?"

"I can't handle more than one tonight." She snuggled closer and draped her leg over his.

"I brought Jem a jersey. That's one thing. And the other stuff is books. But—" He paused. "He can see them when he opens them, I guess."

"Books, I'm impressed."

"Why?"

"Picking out kids' books can be tough. Basketball jerseys are easier."

"I like books." He stroked her arm lightly. "I like them a lot. Like kids, too."

Rhian almost drifted off. The gentle touch of his hands on her arm was so soothing and she was utterly cozy. But this was probably her last night with him. She didn't want to waste it sleeping. "Do you want to see something cool?"

"Is it another interesting shirt?"

"I said cool, not perverted."

"Right." He heaved himself up to sit next to her. "I was thinking of sleep, but hell, it's only—" he glanced at the clock "—3:17 in the morning."

She slid on top of him and then off the other side onto the floor. She looked at him and raised her eyebrows.

"This isn't a cool thing you can show me while I'm in bed?"

She shook her head and turned to the window.

He pulled his jeans on. When he looked up she had the window open and was waiting next to it. He took a deep breath and then followed her onto the roof.

Rhian was sitting on the lower edge of the roof, the long jersey wrapped under her and her hands clasped around her knees. "I never came out here barefoot. It's rougher than I expected."

He positioned himself behind her and then pulled her into his lap. "Next time wear shoes. And pants." He pressed her gently to his chest. "Is this okay?"

"Perfect," she murmured. "Now look."

The view was amazing. A long sweep of dark night, broken only by the glow of streetlights in the park down the street. The sky was clear and full of stars. Then he saw a shooting star and another before he had fully registered the first.

"Did you see that? I've never seen a shooting star in my life." He was amazed.

"There's a meteor shower every year in August."

She leaned into his arms and they both watched the sky in silence. "Did you know that's Jupiter over there?" she asked.

"Where?"

She took his hand and raised it to point to the planet. "The one that's so much brighter."

"How can you tell?"

"Planets don't twinkle."

He snorted. "Is that a scientific fact?"

"Did my technical vocabulary throw you off?"

"I never knew that."

"I didn't, either," she admitted. "After I came out here the first time I looked up the stars on the Internet."

She focused on the star to the right of Jupiter and wafted a silent wish into the night sky. *Let this thing be something we can figure out.*

"Now that you've shown me this cool thing, and I do agree that it's cool, do you want to hear a weird thing?"

"Shoot."

"I drew this."

"What?" She twisted so she could see his face, and his lips were there to meet hers.

"I drew this. You and me, on the roof, in the night. We were standing up in my picture but otherwise…"

"How could you know?"

"I don't know where it came from."

"I don't know what to say."

"Say you'll remember this tomorrow, when we talk."

I'll remember this forever.

"Promise."

They sat in silence as the falling stars streaked down around them.

CHAPTER SIXTEEN

"RHIAN. RHIAN, wake up," Nathan's voice was low but urgent in her ear. She was still mostly asleep. She snuggled closer to him and he wished he would wrap her in his arms and keep her there. But…

"Rhian, wake up. We overslept and someone's downstairs. I think Jem's home."

Her eyes snapped open. She pushed herself up and out of the bed so quickly he would have sworn she had been faking sleep. But that wasn't it. This was Rhian in mama mode—focused and in charge.

"Crap, what time is it?" She glanced at the clock even as she was stepping into the jeans he'd helped her out of last night. "You wait here until I come back. Don't make any noise. Don't move." She eyed him critically. "Get dressed, and then don't move."

He saluted, but she was already gone.

PLEASE LET IT not be Jem, she thought. She'd done everything to keep this thing from him and the idea that it might be screwed up because she'd overslept was too stupid.

She rounded the corner into the kitchen and stopped short. She took two steps further into the kitchen and said, "My God, Min. You did it."

Min's mink-brown hair was now bright, surfer blond, streaked with light, delicate caramel. With her cinnamon eyes the effect was arresting. "You look phenomenal."

Min had been getting out a bowl for cereal, but she abandoned it on the counter as she crossed to hug Rhian. When she released her, Min blushed as she used her hands to fluff the bottom of her hair. "It's so weird. I'm almost used to it, but it still surprises me sometimes." Min gestured at the pizza box and stack of packages on the table. "Did we have a party?"

"No." She stopped, unsure what to say about what she had done with Nathan. She had hope but not much. More than yesterday, maybe? But still, it didn't seem possible he could change enough. Before she could say anything Min lifted her chin and said, "Nice shirt."

Rhian flushed. She was still wearing the Knicks jersey. "It was a gift." She sighed. "Long story."

Rhian lifted one eyebrow. "I've got coffee on."

"Um. I have to do something." Rhian paused but decided not to tell Min Nathan was there. She'd never had anyone stay over and couldn't stop feeling like a teenager caught by her parents. "I'll be right back."

When she got back to her bedroom, Nathan was dressed and standing by the window. "It's Min, not Jem?" he asked.

"Thank God," she answered. "You have to go now, though."

He looked out the window again, his expression unreadable. "You think we're done, don't you? You've already made up your mind."

Her mind and her heart were knotted up. Nothing made sense. "I never want to feel that again. I might have hurt Jem by not paying enough attention."

He nodded seriously. "Okay. But promise we'll talk later. I have stuff I need to tell you."

She nodded.

Min screamed.

Rhian was halfway to the door before she realized the scream meant *I'm excited*, not *I'm dying a violent death at the hands of a lunatic killer*.

"Stay here," she motioned to Nathan.

Min was crouched in front of the TV where a commercial for paper towels was ending. She was jamming a videotape into the VCR and yelling Rhian's name. Rhian wondered if the president had been killed or if—God forbid—there'd been another terrorist attack.

"What's wrong?"

"Oh. My. God. She found him!"

A commercial for a new TV show called *Hide and Chic* was on. The host looked familiar, but Rhian couldn't place her.

"What?"

"Chris Senso. Lindsey Hall. She's going to see him right now. They're on a bus."

Rhian momentarily forgot about Nathan. "She's not!"

"You have to call Jem," Min said as she jabbed the record button.

The front door was flung open and Jem pounded into the living room shouting, "Turn on the TV!" He skidded to a stop when he saw them. "Oh. You know. I ran home to watch with you."

Morning Lindsey! came back on and sure enough, the broadcast showed the interior of a bus and then a line of four more buses traveling together down a street.

Lindsey was more hyper and shrill than usual as she

shouted over the noise of the bus. "We're three minutes from Chris Senso, folks. The Hall Heads are wild to meet him." A roar went up from inside the bus where at least fifty wig-wearing Lindsey impersonators were chanting and clapping. Lindsey turned sideways and pointed to the seat behind her. "Here's someone who's dying to meet Chris!" The cardboard silhouette, wearing the Lindsey! baseball cap and holding a balloon bouquet was propped in the seat behind her.

"We owe this moment to my friend, Patricia, the host of the new show *Hide and Chic*."

Rhian edged toward the doorway. She had to get upstairs. She could smuggle Nathan out while Jem was absorbed in the show. But her attention was caught by the TV again when the camera moved left and she saw the woman next to Lindsey. No longer just vaguely familiar, Rhian recognized Pretty Patty, her new neighbor.

"Tell the fans how you found Chris Senso!" Lindsey said.

Rhian's stomach turned when she heard the woman's first words.

"I thought I was close, but I confirmed my hunch last week. I met with a woman who has original Chris Senso drawings. She and Chris spent quite a lot of time together this summer. Maybe I should be jealous! Anyway, she gave me his address. And here we are!"

Rhian couldn't breathe. She was in shock. Nathan couldn't be Chris Senso. How could that be the secret he'd been hiding?

"That's the lady who came to our house." Jem's voice was shrill. "Do we have Chris Senso drawings?"

"She's talking about you? About you and—" Min's eyes were huge and horrified "—Nathan?"

On the TV, the buses stopped outside Nathan's apartment building, the peach lilies and lobelia looking serene and normal in the midst of the chaotic unloading. "This is it, folks! The hidden lair of Chris Senso!" Lindsey flipped her hair and Rhian's stomach pitched. "Let's see who's behind door number one."

There was a close-up of her finger on the doorbell and a slow fade to a commercial.

Rhian knew no one was going to answer. The person who lived there was upstairs in her house, with no idea that his secret identity was no longer a secret.

"Rhian, is that Nathan's apartment?" Min asked, her eyes wide.

"He's not really Chris Senso, is he?" Jem was bouncing up and down. Rhian put her hand out to make him stop.

"I think." She paused and then continued, "I think he might be."

Oh, Nathan. Why hadn't he told her? She remembered every detail he'd told her about the way fame derailed his life. She knew how much he'd wanted to put that behind him. She felt like vomiting when she realized she and Jem were partly responsible for this shattering of his carefully built secret.

On the TV, the talk-show host was on the steps of Nathan's apartment, Patricia close behind. But Lindsey's face was no longer excited. "Humph. Mr. Chris Senso isn't answering the door."

Rhian had the distinct impression that if the cameras were turned off, Lindsey Hall might throw things, possibly right at Patricia.

Jem did a victory dance around the kitchen. "Chris Senso was at my party!"

"Jem!" Rhian's voice was sharper than usual, sharper than she intended. "He's not Chris Senso. He's just Nathan. This is awful for him."

She saw that she'd hurt Jem's feelings and held out her arms. He walked into her hug and pushed his face against her chest. "But he's famous. He'll be on TV. What's awful about that?"

She smoothed his hair and met Min's eyes over his head. "He doesn't want it. It's why he doesn't use his real name or tell people who he really is."

"I don't understand." Jem's reply was muffled.

"It's hard to explain. But he doesn't want that." She turned him around so he could see the TV again where people were jammed onto the sidewalk in front of Nathan's building, chanting and carrying signs. The jarring blond wigs bobbed in the crowd as the Hall Heads surged toward the cameras.

Lindsey Hall put her arm around Patricia and leaned in so they could be heard. "More reconnaissance, Ms. *Hide and Chic*! What else do you know about the man who won't be found?"

Patricia straightened and looked into the camera. "What I know about Chris would take all day to tell—and some of it is *not* suitable for daytime TV. But here's a tidbit, he loves women with long hair." She swung hers off her shoulders.

Rhian suddenly *hated* women with long hair.

Patricia went on, "What's got me intrigued are those drawings. The woman who owns them told me Chris's address, but she was *very* possessive about the drawings. I happen to know that she's a writer. Putting two and two together, is it crazy to guess that I was the first person to see scenes from the next Chris Senso project! A collaboration perhaps?"

The camera swung to Lindsey Hall, whose eyes gleamed. "Shall we go have a look?" she asked. She turned to the crowd behind her and swept her arm in a big circle. "To the buses, Hall Heads. We're off to see the pictures!"

There was silence in the room while the three of them stared at the TV in shock.

"She's coming here?"

"She's bringing those people to my house!"

"We're going to be on TV!"

Rhian and Min turned on Jem in unison. "No, you're not!"

His eyes filled with tears. "But they're coming here!" he wailed.

Rhian knelt down so they were eye to eye. "Honey, Lindsey Hall doesn't care about us or about Nathan. She only cares about her show. We don't know what crazy thing she's going to do or say and I don't want her to come anywhere close to you."

She stood up and looked at Min. "Call the police. This ends. Now." She tried to send Min a secret message with her eyes. "I have to take care of one thing. Don't let Jem out of this room." Rhian ran out of the living room and up the stairs. She tripped on the top step and almost went sprawling on the landing but managed to fling one arm out and catch herself. When she looked up, she saw Nathan in the doorway of her bedroom, staring at her with accusation in his eyes.

AFTER RHIAN HAD GONE downstairs, Nathan sat down in the chair in front of her bedroom window. When his cell phone rang, he jerked it out of his pocket. He was pretty sure he'd heard Min's voice downstairs, but he didn't want to chance being discovered. The oversleeping had messed Rhian's head around and the balance of "okay to stay" or "got to go" was delicate now.

He heard Matt yelling as soon as he clicked the phone on. "Nathan! She found you. Get out!"

"What? Matt, stop shouting."

"Patricia and Lindsey Hall, the whole freak show, they're coming. You need to be out of there. They're going to be at your front door in three minutes or less."

Cell phone jammed to his ear, Nathan jumped up and started for the door. This couldn't be happening. Not today. Not before he'd had a chance to straighten things out with Rhian.

Adrenaline surged through him. He felt as if he could run…fly. But there was nowhere to go. No time now to tell Rhian what he wanted her to know.

"How the hell did they find me?" Nathan whispered.

"That doesn't matter. You have to go."

"I'm not at my place. I stayed at Rhian's last night."

"Okay, um, that's really bad."

"What?"

"Did you do some drawings for her?"

"I told you about them. She's writing a book, remember?"

Matt's silence was loud. Nathan thought he could hear his own blood fueled by anger and desperation hammering in his veins.

"God…Nathan. I'm sorry. Patricia got your address from Rhian."

The air in front of Nathan's eyes went dark and his head spun.

"Nathan?"

"I heard you." The adrenaline drained away with Matt's statement. He wanted to sit down, never move, think or feel again. He'd been so damn happy when he gave those drawings to Rhian. When would he ever learn?

"I'm sorry."

"Me, too," Nathan ground out. "I have to go. I'll call you from the road. I'm not letting those bitches see my face."

He punched the button on his phone and stuck it in his pocket. He knew what he needed to do—get out of this house, this town, this life.

When he forced himself to start moving, he got to the door and saw her. Rhian was in the hall, staring in. His Rhian, the woman he'd made love to not many hours ago, and now he wasn't sure he even knew her.

"How could you?" His voice was low and shaking with anger. She went cold as she got back to her feet and faced him.

"You know?" She should have guessed someone would tell him. She'd gotten so used to him this summer as Nathan Delaney, the man with no home, that it hadn't sunk in yet that he had a whole life she knew nothing about.

"Surprised?" He bit the word off with harsh emphasis. "The way you were hoping to surprise me? You and Lindsey Hall and Patricia." He walked stiffly down the hall toward her.

He thought she'd turned him in on purpose. She was ready to take the blame for letting Patricia see the drawings, for telling her his address, for talking to the woman in the first place. But not this.

"Nathan, I wouldn't have told that woman anything about you." She held her hands up as if to show her innocence. What she wanted more than anything was to ask him why he hadn't trusted her.

He was next to her now, looking down at her. His fury

was complete, and she was shaken. "Will you answer a question? When did you know? Before or after you seduced me into giving you a Chris Senso original drawing?"

The bitterness twisting his face cut the heart out of her.

"Nathan, I know you're hurt." He laughed derisively but she went on. "I know you must be out of your mind, but I didn't tell her. I wouldn't do that."

There was a silence and then the sickest, saddest laughter she'd ever heard. His eyes were dark with pain and his mouth was tight and hard.

"That's why you made me stay last night. You knew they were coming." He put one hand on the banister and leaned closer. "I can't believe anything you say. You knew what my privacy meant to me…" He faltered. "You talked to *her* of all people. Brought her straight to me."

He brushed past her and started down the stairs. He didn't trust her. Wouldn't trust her. He didn't know her at all. And now he was leaving again.

She ran after him, skidding and jumping down the stairs, trying to get in front of him so she could make him listen.

"Hey!" she shouted. "I thought your name was *Nathan Delaney*. I didn't know that you were Chris Senso, until I heard it on my TV this morning. You certainly never told me."

He stormed on. Not believing her. Still two steps ahead when they hit the downstairs hall. "Was sleeping with me part of the marketing plan for your book?" he asked.

She was shocked enough that she stopped following him. "That's not fair."

"Fair," he snorted. "I hope you get what you wanted."

She opened her mouth to snap back at him but realized

that Jem was standing in the living room doorway, staring at them. When she and Nathan looked over, the boy raised one hand in greeting and smiled hesitantly. "Hey, Nathan."

Rhian pushed her hair off her forehead. This was turning from horrible to…what was worse? Out-and-out hell? Fine. At least she wouldn't drag her kid into it. She pointed at Nathan's chest. "Outside. Now."

"I'm already gone." The muscles in his forearms twisted as he wrenched open the heavy front door. He took the front steps in two strides, Rhian right on his heels.

"You don't get to run away without talking again, Nathan," she snapped. How could he have spent all that time with her and not know her enough to realize she wouldn't do that? He didn't slow down. "I'm telling you that I did not know that woman had anything to do with Lindsey Hall. She asked who painted my house. I gave her your phone number. It was business."

He halted briefly, his eyes searching her face, but then his mouth twisted again. "No. That wasn't it. She knows about the drawings."

She wanted to stamp in frustration. "Damn it, Nathan! She used the bathroom! She saw them on the wall."

He turned away from her, walking away again.

Rhian was almost shouting. "I knew you were a bad idea. That's why I wouldn't date you when Jem was here. But I thought it was because you wouldn't commit. Turns out you're a bad bet because you never trusted me. Everything we had was a lie because you were too scared to tell me what you do for a living."

He was almost at his truck and he didn't actually stop walking when he answered her. "I didn't trust you. You didn't trust me. Looks like we were both right."

Before she could think of anything to say, she heard the rumble of the bus caravan pulling onto her street.

She put her hand to her mouth. "Oh, God. They're here."

His eyes snapped up. "What?"

She pointed over her shoulder where the media wagon train was starting to pull over along her fence. She felt the same sick anxiety she remembered from the day she and Jem left their apartment, following the movers and their stuff and leaving Stupid Len behind.

And then she looked at Nathan's face and this was worse, so much worse. Min and Jem were on the porch, calling out to them.

Nathan bent at the waist and retched into the bushes next to her fence. She watched his back twist as the dry heaving tore him. Her heart broke for him. Mad or not. Crazy or not. Messed up or not, she couldn't leave him here to be devoured by those vultures. He was so alone.

"They're coming. We need to go back in."

He looked from the buses to his truck and then down the driveway where a camera crew was running full tilt toward them, Lindsey Hall's hair brightly visible at the front of the pack. The entrance to the driveway was entirely blocked by buses and vans driven by other news hounds. Word had spread.

"Shit. Shit," he yelled, fists balled at his sides. "Not here, not now."

He grabbed her arm and, keeping an eye over his shoulder, guided her quickly to the house. On the porch he herded Min and Jem inside. Rhian closed the door, leaning into the wood to turn the dead bolt. When she turned Nathan was watching her.

Jem stared at him, but thankfully, he was quiet. Min put

her hands on Jem's shoulders and looked to Rhian, waiting for a cue.

"Nobody opens that door until we figure out a plan," Nathan said. "I'm making a call."

He bounded up the stairs two at a time and slammed the door to her room.

The three of them stared at one another, silent and stupefied. Against her back, she felt the first knocks through the wood even as the doorbell tinkled brightly.

The drawbridge was up. She wished she knew if the four of them were saved or trapped.

NATHAN BRACED both hands on the wall and leaned until his forehead touched the cool plaster. It was happening again. Just like college. This summer with Rhian he'd been taken at face value and accepted for who he was. But now, he was back in the center of a storm. And he'd managed to drag Rhian and her family into this whirlwind with him.

Shit.

He flipped his phone open and hit Matt's number. "Matt," he said. "I…" He didn't know what to say. He was completely at a loss.

"What happened?"

"They came to Rhian's. I'm here, inside."

"Hang tight. I'm on my way. We'll figure this out."

"What? No, Matt! I can't stay here. Didn't you hear me? She turned me in."

"I get that, Nathan. But seriously. Can you leave? Is it even possible?"

He walked to the window and lifted the curtain. It was a freaking carnival out there. People and vehicles everywhere. Who was he kidding? He was trapped here like a bug in a jar.

"Maybe in a while."

"Wait for me. I'll be there in less than an hour."

It was a four-hour trip from Boston to Richwoods. When Matt got moving, not much stood in his way, but an hour?

"How?"

"I got on the road early this morning. I was hoping to save your book—now maybe I get to save your butt, too."

WHEN SHE GOT HIM on the phone, the sheriff said he'd put deputies in the driveway to keep the buses from blocking traffic. If Lindsey Hall came on the property and wouldn't leave, she could be arrested for trespassing. But he had no power to keep the woman from coming to the house and trying to talk to Rhian.

"It's a free country, ma'am."

Rhian bit her lip. Of course it was a free country for normal people like her, but crazed talk-show hosts did not deserve the same privileges.

She tried to be polite as she reiterated that she needed the deputies at her house now because there was a *mob scene* on her lawn.

The curtains had been closed and the doors were locked. Min and Jem had dragged the TV on its rolling cart into the living room doorway. They were crouched in front of the front door, watching the outside of their house on TV. It was surreal. Another knock on the door.

"We don't want any," Rhian shouted. Min gave her a giddy thumbs-up.

On the TV, Lindsey Hall smirked for her fans, winked at Patricia and then slid her card under the door. The front listed her name and her contact information and on the back in big, looping handwriting was an offer of an obscene amount of money for the drawings.

Rhian deliberately ripped the card in four pieces and shoved them back under the door. When she reached for the doorknob, Min looked horrified.

"You can't go out there," she said, sounding panicked.

"I have to get rid of them."

"I know that. Of course you're going out there. Just, not like that." Min swung the hall closet open and pointed to Rhian's reflection in the mirror. "Not the image for your TV debut."

Right. She was still wearing the too big Knicks jersey and it was obvious she hadn't brushed her hair since sometime the day before.

Min handed her a zip-front sweatshirt and a baseball cap. *Okay, better.*

Once she was covered up, she slipped out the door onto the porch. *Chaos.* Lindsey and Patricia were made up for the cameras, their faces garish in the morning light. Flashes popped and she lost her focus, stumbling back until her heels met the door. The solid wood at her back reassured her and reminded her of what she was doing. This was her home. Everything she loved was inside behind that door. She would fight to protect her family.

"Ms. MacGregor, what can you tell us about Chris Senso? The two of you spent time together this summer. What happened?" Lindsey was breathless as she rushed the questions out.

Rhian crossed her arms on her chest. "First. I don't know anything about Chris Senso. Second, if you don't leave when I finish talking, the sheriff and his deputies are here to escort you away."

Lindsey's eyes gleamed and she glanced over her shoulder to be sure her crew was getting all of this. Patricia edged closer, angling to be in the frame of any lens trained on Rhian.

Rhian focused on Patricia first. "The idea that you're performing some kind of public service by turning my life upside down is sick. You ought to be ashamed. I hope to heaven your show is canceled the first week."

"And *you*." She turned the full force of her glare on Lindsey Hall. As a veteran of little-boy birthday parties and afternoons as a playground monitor, her glare was quite effective. The camera operator stationed behind the talk-show host took a step back, but Lindsey Hall was not affected.

"Any nitwit, any complete idiot, even any *talk-show host* should have been able to figure out by now that Chris Senso does not want to be found." Her voice rose as she thought about Nathan and everything they'd lost because he hadn't felt he could share his real life with her. "Chris Senso has given us David Dale. He doesn't owe me—" she swept her arm out over the crowd "—or you, and certainly not you—" she narrowed her eyes at Lindsey "—his personal life. Your hunt is twisted stalking. You're sick."

Rhian started to turn away to go into the house. Before she could get inside, Patricia cleared her throat.

"There *is* a liar on this porch, Lindsey. But it's not me and it's not you."

Rhian turned slowly. The woman pointed to the driveway. "That's Chris Senso's truck. I don't know who you're trying to fool, but professional celebrity hunteresses do not overlook details like that."

Lindsey's expression turned almost feral. "He's here?" she breathed.

Rhian felt like a hot-fudge sundae surrounded by ten-year-olds. Min yanked the door open and Rhian stumbled back inside. She leaned against the door, sick at heart.

CHAPTER SEVENTEEN

LINDSEY HALL, her crew, her fans and Patricia retreated to the end of the driveway. Rhian and her family hid inside away from the windows. Min decided they should all have a bowl of Cap'n Crunch to calm themselves down. Rhian ate hers, but her mind was on the man upstairs in her bedroom. She was running through what she could say, ways she could help, but all she kept coming back to was he was leaving anyway. Didn't trust her. Had never trusted her. Figuring out the steps to take in a situation required knowing the facts. Up until this morning, Rhian would have said she knew Nathan fairly well. Now? No way.

She'd had a fling with Chris Senso and she'd never known. So much made sense now—his reluctance to open up. His drawings. The mysterious source of money. His interest in her writing. My God, she thought, I spent the summer talking over my book with one of the most famous authors ever. She couldn't believe he hadn't told her, but she was equally floored by his generosity to her.

The Cap'n Crunch helped, but they were all still seriously on edge when there was a tapping on a living room window.

"As soon as I can get out of the house I'm buying a shotgun." Rhian pushed Jem toward Min. "Call the sheriff. Tell him someone broke the perimeter."

Rhian wondered if John Wayne had needed to be mad to reach his level of manly kick-buttness. Because she was seriously angry and could imagine how very satisfying it would be to have Patricia or Lindsey at the mercy of her butt-kicking skills. Not that she had any such skills, but at this point, she *felt* she did.

A man crouched in the bushes under the window on the park side of the house. He must have come up through the park and climbed the fence behind the forsythia bush. His auburn hair was covered by a Red Sox baseball cap. Dark sunglasses hid his eyes. The hat and his position in the dirt contrasted sharply with a dark business suit, crisp blue shirt, and expensive-looking leather shoes. He smiled when he saw her and put a finger to his lips as if to ask her to be quiet.

Ha.

"Get the hell out of my yard before the sheriff shoots you," she yelled through the glass, enunciating clearly in case he wanted to read her lips.

The man shook his head frantically. He dug in his breast pocket and she braced to whip the curtains shut, certain he was looking for a camera. When he pulled out his wallet, he smiled at her again and held up one finger.

Sure, she'd wait. Long enough to watch him get cuffed and slapped into the squad car.

He pulled a business card from his wallet and held it up. She frowned and squinted.

Matt Callahan. How did she know that name?

Then she read the next line. *Literary agent.*

Oh God. Nathan's agent. Lindsey Hall had been stalking this guy for weeks. And, she remembered now, he was The Reference. She'd called Chris Senso's agent for a reference and their conversation had almost convinced her *not* to hire the guy. If she were going to sell her story to the tabloids, that would make a nice sidebar.

She unlatched the lock on the window and pushed it up. Then she raised the screen. "Your client is sulking in my bedroom," she said.

Matt raised his eyebrows. "He's temperamental that way."

He put his hands on the window ledge and levered himself up. She stepped back to give him room. As he balanced on the sill, the sheriff came around the corner of the house.

"Freeze!"

Rhian yanked Matt inside, stepped around him as he sprawled on the floor, and then leaned out to smile at the sheriff. "It's okay. He's delivering a pizza!"

She was a very bad person, but it was worth it to see the baffled look on the sheriff's face. *Free country*. She waved before slamming the window shut and pulling the curtains closed again.

"So," she said as she looked him over carefully. He was tall, not as tall as Nathan but definitely over six foot. Hadn't Nathan mentioned that they'd played basketball together? His clothes reeked of success, but the deep laugh creases around his eyes and mouth coupled with the freckles sprinkled across his nose toned down the intimidation she might otherwise have felt.

Min and Jem appeared in the doorway. Matt gave a dorky wave. "Hey."

Jem waved back.

"You're Matt Callahan," Min said. "I recognize you from Lindsey Hall."

"Are you here to help Nathan?" Jem asked.

Matt nodded, the creases around his eyes crinkling

when he smiled. He turned to Rhian. "So my buddy is sulking where?"

She pointed toward the ceiling. "Straight ahead up the stairs."

Matt started out of the room but then stopped. "Your house looks great. I guess that painter I recommended did good work?"

"Yeah, he did quite a job." Rhian said. *And not just on the house.*

Everything was messed up.

How had the thing he'd wanted to do with David Dale—reach out to kids and give them a magical journey to a place where they could discover things about themselves—have turned into this nightmare? He'd been too successful and now he was being stalked, not because of anything he'd asked for but because of who he was and what he could do.

Being good at things—basketball, writing—had never brought him anything but trouble. Heartache and worry and people who wanted to use him.

He raised the edge of the curtain again. He couldn't see individual people even though he stared hard, looking for Patricia. It didn't matter anyway. Every person out there was waiting to pounce.

There was a knock on the door and then Matt poked his head in. His friend hesitated inside the doorway. "Hey, Nathan."

"She let you in?" Nathan snapped.

"About that, we need to—" Matt began, but Nathan cut him off.

"No," he said. He'd had some time to think about this.

"This is the deal. I came back to Richwoods to destroy my book. To end this thing. And that's what I'm doing. No more books. No more bullshit. I'm done."

Matt moved into the room, closing the door softly behind himself. He opened his mouth to speak, but Nathan plowed on.

"The only job you have left to do is to tell all those people out there to get lost because Chris Senso is retired or dead or terminally pissed off or whatever you have to say."

"I like your girlfriend," Matt said.

Nathan wondered if it was possible for a person's head to spontaneously explode.

"She turned me in, for God's sake. Pay attention."

"I think Patricia lied about that. Rhian's as pissed as you are. When she went out there, she really stuck it to Lindsey."

Nathan felt the ground pitch under his feet. "She went out there?"

"Tried to throw them off the scent. Didn't work, but she got some good lines in." Matt shrugged. "My intern Jerry taped it. He sent the clip to my phone. Want to see?"

Nathan scrubbed his hands across his face. He hadn't gotten much sleep last night and needed a shower.

"So one minute you're telling me she turned me in and the next minute you're saying she's defending me. Which is it?"

"You're the one who'd know for sure. Would she turn you in? Work with Patricia? Is that her?"

Nathan shook his head, sick at heart. Of course she wouldn't do that. He was a fool. He'd said such foul things to her. It seemed he was terminally incapable of acting right around her.

"That makes this all worse. I've got to get out of here."

"Why?"

"Because," he spoke slowly, making sure that Matt could understand, even though he'd apparently turned into an imbecile. "Who would want to have me inside their house right now? I'm like a media epidemic."

"Madonna?"

"You're making *jokes?*"

"No. I mean, yes. But I'm stopping. We need to calm down." Matt held his hands up defensively—maybe the murder he saw in Nathan's eyes had something to do with that. He pointed out the window. "Burning your book is not going to stop that. Breaking it off with Rhian isn't going to protect her. The only thing that will stop this is if you come out. You've got to tell your story, defuse the mystery, let people move on."

"No."

"Then it's never going away."

Nathan looked from the unmade bed to the window behind the chair to the silver-framed photos on the dresser. "I at least have to get out of here so they'll leave Rhian alone. She doesn't deserve this."

Matt nodded. "We can do that. But I think you're under-estimating her. Sure you don't want to see that clip?"

"I don't want to talk about her with you anymore. I don't want to watch movies on your phone. What I want to do is get out of here and take this freak show with me. Got any plans?"

Matt nodded. "We sneak. My car's stowed in the park. I came in over the fence. That is one huge bush she's got out there. It's almost like she knew she'd need cover someday."

Nathan wasn't really listening. "Let's go."

Matt stood his ground. "I want to be clear that leaving

her house isn't going to fix this for her. She's part of the story now. If you think she needs saving you're going to have to put more effort into it than sneaking away."

"I'm the problem. I go, they forget her."

Matt looked skeptical but didn't raise any more objections.

They headed downstairs, but Nathan stopped when he saw Rhian, Min and Jem gathered silently around the TV in the hall.

Rhian looked over her shoulder at him and her mouth twitched with held-in tears. She looked back at the set. Plastered over the logo for the Lindsey Hall show, he saw a headline, "The Heartbreak Couple." A picture of Nathan in his Maryland basketball uniform with his arm around his dad appeared on screen next to a photo of a smiling young couple. Nathan recognized Rhian's sister and her husband.

Lindsey Hall, standing outside Rhian's fence, said, "We continue to bring you live coverage of this developing story. Research has turned up tragedy in the backgrounds of both Nathan Delaney and Rhian MacGregor. Could these two have been drawn together by their sorrowful pasts? Stay tuned while we find out."

He was in shock. How quickly had the press rummaged through her personal life? He saw Rhian and Min look at Jem, whose face had gone pale.

"Why did she show my mom and dad?" He turned to Rhian with bewildered eyes and she pulled him closer. "Does she know about them?"

"I'm sorry, Jem. I think she does."

Jem's voice was full of unshed tears. "I don't want her to talk about my mom and dad. What if people watch her show and ask me those questions? I hate those questions."

Nathan knew the questions Jem meant, because he hated them, too.

Min stood up quickly from the floor. "I'll get us all some water," she said and then, somehow, as she went past the TV she bumped it with her hip and it was off the stand and lying on the floor. There was an electric pop and a brief spark and then nothing. "Oops. Sorry about that."

Rhian met Min's eyes over Jem's head and smiled her thanks even as Jem rushed to see if the set was totally broken.

Nathan knew Min had done that on purpose. He loved seeing that Rhian had people protecting her. Min understood and stepped up to bat. He went the rest of the way down the stairs, Matt close behind him.

"I'm so sorry," he said.

Rhian and Jem looked up.

"I never wanted this to happen," he said. "We're leaving now. We'll make them leave, too."

"What? You're leaving?" Rhian stood up, holding Jem next to her. The kid was staring at him like he was an exhibit in a museum, not a guy he knew from around town. He hated this.

"I'm quitting. Matt's going to figure out how to announce it, a press conference or something. I'm going to tell them that I'm not writing anymore. Chris Senso is done. End of story, end of craziness. They'll leave you alone once I'm gone."

Jem looked from Rhian to Nathan. "You're not going to write anymore?"

Nathan shook his head.

"But how will we know what happens? I mean, the new book, David Dale was supposed to get a new power and I heard Silvertip almost dies or something. What about the story?"

Rhian stroked her hand down Jem's arm. "Hush, honey. I don't think Nathan wants to talk about it right now."

"But I don't get it," Jem said. "How can you quit?"

"Jem, it's complicated," he started to say. But the boy shook his head. The kid had tears in his eyes.

"It's not. It's not complicated. It's dumb."

"Jem," Rhian spoke sharply. "Apologize."

Nathan held his hand up. "It's okay. He's fine."

"No, he's not fine. We don't speak to people like that."

"Sorry," Jem muttered.

"For what it's worth, I think it's dumb, too," Matt offered from the stairs behind him.

Rhian glared at him and Jem stared as if he couldn't believe a grown-up had broken ranks.

"I can make you apologize, too, pal," Nathan threatened in a low voice.

"Any time you want to try," Matt countered.

Rhian took a deep breath. "Min, can you and Jem take Matt to the kitchen. Maybe he'd like some breakfast? Or lunch?"

Min swept her arm regally toward the kitchen doorway. "How do you like your Cap'n Crunch, sir?" she asked. "With milk, or dry?"

When they'd left, Rhian said, "I have something to say to you. Upstairs."

"I don't have time," Nathan started to say, but Rhian cut him off. She walked up close to him and he saw that although her jaw was tight, her clear blue eyes were swimming with tears.

"You owe me this."

He almost didn't go, but she walked past him and up the

stairs without another word or glance. She trusted him to follow. He'd see it through to the end this time. She deserved that.

SHE WALKED PAST HIM as if she had no doubt he'd follow her, but the truth was, she didn't have any idea what he would do.

In her bedroom, she walked to the window and opened it. The screen was still off from when they'd come back in close to dawn that morning. It had only been a few hours, but the night felt fuzzy to her. How could they have shared so much and he hadn't trusted her with the most basic facts about himself?

She took a deep breath and turned to face him. It was just the two of them in the room, separated by about ten feet but locked together by their stares.

Nathan spoke first. "I'm sorry, Rhian. Sorry for so many things. I never would have wished this on you."

He looked exhausted. He sounded more than exhausted. He ran his hands through his hair. "I swear I'll make this stop. Quitting should end it, but if not I'll think of something."

She couldn't believe he thought she cared about his PR plans.

"You're leaving," she said in a flat voice.

"Rhian, I have to. You saw what this is like and it's just starting. You don't want to live like this! No one would."

Which made her angry again. "You know what? You don't know anything about me. You might know my real name, but that's about it." Her voice rose. "All the time we spent together this summer and you've still got me wrong."

"What?"

"First you thought I turned you over to those people. You

accused me of working with them! Me, with those Holly-wood people. Come on."

He closed his eyes. "I'm sorry about that. I know Patricia. I should have known how sneaky she can be, but I think some part of me doesn't want to admit how horrible she is. It's embarrassing to see how much of a fool I was."

Rhian sucked in a breath. Oh. *That* she hadn't realized. "She's your Patricia? Ex-fiancée Patricia."

He squinted at her. "You didn't know?"

"Seems like there's a lot I don't know, Chris." She sat down, shocked by the revelation.

"Don't call me that."

"Why? You're not him?"

"Rhian, he's made up. My name is Nathan Delaney. I draw. I write. I like to go dancing. I like kids. You know me."

"I didn't know you were Chris Senso."

"He's not real. He's for them—those people out there." His voice softened. "He's not me."

"But he's part of you." Her voice was rising. She felt tears come into her eyes, thinking about how he hadn't trusted her. "You made him. Your talent, your heart and goodness, are in the books his name is on. All that time we spent together and you never even hinted that you wrote them."

"I wanted to tell you, Rhian." He stepped closer. "But Lindsey Hall had that damn search on and I was worried about exactly this." He waved his hand to the window and the street where the media encampment had become a dull background thrum. "I wanted to head that off. Keep it from you."

"You didn't trust me. And then you ran. You never meant to stay."

He closed his lips tight and tipped his head back. "You're right. I didn't trust you at first. I haven't trusted anyone in so long. But I changed. I wanted to tell you. Last night I tried to tell you so many times, but you asked me to stop. I should have done it anyway. I knew how important it was. But I didn't."

He *had* tried to tell her. He had trusted her enough then; it was her who hadn't trusted him. Or trusted what they had. If she'd let him talk last night would today have been different?

"Rhian, what we had was crazy. I never felt that way about anyone. The day I met you, it was like I knew you. We were going so fast and it was all good, but that doesn't happen to people. To me. Since high school practically every person I ever let close to me wanted something from me. I knew we were different, but it was hard to believe it. I wanted it, but I couldn't take what you were offering me. I was scared."

She remembered the look in his eyes the night he told her about his college trouble. He'd been hurt, but baffled, too.

"I didn't trust you, either," she admitted quietly. "Last night I didn't want to talk about reality because I was sure reality would mean that you weren't right for us. I thought you'd never stay."

"And now it's too late."

"Because you're leaving."

"Because I'm leaving."

Her heart sank. She'd known he was going, but hearing him say the words…

When he went on, his voice was anguished. "Because I can't drag you through this with me. You need to protect yourself and Jem. You don't want this."

Sometimes people left because they didn't care. But Rhian saw now that sometimes they left because they cared too much. She saw how it made sense that he should abandon what they had to protect them both from the prying and gossip. If someone were writing a plan for his life, leaving her would make a logical first step.

But logic and plans could only get a girl so far, she'd learned. Sometimes there had to be luck. Blind faith. Attitude, desire, belief. Sometimes there had to be trust.

"Why can't I decide for myself what I want?" She took a step closer to him. "I spent a lot of years closing doors and building walls. And I was safe, but what else did it get me? Nathan, I never wanted to be famous." She took a deep breath. "But I'd like to be with you. If fame comes with that, then I'll figure out how to deal."

"But Jem," he said softly. "You saw what she dug up already."

"He's strong. We can protect him. You and me. Min. Matt. We have people on our side. You have people on your side. If you want us."

She saw tears in his eyes. A muscle jumped in his jaw. "Why?" he finally asked.

She came all the way to him. "Because I know you. You're Nathan Delaney. You draw. You write. You like to go dancing. You like kids. I love you."

Saying it out loud wasn't as hard as she'd thought it would be. Watching his face, seeing the answer in his dark blue eyes was more amazing than she could ever have imagined.

He put his arms gently around her and rested his head on top of hers. She almost didn't hear him when he spoke. "I love you, too, Rhian."

They stayed like that for who knew how long. The exhaustion seeped away and for the space of the embrace they were warm and comfortable and home with each other. No one else existed. No one else mattered. Here and now. Rhian and Nathan. Home.

Finally he spoke, breaking the moment. "You won't mind being with a plain old housepainter?" he asked.

She pulled back. "What?"

"I can't sit around all day. I'll need a job."

"You're still quitting?"

"I have to." He looked desperate. "I can't ask you and Jem to go through this every day so I can write books. If I quit, once this hysteria dies down, I'll be just another painter."

"God, Nathan. You can't do this to yourself."

"What?"

"You can't let them take that from you. You gave up basketball, and you almost gave up me. You can't give up writing—not because of them."

"If I don't, this will never end."

"Who cares? We'll figure it out. We'll figure it out together."

"I can't ask you to do that."

"But you'll ask me to be with you knowing that you gave up your life to keep my life normal? How long do you think that would last before the guilt took every good thing we ever had?"

"What are you saying?"

"I'm saying what everyone told me this whole summer long. Go for it. Take a shot. Live, Nathan. Do it."

He stared at her and then he reached out and cupped her face, roughly, almost fiercely before pressing his mouth against hers with the full fire of his need burning into her lips.

"I can't believe I found you," he murmured through the kiss.

"I can't believe I almost let you get away," she answered.

RHIAN WENT DOWNSTAIRS, leaving Nathan in her room. Jem and Min were watching Matt eat his third bowl of Cap'n Crunch. Thank goodness, she'd bought the industrial-size box. Min glanced at Rhian's face and then she smiled.

"Are you two finished talking?" she asked with a sly smile.

"Yes, ma'am," Rhian answered.

Matt pushed his bowl away and raised his eyebrows.

"He's upstairs. I have to talk to Jem, and then we'll be right up."

She lofted a prayer, *let this be the right thing*. Wrapping her arm around Jem, she led him into her office. He stood expectantly in the doorway while she leaned back against her desk. It wasn't exactly the birds and bees, but she had no experience telling her eight-year-old that she was dating someone. She wasn't prepared for how embarrassed she felt. Which was ridiculous.

"I need to tell you something. And then I hope you'll talk to me about any concerns you have or…anything." She met his eyes. "Because you know you're always most important to me. Always."

Jem nodded, his face serious.

"I'm dating Nathan. We've…dated…this summer. Which is something I think we're going to continue."

"Duh!" Jem rolled his eyes.

"Duh?" Rhian repeated.

"Yeah, duh." Jem shook his head, making Rhian feel that somehow their roles in the family had been reversed.

"Well." She didn't know what else there was to say. After "duh" and all the well-adjusted acceptance it implied, did they need anything else? "Okay."

"You think he can teach me how to shoot a hook shot?"

"I bought that book. When this is all taken care of, *I* can teach you."

"From a book? When Nathan Delaney is right there?" Jem looked appalled. "He played at Maryland, Rhian. He was in the Final Four. I saw this thing on ESPN one time, like a history show from way back when he was in college, and he was awesome."

"History show, huh?" She opened her arms and Jem walked into them, wrapping his own around her waist. This part at least was going to be okay.

THE PLAN came together over the course of the morning. It turned out that Matt's long history of mischief and his recent professional experience with the press meshed nicely with Min's sense of the ridiculous, Jem's intimate knowledge of kid culture and Rhian's ability to hold nineteen details in her mind while she sorted out the best way to get from Point A to Point B. For a while Nathan thought he could contribute, but in the end his main usefulness was as a plaything for the master plotter and his minions.

Matt started with a press conference. Jem thought of using kids. Rhian reminded them that freedom for Nathan needed to be simultaneous with humiliation for Patricia and Lindsey. Min threw Chet and a Chris Senso T-shirt and Lindsey Hall wig into the mix. Jerry the intern, working remotely from Boston, proved vital with his expert knowledge of Web casting and video hookups.

By 1:18 p.m. (Min tried to convince them to use military time but Rhian kept getting confused) they were ready to move. It was possible they could have called the sheriff and asked for an escort out the driveway. But none of them had gotten much sleep the night before and all of them had consumed unholy amounts of sugar, with the adults adding several cups of caffeine-laden coffee to the mix. Matt didn't have to work too hard to convince them to go "over the fence."

They paused deep in the forsythia bush fort to take a group photo with Matt's phone. Jerry got the shot two seconds later and within minutes he'd posted it to the Internet. The photo whipped an already insanely curious fan base into a frenzy.

Their first stop was Chet's and a supersecret meeting with Rachel, Diane, Denise aka Mrs. T, aka Jem's teacher, Brandon and his parents and Chet. Final plans were made and secret handshakes (Min's choreography) exchanged.

Jerry posted more photos. Hysteria bloomed.

At 4:21 p.m., the doors of Jem's elementary school opened and Mrs. T let the conspirators inside. At exactly the same moment, Patricia answered her cell to hear Nathan's voice.

"You win," he said.

"Nathan?"

"You've got me. I'm going to do your show—you and Lindsey both."

"You're joking."

"No. I'm going to do it. But you have to promise that you'll leave Rhian alone. Pack up your cronies and those impersonators and whoever else and come meet me."

Patricia sounded confused. "Meet you? In the house?"

"For a celebrity hunter you're awfully slow. I haven't been in there for hours."

"Liar."

"Don't believe me, see if I care. But we have a Web site up—there are pictures. Anyway, put Lindsey on, because I need someone to do my exclusive interview."

Patricia did not relinquish the phone. Seconds after she hung up, she and Lindsey were screaming for makeup as the Hall Heads packed onto their buses and the caravan swung through Rhian's neighborhood and back downtown. The interview was being held in a "location known only to the planners and certain invited guests" in order to keep people from overrunning the site.

Patricia was nonplussed by the outside of Chet's, but Lindsey barged in so she had no choice but to follow.

Rachel's band was set up on the stage and three folding chairs had been arranged front and center. Chris Senso was printed in block letters on a paper napkin taped to the middle chair. The right and left chairs were marked for Lindsey and Patricia.

Camera crews arranged themselves on the dance floor. Hall Heads climbed on tables and crammed every booth. The band launched into a rollicking rendition of "Rosa-lita."

Rachel called for Lindsey and Patricia to join her onstage. The drummer gave a long drumroll. Chet strolled onstage, wearing an I Want My Chris Senso shirt (lime-green with rasta hair) and a platinum Lindsey Hall wig. He sat in Chris Senso's chair.

Lindsey looked from the wig, to Chet's stubbly jowls, to the T-shirt straining over his ample belly, to his super-size butt hanging over the edge of the seat.

"That's not him," Lindsey hissed to Patricia.

"Of course not," Patricia answered, although she looked as if she would like to poke Chet to see if Nathan wasn't hiding inside somewhere.

"We were promised an exclusive interview with Chris Senso," Lindsey said.

"Ask away, darling," Chet drawled. "Time the world got to know me."

That was the last civil word spoken on the stage at Chet's.

AT RICHWOODS ELEMENTARY, the kids were flooding in. Jem had started a phone chain with his soccer friends. They'd been sworn to secrecy. They were warned the event would be canceled at the first hint of an official press person. This thing was kids only.

Chet had sent a dozen of the bigger guys from his dart league to work the door. Anyone under the age of fourteen was allowed in. Above that and you were out of luck.

Backstage Nathan leaned against a wall and watched as Mrs. T worked with the janitor and three members of the AV club to set up the equipment Jerry the Intern recommended for the Web cast. Rhian stood next to him, leaning back, her shoulder tucked against his side, his arm draped around her neck.

"You're trembling," she said.

"I'm nervous," he admitted.

"Afraid of the kids?"

"The kids, the cameras, the idea that I'm going to walk out there and suddenly be Chris Senso."

She wiggled her arm behind his back and squeezed him closer. "You're going to be fine. They're your fans. Not wild dogs."

"Yeah, well, I never really asked for fans partly because they scare me more than wild dogs."

"What doesn't kill you will set you free," Rhian murmured.

"Did you make that up?"

"Maybe. But if it's not an old wise saying, it should be."

"It's been quite a ride today, huh?"

Min stuck her head behind the curtain. "Three minutes, Mr. Senso."

"You have so made her year," Rhian laughed. When he didn't answer she tilted her head to see him. His face was white and drawn. "Are you going to vomit?" she asked.

"I'm not sure," he said without a trace of humor.

"Rhian!" Jem skidded up to them. "It's totally packed. There's, like, every kid from this school and then all these other kids I don't even know. They must be from other places—not even Richwoods."

"Oh God," Nathan muttered.

Rhian pushed herself off the wall. "Jem, go help Mrs. T with the sound check."

He was gone before she finished speaking. Rhian reached up and put her hands on either side of Nathan's face. "You're going to be fine, Nathan. They aren't really here for you. They want Chris Senso. They want David Dale. Those kids don't care about Nathan Delaney. Give them what they want. You love David Dale, too, and they'll get that."

He took a deep breath and for the first time since Matt had called that morning, he was entirely sure he was *not* going to vomit. She was right. He had what they wanted. And he actually didn't mind sharing those things. At least not with this audience.

"Showtime," Matt called.

Nathan looked down at Rhian and saw the love in her eyes. He felt it all around him, in this group of people who'd come together, no questions asked, to help him do this thing. Leaning down, he kissed her, full and fast on the mouth. Then he lingered, savoring the idea of Rhian, of them, of years to spend discovering each other.

"Nathan," Matt called again.

Rhian walked with him to the curtain, holding his hand the whole way. He found the opening in the fabric and stepped onto the stage, facing an auditorium full of several hundred kids. The hush was immediate. He blinked in the light and then thought about what Rhian said. The kids had come here to meet Chris Senso and that's who he'd be. Nathan had the feeling Chris Senso liked crowds. Summoning up a big smile, he strode to the microphone stand placed next to a stool at center stage.

"Hello," he said. "I'm Chris Senso. Delighted to meet you. Who's got a question?"

Hands went up all over the room. For a second he thought about turning tail, but he made himself remember who he was doing this for. Himself, but also Rhian and Jem and the hope that they'd be able to find a way through to a normal or at least normal-for-a-celebrity-author life together. He glanced to the side of the stage and saw them all there—Rhian, Jem, Matt, Min, Mrs. T, the dart league guys and the AV club boys, the family he'd found and people he could trust, standing with him.

"Yes." He pointed to a small girl with brown pigtails and freckles. "What do you want to know?"

Six answers in, he felt steady enough to take the microphone out of the stand and hold it without trembling. After the room howled with laughter over his description of Silvertip as a puppy, he sat on the stool and noticed that his knees had stopped shaking. By the time he started enjoying himself, Chris Senso and Nathan Delaney were working together for the first time ever. He glanced into the wings and saw his cheering section beaming at him. Everything was good for him right now. It was all good.

AFTER BOTH INTERVIEWS had broken up, one with considerable police involvement and some nasty, unladylike language, the other with a promise to return to Richwoods Elementary the following year for ChrisCon II, Nathan and Rhian, Jem, Min and Matt slipped out of town. Jerry the Intern had become Jerry the Permanent Employee after the brilliant suggestion to take the David Dale Stealth Tour on the road. The Web casts and camera-phone photos were an Internet phenomenon. Kids in ten states and twenty-seven cities and towns were thrilled to meet their favorite author at secret locations. The Stealth Tour team bought themselves an RV and lived life to the fullest on the road for three weeks. Finally they packed it in to return to reality with promises to reconvene the next year.

EPILOGUE

FAME DIDN'T GO AWAY, but it didn't bother them, either. Not much. Rhian and Nathan got married that fall in the yard at Rhian's house, their home now, next to the forsythia bush with a pair of cardinals swooping back and forth protesting the disruption.

Min stood up with Rhian and Matt stood up with Nathan. Jem stood in the middle of everyone. There never was a happier wedding party.

Min gave them a week of babysitting as a wedding present. She was finished with her dissertation and had accepted the job she wanted. She had moved, leaving them with tears but promises to come back every summer.

Matt gave them the keys to his parent's cabin in Alaska as his gift. They'd have to hitch a ride on the weekly mail plane to get to the place, but he figured it would keep the press out.

Jem gave them a picture he'd drawn. It was the three of them playing basketball in the driveway. The love they shared shone from it so clearly that neither of them said a thing about the fact that Jem had drawn himself in the middle of a stupendous, physically impossible, slam dunk.

Each of the guests received an autographed copy of the fifth David Dale book, complete with happy ending.

They gave Matt Rhian's book and the illustrations

Nathan had worked up for it as their gift to him. He sat
down at one of the round tables in the yard and spent the
rest of the reception reading. Min sat next to him and kept
nudging him to hurry up and pass the pages over.

The best man and maid of honor stopped reading twice,
once to toast Rhian and Nathan, and once to dance a slow,
close dance together. The bride and groom exchanged a
significant glance but knew better than to comment.

Rachel and her band played a straight set of Springsteen
covers, Chet set up his fryer and served piping hot fries
with gravy. The wedding was a wild success.

When everyone had gone home and Jem was asleep and
Min and Matt had disappeared somewhere to talk, Nathan
and Rhian climbed out the window onto the roof with two
sleeping bags and a bottle of champagne. First they toasted
the stars, then they toasted each other. Then they lay down
and very quietly, very carefully, made love to each other
under the early-morning sky.

* * * * *

THE ROYAL HOUSE OF NIROLI
Always passionate, always proud

The richest royal family in the world—united by blood
and passion, torn apart by deceit and desire

Nestled in the azure blue of the Mediterranean Sea, the majestic
island of Niroli has prospered for centuries. The Fierezza men
have worn the crown with passion and pride since ancient
times. But now, as the king's health declines, and his two sons
have been tragically killed, the crown is in jeopardy.

The clock is ticking—a new heir must be found before the
king is forced to abdicate. By royal decree the internation-
ally scattered members of the Fierezza family are summoned
to claim their destiny. But any person who takes the throne
must do so according to The Rules of the Royal House of
Niroli. Soon secrets and rivalries emerge as the descendants
of this ancient royal line vie for position and power. Only a
true Fierezza can become ruler—a person dedicated to their
country, their people…and their eternal love!

Each month starting in July 2007,
Harlequin Presents is delighted to bring you
an exciting installment from
THE ROYAL HOUSE OF NIROLI,
in which you can follow the epic search
for the true Nirolian king.
Eight heirs, eight romances, eight fantastic stories!

Here's your chance to enjoy a sneak preview of the
first book delivered to you by royal decree…

FIVE minutes later she was standing immobile in front of the study's window, her original purpose of coming in forgotten, as she stared in shocked horror at the envelope she was holding. Waves of heat followed by icy chill surged through her body. She could hardly see the address now through her blurred vision, but the crest on its left-hand front corner stood out, its *royal* crest, followed by the address: *HRH Prince Marco of Niroli...*

She didn't hear Marco's key in the apartment door, she didn't even hear him calling out her name. Her shock was so great that nothing could penetrate it. It encased her in a kind of bubble, which only concentrated the torment of what she was suffering and branded it on her brain so that it could never be forgotten. It was only finally pierced by the sudden opening of the study door as Marco walked in.

"Welcome home, *Your Highness*. I suppose I ought to curtsy." She waited, praying that he would laugh and tell her that she had got it all wrong, that the envelope she was holding, addressing him as Prince Marco of Niroli, was some silly mistake. But like a tiny candle flame shivering vulnerably in the dark, her hope trembled fearfully. And then the look in Marco's eyes extinguished it as cruelly as a hand placed callously over a dying person's face to stem their last breath.

"Give that to me," he demanded, taking the envelope from her.

"It's too late, Marco," Emily told him brokenly. "I know the truth now…." She dug her teeth in her lower lip to try to force back her own pain.

"You had no right to go through my desk," Marco shot back at her furiously, full of loathing at being caught off-guard and forced into a position in which he was in the wrong, making him determined to find something he could accuse Emily of. "I trusted you…."

Emily could hardly believe what she was hearing. "No, you didn't trust me, Marco, and you didn't trust me because you knew that I couldn't trust you. And you knew that because you're a liar, and liars don't trust people because they know that they themselves cannot be trusted." She not only felt sick, she also felt as though she could hardly breathe. "You are Prince Marco of Niroli…. How could you not tell me who you are and still live with me as intimately as we have lived together?" she demanded brokenly.

"Stop being so ridiculously dramatic," Marco demanded fiercely. "You are making too much of the situation."

"*Too much?*" Emily almost screamed the words at him. "When were you going to tell me, Marco? Perhaps you just planned to walk away without telling me anything? After all, what do my feelings matter to you?"

"Of course they matter." Marco stopped her sharply. "And it was in part to protect them, and you, that I decided not to inform you when my grandfather first announced that he intended to step down from the throne and hand it on to me."

"To protect me?" Emily nearly choked on her fury. "Hand on the throne? No wonder you told me when you first took me to bed that all you wanted was sex. You *knew* that was the only kind of relationship there could ever be between us! You *knew* that one day you would be Niroli's king. No doubt you are expected to marry a princess. Is she picked out for you already, your *royal* bride?"

* * * * *

Look for
THE FUTURE KING'S PREGNANT MISTRESS
by Penny Jordan in July 2007,
from Harlequin Presents,
available wherever books are sold.

Experience the glamour and elegance of cruising the
high seas with a new 12-book series....

MEDITERRANEAN NIGHTS

Coming in July 2007...

SCENT OF A WOMAN

by

Joanne Rock

When Danielle Chevalier is invited to an exclusive
conference aboard *Alexandra's Dream,* she knows it
will mean good things for her struggling fragrance
company. But her dreams get a setback when she
meets Adam Burns, a representative from a large
American conglomerate.

Danielle is charmed by the brusque American—
until she finds out he means to compete with her bid
for the opportunity that will save her family business!

Silhouette®

Romantic
SUSPENSE

**Sparked by Danger,
Fueled by Passion.**

Mission: Impassioned

A brand-new miniseries begins with

My Spy

By *USA TODAY* bestselling author

Marie Ferrarella

She had to trust him with her life.…
It was the most daring mission of Joshua Lazlo's
career: rescuing the prime minister of England's
daughter from a gang of cold-blooded kidnappers.
But nothing prepared the shadowy secret agent
for a fiery woman whose touch ignited something
far more dangerous.

My Spy

#1472

Available July 2007 wherever you buy books!

Silhouette®

nocturne™

DON'T MISS THE RIVETING CONCLUSION TO THE RAINTREE TRILOGY

RAINTREE: SANCTUARY

by *New York Times* bestselling author

BEVERLY BARTON

Mercy, guardian of the Raintree
homeplace, takes a stand against
the Ansara wizards to battle for
the Clan's future.

On sale July,
wherever books are sold.

SNRT2

THE GARRISONS

A brand-new family saga begins with

THE CEO'S SCANDALOUS AFFAIR

BY ROXANNE ST. CLAIRE

Eldest son Parker Garrison is preoccupied running
his Miami hotel empire and dealing with his recently
deceased father's secret second family. Since he has
little time to date, taking his superefficient assistant
to a charity event should have been a simple plan.
Until passion takes them beyond business.

Don't miss any of the six exciting titles in
THE GARRISONS continuity, beginning in July.
Only from Silhouette Desire.

THE CEO'S SCANDALOUS AFFAIR

#1807

Available July 2007.

REQUEST YOUR FREE BOOKS!
2 FREE NOVELS PLUS 2 FREE GIFTS!

HARLEQUIN®

Super Romance®

Exciting, emotional, unexpected!

YES! Please send me 2 FREE Harlequin Superromance® novels and my 2 FREE gifts. After receiving them, if I don't wish to receive any more books, I can return the shipping statement marked "cancel." If I don't cancel, I will receive 6 brand-new novels every month and be billed just $4.69 per book in the U.S., or $5.24 per book in Canada, plus 25¢ shipping and handling per book and applicable taxes, if any*. That's a savings of close to 15% off the cover price! I understand that accepting the 2 free books and gifts places me under no obligation to buy anything. I can always return a shipment and cancel at any time. Even if I never buy another book from Harlequin, the two free books and gifts are mine to keep forever.   135 HDN EEX7 336 HDN EEYK

Name   (PLEASE PRINT)

Address   Apt.

City   State/Prov.   Zip/Postal Code

Signature (if under 18, a parent or guardian must sign)

Mail to the **Harlequin Reader Service**®:
IN U.S.A.: P.O. Box 1867, Buffalo, NY 14240-1867
IN CANADA: P.O. Box 609, Fort Erie, Ontario L2A 5X3

Not valid to current Harlequin Superromance subscribers.

Want to try two free books from another line?
Call 1-800-873-8635 or visit www.morefreebooks.com.

* Terms and prices subject to change without notice. NY residents add applicable sales tax. Canadian residents will be charged applicable provincial taxes and GST. This offer is limited to one order per household. All orders subject to approval. Credit or debit balances in a customer's account(s) may be offset by any other outstanding balance owed by or to the customer. Please allow 4 to 6 weeks for delivery.

Your Privacy: Harlequin is committed to protecting your privacy. Our Privacy Policy is available online at www.eHarlequin.com or upon request from the Reader Service. From time to time we make our lists of customers available to reputable firms who may have a product or service of interest to you. If you would prefer we not share your name and address, please check here.

HSR07

Do you know a real-life heroine?

Nominate her for the Harlequin More Than Words award.

Each year Harlequin Enterprises honors five ordinary women for their extraordinary commitment to their community.

Each recipient of the Harlequin More Than Words award receives a $10,000 donation from Harlequin to advance the work of her chosen charity. And five of Harlequin's most acclaimed authors donate their time and creative talents to writing a novella inspired by the award recipients. The More Than Words anthology is published annually in October and all proceeds benefit causes of concern to women.

HARLEQUIN

More Than Words

For more details or to nominate a woman you know please visit

www.HarlequinMoreThanWords.com

MTW2007

COMING NEXT MONTH

#1428 SARA'S SON • Tara Taylor Quinn
One morning, a young man knocks at Sara Calhoun's door—the son she gave up for adoption twenty-one years ago. The son she hasn't seen since the day of his birth. This meeting leads to the unraveling of other long-hidden secrets and…maybe…to the love Sara's always wanted to find.

#1429 STAR-CROSSED PARENTS • C.J. Carmichael
You, Me & the Kids
What if Romeo and Juliet had been children of single parents? And what if those parents had fallen in love, as well? Leigh Hartwell can't believe her daughter Taylor has run off to be with a boy she met on the Internet. Which is why she drives several hundred miles to drag the girl home. But Taylor has other ideas…and so does the father of the boy she's gone to meet.

#1430 THE SHERIFF OF SAGE BEND • Brenda Mott
Count on a Cop
Lucas Blaylock, sheriff of Sage Bend, Montana, can't ever forget that he's the man who broke Miranda Ward's heart when he jilted her at the altar. He won't let himself forget it, because someday he might prove just as bad as his criminal father and abusive brother. But for now, he'll do anything he can to help the woman he loves find her missing sister….

#1431 THE OTHER WOMAN'S SON • Darlene Gardner
Jenna Wright can't say no when a handsome stranger hires her rhythm and blues duo to a long-term gig on Beale Street. But she soon finds out that Clay Dillon is keeping a secret from her and that his offer really is too good to be true. Seems she and Clay have something in common—his half sister, a young woman who desperately needs what only Jenna can give her.

#1432 UNDERCOVER PROTECTOR • Molly O'Keefe
FBI agent Maggie Fitzgerald has never had a problem being undercover…until she's assigned to investigate journalist Caleb Gomez. She needs to focus on extracting his information about a drug dealer. But Caleb's charm is reminding her she's a woman first and an agent second.

#1433 FATHER MATERIAL • Kimberley Van Meter
9 Months Later
Natalie Simmons books a rafting trip hoping to reconnect with her ex-fiancé, but instead she has one night with river guide Evan Murphy—and leaves with more than just memories. When he finds out she's pregnant, Evan is determined to show her he could be a good dad. Too bad Natalie is convinced he's not father material.

HSRCNM0607